C000071670

The Emerald Eye

Robert Lewis Lambert

The Emerald Eye

Paperback Edition First Publishing in Great Britain
in 2014 by aSys Publishing

eBook Edition First Publishing in Great Britain
in 2014 by aSys Publishing

Illustrations by R Lambert

Front cover design by R Lambert and painted by Paul Stanley

Disclaimer

ISBN: 978-0-9929796-8-3

aSys Publishing
http://www.asys-publishing.co.uk

Dedicated to:
Christopher, Richard, Ashleigh, Murray,
Alexander, June and Mae.

Special thanks to Ronell Lambert for the editing and
support on the production of this book.

Contents

Chapter 1

Craig looked on helplessly at his sister Hollie who was in the clutches of the tall thin man, holding a knife at her throat. His sunken eyes glared at Craig like black wet coals. His teeth ground together making saliva form in the corner of his mouth, making Hollies' skin crawl. Cradled in her shaking hands was a bag of gold coins, which the man was going to steal and escape through the Summerhouse. Sweat ran down her face and mingled with her tears. Hollies' young life flashed before her as the end drew near as she shook uncontrollably. The Templar Knight stood towering in front of her, his sword drawn, pointing it at the man's chest who snarled with contempt at his noble gesture. It was like a scene from a nightmare, but it wasn't, this was very real. Craig, with fists clenched, watched with others wishing the nightmare to end. He also wished he could turn back the clock, because three weeks ago they were safe. Happily driving to their new home with their parents Simon and Shirley Templeton.

It had been many years since their father, Simon, had been in picturesque Malvern. He had been a student living with his friend, Samuel, both studying medicine. One day Samuel went through the doorway of the Summerhouse, not to return. Years later on a visit from London Simon went with an estate agent to view the house which was up for sale. Wendy handed her business card to him,

"Thank you Wendy . . . House! . . . Your name is Wendy House?"

"Yes it is! . . . Really! . . . I know, I have heard all the jokes."

After seeing inside the Victorian house they went into the garden, Simon walked down the long path to the Summerhouse and opened the doors,

"Well old friend, you're still here."

Wendy looked confused, "Who's here?"

"Oh! No one.'

Now they were moving to the house, 'The Brant'. Down the road lived another family who had two sons, Daniel aged 17, was looking for his first job and his younger brother, Alex, aged 10, was looking forward to having new kids living in the same road. He was keeping an eye open for the new people who were moving into the house that everyone locally called, 'Spook House'.

The old house was imposing with a gate that creaked. Craig and Hollie looked up at the hills that had once been occupied by the Romans. The hills had provided inspiration for the music of composer Edward Elgar. Tolkien dreamed of Hobbits, and a Lion, a Witch and a Wardrobe found fame in a book.

Two young boys passing asked, "Are you the new people moving into Spook House?"

"Yes." replied Hollie.

Craig asked, "Why do you call it Spook house?"

The boy smiled, "You will find out soon enough."

Then they both ran off down the road, leaving Craig and Hollie pondering. He turned to Hollie and chirped, "They're just winding us up. Come on Hollie I'll race you to the bedrooms—winner gets first choice."

Craig won and claimed the bigger bedroom. Hollies' was not much smaller and had a lovely big sash window overlooking the back garden which was overgrown.

The house had a musty smell. A wide staircase led the way to the bedrooms. In the bathroom Simon gazed deep into his reflection in a cracked mirror, 'Well' he said to himself, 'This is another fine mess you have got me into!' He pulled a face at himself and replied, 'This is going to be our home and I expect you to have it finished in twelve months . . . fat chance! . . . But first, fit a lock to that Summerhouse last thing we need is ghosts of the past running amuck around here.'

Simon went back to the car and got his tool box, and went to the Summerhouse to fit a lock, he felt that all the time he was being watched! He took a latch and screwed it to the doors, then fitted a padlock. Back at the house he called out to Shirley, "I have put a lock on that old Summerhouse at the bottom of the garden as it's not safe, don't want the kids hurt!"

"Ok, good thinking my love."

Craig and Hollie heard this and pondered over it for a moment, old Summerhouse . . . locked up . . . made it sound interesting!

Whilst Simon and Shirley went about sorting out boxes, Craig and Hollie ventured out to the garden which resembled the Amazon jungle. It was enormous, wide and very long, Craig suggested,

"We must investigate that Summerhouse that Dad locked up." Hollie looked at Craig with raised eyebrows and replied,

"And I suppose this means you can get off from helping Mum and Dad in the house."

Craig looked and smiled. "Of course Hollie! Come on you know very well they will be so engrossed in organising and planning, that we would be in the way. So it makes sense to let them get on with it, leaving us to do what we are good at."

"But Craig, that's rubbish and you know it, but OK I like the idea! Let's go before they call us."

They ran down along a path of worn blue brick, then Craig stopped suddenly, causing Hollie to bump into his back,

"Look Hollie". He whispered.

In front of them hidden in the shadows of an ancient oak tree stood an old house the size of a small black and white cottage. It had unusual double doors with windows either side and shutters that were closed. It had an air of abandonment, with a thatched roof had moss patches growing in abundance. The timber frame was coloured black with wattle and daub walls that were uneven.

"Wow! Hollie, look at this!"

"It's wonderful." she replied.

Craig went to work on the screws with his pocket multi tool, whilst Hollie kept an eye out for their parents, the screws were tight but slowly Craig unscrewed all four screws and put them carefully in his pocket.

They slowly opened the door. It creaked and groaned until they could see inside, but it was quite dark. On Craig's multi-tool was also a torch, he put it on.

They felt a cold shiver creep down their spines as both felt though they were not alone. Hollie froze as she saw a hooded figure standing in the corner, she grabbed Craig's arm who then jumped. She screamed pointing at the figure, Craig instantly ran and jumped at the figure. They both crashed to the ground in a cloud of dust, Hollie dashed over and grabbed the torch and shone down on Craig who was coughing and sneezing, she then turned the torch on the hooded figure, Hollie looked on in amazement and grinned, for she was staring at a dust sheet rapped around an old coat stand,

"Well done Craig you managed to kill a coat stand."

Before Craig could reply they heard their Dad, Simon call, "Hollie is that you?"

Hollie gasped, "Dad, he's coming down, quick let's get out."

They both leapt up and out the door, Craig screwed the latch back fast as he could, then they ran up to the house and straight into their Dad.

"Steady on you two." Simon said in a stern voice, "Your Mum said she heard Hollie scream?"

Hollie thinking fast, "Yes Dad it was me, Craig jumped out from one of the bushes and scared me half to death."

"Really Craig you shouldn't, come on, we have work to do inside."

Simon put his arm round Hollie and led her up to the house, she turned to Craig who followed and stuck her tongue out and winked, Craig returned the compliment.

When they got back to the house, they got another shock, their Dad had a huge list of jobs for the two of them, on it were lots of various chores. Both reluctantly carried these out, however their minds were elsewhere. Both thought that the Summerhouse looked fine, so why did their dad lock it, Hours had passed when Hollie left what she was doing and joined her parents who were in the kitchen having mugs of tea,

"Well we've nearly finished the list of jobs. . . . We were wondering what's wrong with the old Summerhouse at the bottom of the garden to make you put a lock on it."

Simon paused before answering, "It's very old and needs a lot of work, the estate agent said that the building report stated it to be unsafe, so I fixed a lock to it as I don't want either of you two coming to any harm."

"Oh! Right, what's for tea?" Hollie asked.

Simon feeling so pleased with his answer to Hollies' question thought he would celebrate,

"Well being as not everything is unpacked and the kitchen is in such a mess, let's all go out for a curry!"

Shirley looked surprised as Simon was not renowned for spontaneous treats, and Hollie instantly grinned and rushed upstairs to tell Craig the news, "Craig, Dad said that we are all going out for a curry!"

"Dad must be feeling guilty or hiding something, as he never takes us all out for a curry when there's so much to do, unless it's someone's birthday or their anniversary!

The next morning they were all sat in the kitchen with toast and mugs of tea, Simon was writing out lists of jobs, yet again for Craig and Hollie. It had been standard practice for them to have lists of jobs so to earn pocket money over the weekends, however because of the move the lists were four times as big. Simon handed out the lists,

"Craig and Hollie here are your jobs for today, mostly unpacking and moving stuff around. Yes I know there is a lot, that's why you will get some extra pocket money."

Craig nodded with a full mouth of toast and Hollie smiled, "Thanks Dad."

Then there was a knock at the front door, Hollie went to answered it, followed by Shirley. It was the estate agent holding a bouquet of flowers, she smiled,

"Good morning Mrs Templeton these flowers are for you to welcome you to your new home."

"Oh! Thank you, will you come in for a cup of tea?"

"Very tempting, but I do have an appointment I must get to."

"Never mind, please do drop in another day, we are so pleased so far, it's a wonderful house."

"Yes it is a great house with so much potential."

Hollie used this as an opportunity to ask about the Summerhouse. "What's wrong with the Summerhouse? Can it be fixed?"

"Fixed! Nothing wrong with it, we had a structural survey done and it was sound."

"Oh! Great that means we can clean it up."

"Yes! It would make a fabulous den or chill out area for you and your bother, I must be off or I will be late; Bye for now."

Wendy left and Hollie closed the door feeling confused about the Summerhouse, she looked at her Dad,

"I thought you said it was in a poor state, even dangerous!"

Shirley was putting the flowers in water and agreed with Hollie, "Yes Simon, you must have got it wrong, as you said before leaving London, 'A cluttered home means a cluttered mind', and insisted everyone cleared out their rooms. Well now let Craig and Hollie clear out the Summerhouse, that way if we need a little extra storage space later on, then we have it!"

Simon felt cornered by both of them, then Craig made it worse, "That's great Dad, that means Hollie and I can clean it out for us to use!"

Shirley arranging the flowers and placing them in the window agreed once more, "What an excellent idea, Craig. When you've finished your jobs for today I don't see why you can't start work on it, it's a lovely day outside. . . . Good idea don't you think dear?"

Simon gave a reluctant smile.

It took more than half the day to finish the list of jobs but as soon as they had finished Hollie grabbed a broom, "Right Dad, Craig and I are off to clean up the old Summerhouse."

"I will come and remove the lock."

Craig hearing this, realised that he might notice that it had been tampered with so he replied, "It's OK Dad, you are busy, I can do it for you."

"Thanks Craig." He replied with crossed fingers, hoping that all would be alright.

It wasn't long until Craig was removing the lock and opening the doors once more. The light shone through and lit up the stone fireplace, they stood in silence as if to listen to the memories that haunted the house. A shelf was to the right of the chimney breast, with a large leather bound book. It had an unusual design of a man's head with tree branches that were embossed around it. The floor had large Elm floorboards a foot wide, and in the corner stood an old broom, like the ones witches would use for flying.

Craig imagined Hollie riding it and quietly laughed to himself, "I see you brought your transport".

Hollie stuck her tongue out and replied, "For that remark you can use it to sweep out the dirt.'

Hollie sneezed and said "So much dust! Worse than your bedroom Craig!'

Several hours passed and gradually the Summerhouse was looking better. Craig moved a lot of rubbish to the skip and Hollie had swept all but one corner. Craig was eager to finish and go on his computer and email his friends in London.

'That's it I've had enough.'

"Oh! Craig we've done so much and there must be an hour of daylight left yet!"

"Exactly Hollie we've been at it all day, I'm worn out, aren't you?"

"Well yes I suppose so."

Hollie walked over to a wall of old planks of wood and a door leaning against it and took hold of a large plank but it was just too big and awkward, "Craig . . . give me a hand to move this wood. I thought we could move all this wood out. I expect Dad might be able to use it."

"Ouch!" cried Hollie as a splinter jabbed into her finger.

She put the finger into her mouth and the heavy wood toppled back towards the wall and hit it braking through, making a hole. Clouds of coloured dust burst out of it, as though it had waited hundreds of years to escape from the hidden depths.

They both looked at the hole and were puzzled by it, Craig stepped up to the wall,

"It's a false wall, I wonder what's behind it". He looked but the light was fading and he could not see so he suggested, "Let's come back in the morning, I can't see in this light."

Hollie replied, 'Use your torch'

"But Hollie . . . "

"Oh! Come on Craig where's that sense of adventure you had earlier today?"

"It's sleeping I think. . . . "

He took the torch and shone it through the hole, and they moved. They could just make out a wood carving, they started to tug and pull at the other timbers, which sent splinters and cobwebs flying.

Gradually carving was uncovered, until a face of a man surrounded by leaves and branches was revealed. The sculptured head had a hole where the right eye should be, to match the other green eye which seemed to stare at them. It was set inside several pale green dials which were so dirty it was impossible to read the writing on them. Craig touched the dials, then tapped with his knuckles. They twanged, and Craig realised they were made of copper which had oxidised giving them the pale green colour.

"It's copper, turned green just like the statue of Liberty and the roofs of those churches that Dad drags us to. Castles and Churches full of dead people: he called it Fascinating History." Hollie replied, "Yes I remember . . . you called it something else."

Craig grabbed the broom and began to brush away years of grime. Gradually the man's face became clear as did the writing. He was mounted onto a large copper dial which seemed to be set onto three other copper dials each being smaller than the previous one. On each one was a large knob with an arrow pointing in an anti-clockwise direction, the large outer dial were years. On the next smaller dial were the months and the next 1 to 31 for the days. On these three plates the number and months were marked with a green crystal, and in the centre was the face of the man. Then he realised he had seen this before and turned to the old book. Hollie turned to

Craig, to see him sitting on a box, "Look at this Hollie." Craig said all excited, "It's really old and has that guy's head on it."

Craig started to read aloud the contents of the first page,

To whomsoever be concerned—
Respect this cot and treat it gude,
And forbye ye may be forewarned
that if ye do the things ye should—

To close and lock the shutters tight,
And set ye copper dials with care—
That Time itself will take to flight,
And great adventures follow there.

"Do you think it means this house?" Hollie asked,

"Well it's got shutters, and it's probably as old as that book." Craig chuckled "It's older than Dad! . . ."

'So is that joke!' Hollie replied, "Well I suppose it could have been here before the house, and they built around it, so it could be used as a Summerhouse. Remember Mr and Mrs Davis back in the city? They had that Summerhouse built in their garden, it was huge."

Craig grinned, "And Dad called it a monument to a city banker's opulence. . . . Dad didn't care much for show-offs, especially when he asked Mr Davis if he would help out at the local charity event and he said 'No' he was busy making money, but turned up to the event with his stuck-up wife dressed up like a wag, and paraded around like a lord."

Hollie added, "That's right. Just like a lord . . . which is ironic considering that a real lord, Lord Bray was there helping out on the Bring & Buy . . . he was a lovely old man liked a good laugh!"

Craig scanned more of the writing in the book, "Treat this place well and adventures we will see. . . . So far that's been half a dozen spiders and a disgruntled mouse, who we evicted."

Craig rubbed his eyes, "It's all too much. I think we had better get back to the house. It will be dinner soon, and Mum and Dad will wondering where we are. Let's come back tomorrow, the sun's starting to fade now anyway and I have to check my emails."

Hollie nodded in agreement, and the two left closing the door behind them, then Craig said,

"Hold on if Dad sees that hole he will not be pleased, we should cover it."

"Yes, I have something we can use, I won't be a moment."

She ran up to the house and her room, then came back with a large wall hanging that she had made at school. She hung it with Craig's help. It was almost perfect, every type of stitch was used in it, Hollie had made it with her Mum for a school project. Much of the material came from their old clothes, so it held many memories. They stood back and felt a sense of achievement, it actually looked great.

Craig picked up the last of the planks which he had been stacking outside and placed it with the others outside, on the path.

Hollie smiled, "Let's come back early tomorrow."

Craig laughed, "Yes! Sure, let's . . . you can evict some more spiders and I will read a bit more of that old book. . . . "

As they walked back up the path towards the house Craig looked back at the Summerhouse and said, "Those boys who called this place Spook house . . . I wonder if they meant that Summerhouse because I get the strange feeling someone is watching us!."

Hollie stopped and looked back, "Why are you scared Craig? . . . Watch out for the bogy man." then chuckled impersonating a witch's cackle.

As they got halfway up the path they met Simon coming down who asked,

"How is it going? Can I see?" asked Simon rubbing his hands together in anticipation. Hollie put her arms round him, "No not yet, Craig and I aren't finished, we want it to be a surprise."

Craig endorsed it, "Yes Dad, it will be a surprise, come and see how much we have cleared out and put in the skip put loads of wood in a pile for you and. . . . "

Simon looked suspiciously at Craig, "What are you trying to hide?"

"Nothing, honestly!" pleaded Craig.

Simon was not convinced, so he manoeuvred out of Hollies' bear hug and started to make his way to the Summerhouse. Hollie ran to the Summerhouse doors and stood in front,

"But Dad it's not ready."

"Let me be the judge of that."

Simon opened the door, his eyes zeroed on the wall straight away,

"That wall hanging." he said pointing, "Why have you put it there?"

Hollie knew the game was up and her shoulders sank, "Well Dad it's like this . . . "

Before she could finish Simon smiled, "You put that up for Mum, because you know she has always loved it, she was so proud when you brought it home from school."

Hollie smiled, "That's why I put it up there as a surprise for Mum."

Craig expanded on that, "That was the surprise Dad, it also hid the ugly wall behind it."

Simon felt awkward that he had spoilt their surprise, "And the whole Summerhouse is so clean, maybe I could see such enthusiasm with your bedrooms?"

Chapter 2

The next morning Craig and Hollie awoke from an uneventful night's sleep, no bumps in the night in spook house, however there was a knock at the front door. Hollie rushed to see who it was, she thought it might be Wendy House calling in for a cup of tea, however when she opened it, standing on the step was a boy of about 11, he smiled, "Hi, I'm Alex, I live down that way."

"I'm Hollie, come in and meet my brother, Craig. He's just finishing his breakfast, and Mum and Dad are about somewhere finding homes for various boxes."

Alex, was short and stocky, and had a round face with freckles over the bridge of his nose. He had light brown curly hair and a cheeky smile. He followed Hollie to the kitchen. Hollie introduced Alex to Craig, and then the three sat at the breakfast table.

"I thought I would come and say hello. I saw you moving in yesterday. So how did the night go? What is it like living here? Have you got a dog, and what about . . . "

Alex was interrupted by Craig, "Hold on Alex. Get your breath. One question at a time,"

Alex paused, "Sorry! It's just that I've waited so long for other kids to move in. It's so boring in our road. Don't get me wrong . . . this is a nice place, and the school is great, it just can be so quiet and boring sometimes. Although last month some friends and I were out at Lye Sinton woods and saw the Black Cat, big Leopard that prowls the area it had been taking chickens from old man Stanley. People said that it doesn't exist! But it does!' He paused, 'This place is full of old people with those walking frames and pavement scooters. By now the three had moved from the breakfast room to the garden. Alex carried on telling them more of what he knew about the house,

12

including stories told to him by his elder brother, Mathew (who everyone called Daniel.

"Lots of people have said that this place is haunted, because of the noises you sometimes hear at night. Then there's the stories of the people who lived here before . . . long ago. They disappeared! . . . an old couple, the Crosby's. No one knows what happened to them. They could have been murdered and buried in the garden, or kidnapped by aliens."

"People don't just disappear, Alex." reassured Craig, "and I very much doubt that intelligent beings from another world, would want to pinch a couple of old age pensioners from the planet earth. They may have just moved away quietly, to somewhere more peaceful."

"No! They didn't. Besides, they left their stuff and why move? It's so peaceful here, there's more action in the local graveyard. Nothing ever happens here," Alex sighed then continued. "It was years before the house was put up for sale, according to my brother Daniel, I can't remember that far back. Anyway . . . "Alex paused, drawing breath, "That's when the last people moved in. Then they went. Now you're here. I hope you intend to stick around a lot longer." said Alex, feeling quite exhausted from his history recital.

"We will, don't worry, Craig and I love it here and now we have a friend. We have something to show you, don't we Craig?"

"We do?"

"You know, the Summerhouse at the bottom of the garden"

Moments later they all stood in the Summerhouse looking at the dials

Alex walked up close and touched it, it was cold and mysterious and yet it seemed familiar, his brother had told him of such a thing from years ago.

They sat in a circle facing each other on the floor. Alex looked all around and told them of another story, told to his brother Daniel by Mr Crosby, before he and his wife disappeared.

"He used to sit on his lap, and old Mr Crosby would tell him stories that he had told his son many years before. His son had died in a war and he said that it reminded him of happier times. He thought he was going to cry, but then he went on to tell him of this place."

"What place?" asked Hollie, mouth wide open.

Alex stood up, and with his arms raised to the roof, he announced like a Shakespearean actor, "The Summerhouse . . . it is truly magical"

Craig laughed, "It's a big old shed, where people many years ago would sit on summer days sipping afternoon tea, reading the daily paper and falling asleep. At least that's what my Dad said, and he's nearly always right. Mind you when he mentioned about this being here before we moved, he did seem to be evasive"

Hollie agreed, nodding at Craig's almost adult way of approaching the facts. Then she asked, "What did Mr Crosby say about this place?"

"He told my brother Daniel that it was magical, and that it had amazing powers."

Craig roared with laughter, "We are away with the fairies now."

"No honestly." replied Alex with conviction. "According to Daniel, Mr Crosby would never tell a lie, he really meant it, but he never went into great detail because he said Daniel was too young and wouldn't understand,"

"Did Mr Crosby ever show him this book? We found it in here yesterday. Read this first bit here." asked Craig

Alex read the first passage, "I it sounds like a riddle but I don't know what it means."

Craig took it back and continued to read out aloud.

**"As many years as there has stood
this cottage here . . . for just so long
A span of years the owner could
Go back in time . . . but right no wrong
That you discover in the past:
What has occurred is hard and fast!**

Craig continued, "The last few lines though have been torn out. . . . Damn! But maybe there isn't anymore, and it's just a damaged page. All the other pages in the book are blank! . . . Odd that! But it sounds like time travel to me . . . Which is impossible!"

Craig eyes lit up and he smiled with glee, "Of course" he said "Maybe it's really the instructions for this Summerhouse, maybe it's a time machine disguised as an old shed'

"Now who's off with the fairies Craig." laughed Hollie.

He put the book in front of Alex and Hollie and pointed to each line in turn. "I'm being serious look at this first line, basically it tells us to look after the house and adventure will be our reward. It seems to say that if the shutters are closed, and we wish for something, then it will come true outside."

He paused and blew dust from the page, then continued pointing to each word with his index finger. "It says for as old as the house is, we could go back in time, but we must not meddle with the past, or we end up in a real mess."

"A big pile of smelly stuff'." Alex added with a smile.

All three looked at each other, their imagination's running riot, Craig rubbed his hands together, "Just think Hollie, we may get history lessons for real, better than old Smithies class. The way he teaches history I keep falling asleep . . . boring . . . Alex, did Mr Crosby ever hint on anything like this?"

Alex thought for a moment, "Now you mention it, my brother said that he did say once, if he could change the past, the one thing he would do was see his son again. I said earlier that the son died in the war, Second World War, I think."

The three sat quiet for a moment before Hollie broke the silence. "They went back to him . . . somehow, that's why they disappeared. He said that he wished to go back to happier times. They both went back by using the Summerhouse, and never returned."

Craig shivered, "This is spooky . . . Why didn't they return? . . . I hope that it isn't a case of they couldn't get back . . . The last thing we want is to get stuck in the past, our Dad is always saying how things were different in his day. They were so much better."

He put on his father's voice and started to mimic him. "Craig my boy this world lacks good old fashioned discipline in the schools and streets."

Hollie laughed and replied also mimicking. "Criminals should be punished not rewarded."

Alex looked on at their performance, "Your Dad sounds scary"

Hollie replied, "It's OK Alex, he's a big softy it's just when he watches the news on TV he gets so worked up. He starts to drum into us what life was like when he was young."

Craig started to laugh and added. "That's right and each time he does the stories get more and more absurd."

"Oh! Come on Craig, Dad does have a point."

Craig agreed, looked at the copper dials and said, "Well getting back to this book we will just have to be very careful."

Craig grinned, "Let's give it a go. Come on Hollie, Alex we will be OK . . . just once. What do you say?"

All three held hands and said, "Yes, let's do it."

"Hold on" said Alex, "Shouldn't we get supplies and stuff to take with us, that's what they do in the movies."

"Like what" asked Hollie,

"I don't know, Daniel would know . . . He's older, nearly 18 . . . One smart cookie, but don't let him know that I said that, it will only go to his head."

"Go and ask him to come. Even up the numbers! Besides it's because of the stories he passed on to you that we know so much. Maybe he knows even more, but never told you."

"Maybe" replied Alex, "He also knows a lot more about this place than I do. He might even remember how the riddle ended."

Craig closed the book with a thud, and a plume of fine dust engulfed him, he waved his hands around to disperse it whilst coughing and spluttering. Then he notice that now he could read the small print on the cover. It read,

Keepers Key Book.

Year of our Lord 1422.

"Look" announced Craig, "On the cover I think it says it was made in 1422. A real find don't you think . . . "

On that note Alex hurried off to fetch his brother Daniel. Daniel was a tall seventeen year old who was coming to terms with leaving school and entering the big wide world of finding work, making money, and paying his way in life.

Alex arrived back nearly two hours later with Daniel who was tall and dark, dressed in jeans, chequered shirt, brown boots and with a confident smile. Alex introduced them all.

He shook hands with Craig in quite an adult fashion, and then he smiled at Hollie and nodded hello. They all sat inside the Summerhouse and told Daniel all that they knew about the house and the discovery of the book. Hollie wanted to know more about him, "So Daniel you've left school, what's it like?"

"Ok, I guess, but it's daunting, got to get a job, pay housekeeping, it's not as easy as I thought it might be, wish I had done better in my exams now."

"I'm sure you'll be alright, what do you want to do?"

"Building maybe or painting and decorating, working with Dad would be great, it's because of him that I got interested in building."

"Is that what he does?"

"No he's an engineer, he seems to put his hand to anything. He tried to get me a job at where he works, but the company has been going through rough times."

"Are there any jobs going?"

"No. None, he's even worried about his own, he says it's to do with other companies abroad undercutting them, or something like that!"

Craig joined in the conversation, "Our Dad's a surgeon, so no chance of me working with him, I'd end up killing someone!"

"He's a surgeon. Now that's a career." Daniel said with envy.

"Yes, Dad asked me if I wanted to be a doctor, but the sight of blood makes me heave."

Hollie started to laugh, "Not to worry, Craig, Mum says do whatever you're good at and enjoy doing."

Craig smiled, "But I don't know what I like doing."

"Craig mate, you've got time yet to decide. Do as my Dad told me, just do the best you can in everything . . . just wish I had done a bit better."

Daniel's eyes were drawn to the book that Craig was holding, Craig opened the book and showed Daniel the pictures and verse inside. Daniel took the book and sat in the old arm chair and scanned every detail of the book. All the boyhood memories started to come back to him. He closed the book, ran his hand over the leather cover and read the small print. Craig clapped his hands together, "Well are we up for it? . . . as in give it a go . . . see if we can go back in time"

Daniel looked up from the arm chair, "Are you serious?"

"Yes, why not?"

"Because . . . Well. . . . "

Daniel was not sure why not, except it was a little scary, however he could not admit that. The other three said 'yes' with excitement. Then Daniel damped it by saying. "Of course we could try . . . but you might end up being disappointed."

They all stood quiet, then Hollie piped up and said, "Oh! Come on let's do it will be fun, according to Alex nothing ever happens here, so let's go elsewhere and have some fun!"

Then Hollie heard her father calling from the house, she quickly with Craig's help put the wall hanging back, just as the door opened. It was Simon, "Well here you two are, your Mum and I need a hand in the house."

"Alright Dad." said Hollie with a big sigh.

Simon noticed her lack of enthusiasm, "I know you've worked hard for several days now, so tomorrow you can do whatever you want."

This brought a smile to Craig and Hollies' faces, then he asked, "And these boys are?"

Hollie introduced them, "This is Alex and his brother Daniel, they live just down the road."

"Pleased to meet you both. Sorry about breaking up your gathering but we really do need a hand with jobs. Why don't you all come tomorrow?"

Simon then went back to the house as the others said their goodbyes, Hollie grinned. "That worked out perfectly, eh! Craig?"

"It did, now it looks that we have to work all day, so we had better meet tomorrow at nine sharp."

That night the four adventurers lay in their beds making lists of provisions to take in case they did find themselves in another time. Yet in the back of their minds lay the seed of doubt. Craig thought, have I got all that I may need? Torch, penknife . . . my collection of old money, if we are in the past a little old type money may come in useful. His bedroom walls were bare, all his pictures yet to be unpacked, unlike Hollie, who sorted her room out the first night. She was always well organised.

Meanwhile Alex read his list to himself in bed whilst his rather tatty teddy looked on,

"Torch, string, pocket knife, sandwiches and crisps. Now, is there anything else?" He looked at his teddy, "Sorry Ted, you have to stay, I've got to think of my street credibility with the new neighbours. I mean come on let's face facts you really should have gone to the charity shop years ago, but after all we are a team. That's why this time you have to stand guard over my bedroom."

Daniel also lay back in bed looking at his backpack and contemplating its contents. A head lamp, matches, pair of binoculars, bar of chocolate, and bits still in the pack from his last camping trip. Had he taken the dirty washing out of it? . . . No! He got out of bed and picked the pack up, and smelt it, and it was evident that old clothes were still in there. Removing them and put them in the laundry basket out on the landing. He closed the lid quickly as the smell was enough to waken the dead, let alone his parents! Daniel looked at the picture on his bedside table of his dog. A 4 year old border collie, Ben. His bedroom wall was adorned with pictures of motorbikes including his own off road bike. At weekends he and friends would go off road around a mates farm fields. Other posters of rock stars and his Martial Art certificates, his main sport which he took up at the age of nine.

Down the street Hollie lay in bed also making a mental list, my digital camera may come in handy too, take a photo of Daniel. Her bedroom walls were hung with pictures of horses and certificates for riding, show jumping and gymnastics.

At nine the next morning the intrepid four met at the Summerhouse. Simon and Shirley Templeton had already eaten breakfast with Craig and Hollie. Now Simon was stripping wallpaper from the living room walls, while Shirley did the washing up in the kitchen.

"What are Craig and Hollie up to?" asked Simon.

"In the back garden, with two new friends they have made, Daniel and Alex. It's good that they have made friends so quickly."

Craig, Hollie, Alex and Daniel all stood looking at the dials and the green man in the Summerhouse, then Daniel broke the silence, "This brings back all the stories that Mr. Crosby used to tell me, I believed them so much I would dream at night that I could go anywhere in time."

Craig was eager to get started, "Right Hollie close the shutters like the book says."

Alex sat down on the floor, cross legged. He mumbled, "Nothing good will come of this. What am I doing here? We could end up in a world full of monsters."

Hollie looked at Alex and reassuringly said, "Don't worry Alex I will look after you."

She looked out of the window at the overgrown garden. The house could not be seen. She brought the bar down across the shutter, locking it. It went darker inside and very quiet. The breeze outside was the only thing which could be heard. Craig moved the copper dials, to set a date, "Well, the dates on the dials are set to a random date and yet I don't feel anything happening. Daniel do you want to be the first to look outside, to see if we are still here?"

Daniel opened it slightly and peered through it, all eyes were on him to see his reaction to what was outside the Summerhouse. Daniel's eyes widened, his mouth ajar, he looked back at them and said. "You better take a look at this."

Each ran to a window, and in one movement and altogether pulled opened the shutters, as Daniel cried out, "Look . . . nothing." In front of them was the overgrown garden and a dog. Ben his Border Collie. Nothing had happened.

Alex cried out, "Ben what are you doing here, go home!"

Hollie opened the door and let Ben in, "He is adorable" and she dropped to her knees and started to make a big fuss of him, as he rolled onto his back. Daniel joined her, and said, "He must have followed me here. He is very faithful and follows me everywhere."

Hollie looked at Daniel and replied, "Can't say I blame him."

Daniel stood up, not knowing how to reply. Alex made a gesture of putting two fingers in his mouth being sick! Daniel replied with another hand gesture. Then Craig turned to Daniel, "Daniel, nothing's happened. Can you remember if there was any more to this riddle?"

Craig opened the book and pointed out the damaged page. Daniel sat in an armchair, looking at the missing part. It was not a large piece but it may have been a few important lines. Daniel mumbled out loud, "What was it? There was more. Not a lot, but something which I can't quite remember, Mr. Crosby read the whole thing to me on a few occasions. He would stand up, pace up and down, waving his arms . . . all very theatrical." he said with a smile.

Daniel stood up and walked round the Summerhouse in the steps of Mr Crosby as he had all those years before. He moved to each window and shut the shutters and locked them. Checked the door was shut tight, and moved back a step, raising his hand to his rubbed his chin, "What did he do next?" he said out loud.

He stood there for a short while and everybody's eyes fixed on his next move. Daniel smiled, "Of course The Green Man."

"Who?" they all asked.

He pointed to the green man carving in the middle of the dials. "I seem to remember that these dials move. They were set to the dates required and then he would push a lever or something on this wall. Although he never actually did it with me here. He just went through the motions, when telling me the story. This carving of the Green Man, it's an old thing that you can find on buildings, he was the spirit of the forest or . . . life . . . or something like that."

Daniel turned each dial to make sure they moved, studied the wall closely for a lever. Then he ran his hands over the wall saying. "It was here somewhere . . . Come on people give me a hand."

One by one they tried. They found nothing. Daniel was desperately looking for it. He felt as though he had let them all down. He turned and faced them and said. "Sorry guys . . . I thought I could remember."

He stepped away from the dials and looked around, thinking of Mr Crosby's movements. Then he remembered Mr Crosby reaching up to a low beam and bringing down something. So Daniel reached up and felt the something. He brought it down. It slipped from his hand and hit the floor. Ben shot to his feet and picked it up in his mouth. Daniel stooped to retrieve it, but missed! Ben started to run round the room thinking this was a new game, they all tried to catch him but failed. He started to race round the house, avoiding the boy's advances. Then Hollie sank to her knees, put her hands out and called in a soft voice, "Ben . . . Ben come on boy . . . come to Hollie." Like a true dog whisperer.

Ben stopped, looked and paused, then went to Hollie. She put her hand out and Ben gently dropped the object in it.

It was copper shaft with the missing eye on the end. She handed it to Daniel. "Thanks Hollie . . . Ben come sit there and behave."

He gave a large sigh, then took it to the Green Man's head and placed it in the socket. At that moment the stones in the disc's lit up the room in a green glow. Small green balls of light came from the stones and flew in an orbit around the room at speed. There was shaking of the house and the wind grew to a gale outside. The room filled with movement and they felt everything shake. The smells of bygone years twisted in the room like a mini tornado. The noise seem to grow louder, Hollie wanting to make light of her fear, nervously said, "That humming noise is B flat I do believe."

The others either ignored her comment or couldn't hear her. All the objects in the house including the armchairs seemed to fade away as the green light faded and the house settled. The humming stopped, and Daniel looked at Craig with an embarrassed look and said in a whisper, "I think that worked." They both looked at the dials, the dials were on the date 1952 August 06.

Chapter 3

All eyes were open wide when Craig asked Daniel, "Shall you look or shall I?"

They both moved to a window, grabbed a shutter and pulled it open. They looked out and gasped, and Daniel said, in a slow whisper, "Well, either we have moved back in time or in the time we've been in here, your parents have been really busy."

Outside the garden had changed, no longer was the garden overgrown. It was pristine, with lawns, flowering shrubs and bushes. The trees were thirty feet shorter and the cobbled path with blue brick edging looked as if it was new. In fact everything was very different indeed. They all were amazed and felt a little frightened. After all, no one thought it would actually work!

It was just supposed to be a bit of fun. Now the fun wasn't that funny anymore. . . . It was unbelievable and a little scary!

Craig ran his fingers through his hair in disbelief of what took place, "We need to find out if those dials are accurate."

Hollie replied in a frightened, "But how do we get back."

Daniel responded to Hollies' plea for help with confidence, "Don't worry, we just have to set the date to the date we left, and we should end up back at the right place and time."

"Very scientific." Hollie replied with sarcasm.

"I am the oldest so I had better go first."

Hollie grabbed his hand and squeezing it and said, "Please be careful."

Alex looked at his brother and with hand on heart blew kisses at him saying, "Yes do be careful."

Daniel gritted his teeth and replied, "One of these days Alex . . . one of these days"

Craig drew a deep breath, "Wait, I will come with you. Alex you stay here with Hollie."

Alex wished them both luck, and Craig and Daniel made their way up to the house, trying not to be seen by anyone. They got to the side gate and Daniel observed, "It looks deserted. That's lucky for us. Let's be quick. If we go to the local shop, we can find out the date from the daily paper, as long as it's still there."

Craig agreed, after all asking a stranger the date and year would seem a little odd. They walked down the road from the house. Lining the road on the other side were several vintage cars, all black. The street lamps were very ornate. What had been a big tree at the side of the road was now a sapling. Several of the houses had, instead of hedges, white picket fences and others iron railings. Some of the houses Daniel recognised and others, not.

A woman passed by dressed in a tweed pencil skirt and jacket which complemented her very trim figure. She also wore a small hat with feathers displayed in the brim. Her lips were adorned with red lipstick, and she wore lace up shoes with 2 inch heels. Daniel thought it looked dated, but also had a lot of elegance and style which he often thought was lacking nowadays. Both looked back to see her gracefully walk away.

"That actually looks really nice." commented Daniel, then added.

"Beats how some of the girls look now, I must say, and she's well fit . . . "

"Come on Casanova" joked Craig.

A steam train hooted in the distance, the smell of fresh baked bread wafted from an open window. The local shop came into sight, painted white with old fashioned black lettering on the wall above the door. It read, Grinnell's Stores, and outside the window was a display of fresh vegetables with a small hand written sign saying 'Local Farm Produce.' They went inside. Several ordinary light bulbs hung from the ceiling, lighting up the wooden shelves. They spied the papers lying on the bottom self. Craig picked one up and stared at the date. Craig also looked. What his eyes saw confirmed what they had seen so far. The date read 6th August 1952. Craig tugged at

Daniel's arm, hinting with the movement of his eyes and tilt of his head to come outside.

Once outside, Craig studied a newspaper, "The date on that paper said this is 1952. That's before my dad was even born, in fact my granddad who died some years ago, will be about here somewhere!"

Daniel was still taking it all in. then he replied, "I never imagined it would work, but it has . . . and that was the date on those dials. This is amazing! Let's get back and tell the others, then go and explore."

When they got back to the house, they quietly made their way down the garden, making sure to hide behind each bush as it came to hand as they approached the Summerhouse, they noticed that not just one shutter was open, but both. They opened the door and rushed in, to find that Hollie and Alex were gone!

They looked at each other, then Daniel suggested, "We told them stay here! Come on, we had better go and find them, they can't have gone far."

He looked at his watch, "We were only away for twenty five minutes."

They kept their heads low as they passed the back of the house, then by a slightly open window Craig heard Hollies' voice, "We are telling the truth . . . honest . . . aren't we Alex."

Craig froze and signalled to Daniel to listen. Then a woman's voice answered Hollie, saying, "I don't doubt you are telling the truth as unbelievable as it may be. We will wait for your friends to come back and see what they have to say. If it had not been for your dog barking, I wouldn't have known you were there. You are such a lovely dog aren't you my sweet." Then she patted Ben as he looked up at her with obedient eyes.

Craig and Daniel looked at each other, then Daniel said, "Trust Ben to mess things up. We have to knock on the door and give ourselves up. Besides it's not if we have done anything wrong . . . eh! Craig"

Craig nodded reluctantly in agreement but added. "We have trespassed, technically, I suppose, but I shouldn't think it could get us into that much trouble. It does sound like an old lady. Maybe she'll give us a ticking off and a cup of tea."

"You are the ultimate optimist aren't you?" replied Daniel, then he added "Don't tell her we are time travellers, or she will call the guys in the white coats to cart us off to the Looney bin!"

Craig and Daniel went to the front door, drew a deep breath and knocked on the door. Craig looked at the immaculate front door, "Bet my Mum and Dad wished the house looked like this now."

The door opened. In front of them stood a short elderly lady, sprightly looking, with a stern look on her face. "Come in. You are expected. I am Mrs. Bennett, I have two of your friends in the drawing room, waiting." Craig and Daniel walked through. "You can sit there." pointing to two dining chairs. She sat opposite all four of them, "Your two companions tell me that you appeared out of nowhere, and into my Summerhouse. A most intriguing story, I was not born yesterday." She paused for a second, then continued with a firm voice. "You two gentlemen can give me your story, before I call the Police, and have you arrested for trespass."

Both Daniel and Craig had dry mouths. Their hearts were beating so fast that Craig was feeling quite faint. "Well, I am waiting" the lady repeated.

Craig jumped in his chair, and then Daniel spoke. "I am sorry about how this must look, but honestly we mean no harm. What Hollie and Alex told you is true. It sounds mad but it is true. We can hardly believe it either."

Mrs. Bennett's face was unchanged, and she sat with her arms and legs crossed. "I must say, the local constable will have a good laugh at this one."

Now Daniel was having visions of all four of them being stuck in 1952. The situation was getting worse by the minute. At this rate they may never see home again. Daniel took a deep breath and with nothing to lose, told the whole truth to Mrs. Bennett. He told her of all the stories he had heard through Mr. Crosby. Craig, who by this time had regained his composure said, "Yes it's all true. When my sister and I moved to the house we found the Summerhouse and the book . . . "

At that point Mrs Bennett asked, "What book? May I see this book?"

She had suddenly become almost excited, intrigued. "I'll go and get it." said Craig, leaving quickly.

In the Summerhouse the book was the only thing left, everything else that had been there was gone! On his return he handed the book to her. She smiled for the first time. She opened it thoughtfully, she smiled as she looked through the pages, it was as though she had seen it before, "People like you . . . and once . . . I . . . passed through from one time to another."

All looked at her with open mouths. She gently ran her fingers over the open pages and said, "You have been honest with me, and I thank you for that, but I did have to make sure." She continued, "You see, I know it can do these things, because I also have used the Summerhouse for . . . shall we say holidays."

All four listened with deep interest, and she carried on. "When my husband, Alfred, was alive and we moved to this house, the Summerhouse came with it, and this book. However on one of our adventures the book and key disappeared. We don't know how. Years later a good friend of mine and I covered the wall with a false one to keep its secret hidden."

Daniel coughed so he could interrupt her and ask a question. "Sorry, but could I ask you to tell us more about the Summerhouse. All we know is what we read inside the book and that we got here. Other than that we don't know a lot."

Mrs. Bennett laughed, "That's obvious. Let me tell you all about the Summerhouse, the good and the pitfalls."

"Pitfalls! What pitfalls?" asked Craig.

"Yes pitfalls, but let's go one step at a time shall we, from the beginning. There were several cottages built, by Benedictine monks, who lived in a local monastery. They lived a self-contained life, and the only contact with the outside world were the cottages they built. Each year the Monks built a cottage for the three big landowners, for their farm workers to live in. Why some were fitted with the Green Man and the dials I don't know. On the dials in Latin are inscribed the words, 'The Brotherhood of the Green Stone.' The wooden frame of the cottages was made from thousand year old oak trees, and the walls were made from local stone. The green stones in the dials are a mystery. Another good friend of mine, who is an expert on stones, said they were not glass, not emeralds either." She paused, then continued. "The Monks used the money from the sale of the cottages to pay local workman to carry out building work on the Monastery . . . Stone masons mostly. As time went on things changed, and eventually many years later these few cottages were knocked down to make way for new, better houses. Only two survived, including this one, as far as we are aware. Why the Green Man and dials were made and who installed them no one knows, only that they are here and they work as a gateway to another time." She paused and thought for a moment, "Although we did hear on one of our journeys that a fellowship of brothers found the rock, an elder who was a wise man and mathematician, developed the dials and time travelling device."

She sat back and looked at the young faces, as they sat quietly digesting all that they had been told. It felt good for her to unload the secrets she had kept for so long.

Hollie, Alex, Craig and Daniel sat transfixed. She continued. . . . "The other surviving house belongs to a solicitor and antique shop owner, Mr Coombs. He lives just up the road and I believe he knows his Summerhouse's secrets. However I am sure he is unaware that this one has the same power."

Daniel and Craig were now starting to see that time travel was not going to be plain sailing.

Mrs Bennett carried on with her lecture, "Earlier I said that there were pitfalls, some years ago when the original owner of the other house died, Mr Coombs was the solicitor in charge of the dead man's estate. In a position like that he was able to do almost anything. So when he found his client's copy of this book and worked out just what the house could do, he bought the house for himself. He started to use the Summerhouse for his own evil doings, and I think I know how . . . He possibly brought back silver and pottery that were in perfect condition from the past to sell as antiques. His shop has become well known for selling antiques of the highest quality, because they are in such good condition. It made him a fortune as well as his Solicitors business, a business driven by supporting criminals in the dock. Daniel, his son, now owns the house. Mr Henry Coombs now lives in St. Antonin-du-var, in the South of France. You can see there are people who will abuse the Summerhouse. That is why my friends and I planned on taking the secret to our graves, but as long as this man's son has his house I find it hard to rest. He must be stopped. He is as bad, if not worse, than his father. I am sure that the poor Monks are turning in their graves!"

Daniel stood up, walked to the window, then turned to his friends and said, "What do you reckon? Shall we stop this dude or what?"

Craig, Alex and Hollie stood and said together, "Let's do it."

Mrs. Bennett smiled, "That is very kind of you but his name is not Dude, it's Coombs, Mr Daniel Coombs. He lives next door, 200 yards up the road. He is a solicitor as his father was, and he still has his father's antique shop. I know much but can prove nothing.' Now then, you must all be hungry, why don't I make some sandwiches for you all, with a pot of tea."

Chapter 4

Mrs Bennett sat them all at the table in the kitchen. Craig thought, so this is what their kitchen looked like in 1952? Pale green and cream paint work.

Mrs. Bennett prepared ham sandwiches on a large serving plate and a pot of tea. All the crockery was in matching blue and white pattern. Mrs. Bennett looked on as the four tucked in, Alex's eyes bulging, as his stomach rumbled at the glorious sight.

She smiled as memories of her two sons came flooding back. A tear welled in the corner of her eye. Craig noticed this and asked if she was alright. "Yes I'm alright. Watching you reminds me of when my boys were your age".

"Do they live nearby?" asked Craig.

A tear rolled down her left cheek, and she wiped it away and replied, "I lost both of them in the last war. Andrew died in Africa serving with Monty, he and his troop were cut off, surrounded by the enemy for three weeks. Slowly, but surely they fought their way through back to safety, however, sadly Andrew was shot down carrying a wounded friend with only a mile to go to safety. I have his medal in my bedside drawer. His friend, who made it home is, now a policeman like his father, Harry. My other son, William, died in Normandy, one of the first to storm the beaches, but also one of the first to die, so many sons died that day! They were good boys. I'm very proud of them. It's just at times, I wish I had known them for a little longer. I thought life had thrown all the pain it could at me, until I lost my husband eighteen months later, he was also my best friend."

She swallowed hard, and paused then smiled for a moment, then continued,

"The doctor said he died of a heart attack, but dear Alfred was as strong as an ox. He looked after his health, worked hard in a foundry. He was physical fit. I believe it broke his heart when we lost our sons."

She wiped another tear away, then sat upright and said, "But we must not forget, that our freedom was at their cost."

By now their smiles had dropped, as they had never really thought of the impact of such a loss on a person. Hollie remembered an old man on Remembrance Day, and how she had avoided giving her money to the man who held a Poppy Appeal Collection tin. Now she wished she had not. Craig thought of his computer game, about how shooting soldiers during the war was cool. It seemed quite sick and pointless now. Alex however thought only of the last sandwich on the big serving plate, and who was going to get it!

Mrs Bennett brought out some homemade fruit cake, and each had a slice. Alex thought it was Christmas again as the cakes flavour exploded in his mouth. He had cheeks swollen like a squirrel, stuffed with, as he described it, 'the best cake ever', and proceeded to shower everyone with his crumbs as he spoke. This made Mrs Bennett roll with laughter, which brought a smile to everyone's faces.

Daniel helped himself to the last piece of cake, then suggested to the group, "So it seems to me that Daniel Coombs is probably doing as his father did, going stealing collectables from the past, to bring back and sell as antiques, he could put them straight into the shop window in mint condition and sell for huge profit. . . . He's got quite a scam going."

Mrs Bennett clapped, "I do believe he is, but it's proving it. He is in the legal profession and knows the loopholes. You would have to catch him in the act, but you never know how far he will go back in time."

At this, Daniel had an idea, "I've got it Mrs Bennett! What if we hide away in his Summerhouse, and then go wherever he goes."

Daniel thought he had got the perfect plan, but then Mrs Bennett replied, "Oh Daniel my dear boy, I do believe Mr Coombs keeps his Summerhouse very sparse of furniture or anything else, there would be nowhere to hide inside it. Apart from that it's always locked."

Daniel covered his eyes and mumbled, "Needs it empty for all the antiques and money, there has to be a way to get in and hide, because that's the only way we will catch him."

Then Craig stood up and held Hollies' shoulders, "Hollie remember your history. . . . The Trojans who built that horse as a gift and hid inside it, we could do the same."

Daniel looked puzzled, "I don't think our Mr Coombs is the sort who will take in stray wooden horses, and put them up in his Summerhouse."

"No he won't" agreed Craig. . . .

"But he might take delivery of a crate destined for his next door neighbour, who is out."

"That is such a good idea" said Mrs Bennett

"I could have a crate arrive marked 'fragile.' A friend of mine can deliver the crate, with you inside, and have him say it must go behind closed doors. We will have the crate too big to go through the front door, but small enough to fit through the double doors of his Summerhouse. Mr Coombs should fall for it, but I will stay out overnight, well pretend to."

Mrs Bennett paused for breath, and Daniel suggested, "I think Craig and I should be the ones in the box. In fact two boxes, one for each of us. Two of us in one box would be too heavy for anyone to move, and Hollie, not being funny, I'd just rather you stayed with Mrs. Bennett."

Hollie took this as a gesture of endearment and not male chauvinism. Alex folded his arms, looking at the ladies, "Well I suppose being the only other man, I had better stay here and look after the women."

Ben gave a little whine, Alex looked at him, "Yes Ben I'm here for you too."

Mrs. Bennett looked at him and winked, "That's my little hero."

Craig started to show with his hands, how big the boxes should be, we could mark it as furniture, which would account for its size, and their weight. "This size should be OK, with hinges on the inside, so we can open it and close it again. Craig and Daniel shook hands, and drew it out on a piece of paper complete with sizes. They gave the paper to Mrs Bennett.

Mrs Bennett got her coat put the paper in her pocket and told them that she was just off to see a good friend about a box. Craig thought for a second that she may come back with the police instead of a box. No he thought, she's too nice.

Hollie stacked the dirty plates, and took them to the sink and started to wash them up. Out of the window she could just see the road. It was quiet except for the odd car. She thought how quaint it was to see men actually wearing hats as attire, but she had to admit, it did look smart and almost macho.

Alex moved across to Hollie and asked if he could help, "Yes please, Tea towel is just there, you can dry."

Mrs Bennett had been gone a while when Alex started to dry the crockery and place it neatly on the table. "Do you think Mrs. Bennett will be long" asked Alex.

"No I shouldn't think so."

Alex nodded in agreement, "It's just that it seems to have been ages since she went."

Hollie handed the last wet plate to Alex and poured the water away. Alex turned and his eyes caught sight of Mrs Bennett walking back to the house, but she was not alone. Walking alongside her, pushing a bicycle, was a very tall man in dark clothing. As they got closer Hollies' eyes widened as she could just make out an unmistakable policeman complete with a handlebar moustache. Alex ran to the others waving his arms up and down, and Daniel tried to calm Alex down, "Steady on Alex, you'll take off in a minute."

Then Craig followed the direction of Alex's finger, pointing towards the front door.

The door opened, Mrs Bennett walk in, followed by the policeman, who left his bicycle leaning against the front porch. Mrs Bennett took off her coat, Daniel, Craig and Hollie looked on in disbelief, Alex found his voice and shouted, "She's got the cops."

Not a word left the mouths of the intrepid four, whose faces were full of disbelief.

Daniel stepped forward, "We thought you were our friend, now this" pointing at the policeman. Mrs Bennett straightened her cardigan and said, "Now this . . . this is my dearest friend, Harold. . . . I call him Harry."

"Hello son." he boomed and stepped forward and shook hands with Daniel, then Craig, then Hollie. When he got to Alex he said, "Cops is the American force, English police slang is Bobby, but you can call me Harry, pleased to meet you son." They shook hands,

"Sorry, it's just that I thought we were in trouble."

Harry laughed, patted Alex's head. Harry reached down to his ankles and took off his bicycle clips, "Mrs B and I have been friends for many years, her husband Albert, was a good friend of mine. Our sons fought in the war together, in fact my son is alive because of young Andrew's bravery. So when Albert died it was my duty as an officer and a friend to look out for Mrs B in her time of need. A close friend is worth their weight in gold, eh! Mrs B?"

Daniel, Craig, Hollie and Alex sat and listened to what Harry had to say with interest. It was a live history lesson in a way. For Alex it was boring, except he was amazed by the size of Harry's boots, which were enormous!

"When Mrs B first told me of the Summerhouse and its powers, I thought she going quite dotty, but some weeks later she took me on a trip to prove it. It actually changed my life. That is why when she came and told me of you lot I believed her."

He rolled on his seat and leaned forward as though to whisper, "I also know that Mr Daniel Coombs is not straight as an arrow, like a member of the legal profession should be. That is why I am here. If you can bring me the evidence I will arrest him. Your idea using boxes is quite a good one, maybe we could just go through that again?"

After much chat Harry left to see a man about the two boxes, it was arranged that Harry's friend would bring the two boxes by 4o'clock, on a truck, and addressed to Mrs Bennett. With Daniel and Craig inside, it would be delivered, to Mr. Coombs for safe keeping until her return. Mrs Bennett had said that Mr Coombs usually went to the Summerhouse between the hours of six and seven, so this would mean that the boys would have to sit quietly, for at least an hour.

Two hours later there was a knock at the door. Mrs Bennett opened it, it was Harry and a short stocky man. "Mrs Bennett, Constable Harry and I have two large boxes for you.'

"It's alright Mrs B, it's Bill who will be our delivery man." said Harry.

Bill walked in and Harry introduced him to everyone, then Harry proceeded to go through the plan again.

Daniel and Craig followed Bill to the back of the canvas covered truck, making sure that they could not be seen. Quickly they both dived into the back of it, in front of them were two boxes, Bill lifted the lids, "I got two crates as ordered, should fit a young man in each."

The boxes were only just big enough for them to get in, a bit of a squeeze but it meant that they would be held securely in position whilst in transit. Each would fit snugly onto the stacker truck for Bill to wheel it from the lorry to Mr Coombs Summerhouse. They got inside, and Bill closed the lids. They both sat there like sardines in a tin. Then they heard the lorry start up, and move the 100 yards down the road to Mr. Daniel Coombs house. It stopped, and Bill got out. They heard the sound of the garden gate opening, then the faint knocking on the front door. Bill came walking down the path with Mr Coombs, who had fallen for the story. He was going to let them into the Summerhouse. Bill with the aid of a plank, slid the boxes off the back of the truck. He then tilted one onto the sack truck, tilting it back and saying, "This is very good of you Sir, to let me put these in your shed till Mrs. Bennett gets home."

Mr. Coombs, with agitated voice replied, "It is not a shed. It is a Summerhouse. It will be safe, as I keep it locked."

Craig and Daniel were relieved not only that they were on their way to the Summerhouse, but that Mr. Coombs did not smell a rat! Bill had to take them one at a time, and Daniel's crate went first.

The journey up the path in the box, on a sack truck was not Daniel's idea of fun. It was more uncomfortable than expected, and more difficult to keep quiet. Bill made up for any noise he made by whistling, very badly, much to Mr Coombs annoyance, "Can't you can leave the box's here, it's out of sight from the road" asked Mr. Coombs,

Daniel realised that he was not in the Summerhouse, because he could just see through a knot hole in the box.

"It's very kind of you but ... "smiled Bill, Mr Coombs eyes looked to the heavens as he knew the little man was about to add another request, "It's just that if it rains, the pieces of furniture inside will get wet and on my delivery note it stresses that they must not be left outside, it's the finest Walnut you see. Isn't that the Summerhouse you mentioned? It looks as though this box would fit through its doors quite easily"

Coombs rolled his eyes, "Alright, alright, it can go in my Summerhouse. I have the key in my pocket."

A few moments later, they arrived round the front of the Summerhouse. The doors were opened. . . . Bill tilted the box once more, and rested it inside, "It will be quite safe here, and dry". Bill then went back for the box with Craig in, he brought it back to the Summerhouse, he put the crate next to the first. The doors were closed and locked by Mr. Coombs. Daniel and Craig waited a few minutes then carefully opened the boxes, breathed fresh air, and stretched their arms and legs. Mr Coombs, back inside his house was cataloguing the antiques he had stolen on his last trip. Bill returned to Harry and Mrs. Bennett, to report the progress.

"How did it go?" asked Harry,

"OK. The boys are in the Summerhouse."

Mrs Bennett put her right hand on her heart, "Thank goodness for that. Now all we have to do is wait; it's up to Daniel and Craig now."

Daniel and Craig sat in the darkened Summerhouse of Mr Coombes and talked. Daniel asked in a whispered voice, "Do you miss the city life?"

Craig almost laughed, "No, don't miss it, miss my friends though. How about you? What do you want to do? It must be great leaving school . . . being independent."

"It's odd, but for years I wanted to be older, be working and be independent, but now I have it, it's not what I expected."

"In what way?"

"A lot tougher, almost scary in a funny sort of way. Hope Ben's behaving himself this time."

Craig stood up and stretched, "Don't worry Hollie will look after him, I have a feeling she has taken a shine to you."

Daniel did not register the reply, as he was too busy keeping an eye on the house, where Coombs was counting the day's takings from his Antique shop.

For nearly a full two hours Daniel and Craig sat and talked until Daniel saw a torch light heading towards them, "That's our cue. Back in the boxes."

They did so with difficulty and pulled the lid shut. The keys rattled as the door was unlocked, and Mr Coombs entered. Mr Coombs had lived a solitary existence since his father died, he was not the sort of person that made friends easily, as a boy he had imaginary friends, because his overpowering parents would send his friends away, he was not allowed to mingle with the other children of his neighbourhood. He quietly talked to himself, much to the boys interest and good fortune as this enabled them to keep track on what he was doing.

"Lock the doors. Close the shutters. Now where's that spade . . . there it is."

Then the boys heard the sound of the dials being moved and set.

"Right now off back to 1948." he cackled.

Then he went quiet, and all you could hear was the sound of movement. Then he spoke again. Green light beams from the stones on the dials filled the Summerhouse, and penetrated the two boxes telling Daniel and Craig who were inside them that they had travelled in time yet again.

Mr. Coombs spoke, "It's dark. Good."

His voice became a mumble, and the boys could not believe that a person could talk to themselves so much! Daniel did wonder on Mr Coombs sanity and thought to himself, 'Do I ever speak to myself, No! I don't think so!'

The keys rattled, door opened, and he was gone. The boy's eased off the lids very slowly and peered out, they could just make out Mr. Coombs silhouette, as he crept up the path, towards the house. It was in complete darkness, in fact it looked as though nobody was living there. Indeed there wasn't. Daniel looked at Craig and whispered, "That's how he is doing it. He's coming back to a time when no one is living here, so no one can see him come and go. It's perfect. Come on let's follow him."

They crept out slowly, and followed Coombs as he walked out the gate and turned right. He was only lit by gentle gas light, coming from old cast iron lampposts. The moon was full, which helped them see their way along the cobbled path. The roads were empty of parked cars, as Coombs stopped by the local shop, he went in and Daniel and Craig pretended to peruse the evening papers, Daniel looked at an evening paper on a display stand. The front page heading was about President Truman in America . . . another smaller one about Churchill and European unity . . . another article about the progress of the newly nationalised railways. He looked for the date and said to Craig, "It's 1948 November 7th." Craig rubbed his arms and said, "I thought it was cold, wish I had put something warmer on now."

They both admitted that they hadn't thought that they may go back to any of the four seasons of British weather, which was very cold, very dark and a situation that nerve wracking. Minutes later Mr Coombs came out of the shop and started walking at speed further down the road. The boy's followed, keeping a safe distance.

Chapter 5

They had been following Coombs for some time when he suddenly vanished down a pathway, at the back of some houses. It was darker down this path, but they could still make out the figure of Coombs. He was walking at quite a pace, as Craig described it, 'A Man on a Mission'. Then he stopped outside an old shack. Daniel and Craig could just make out in the moonlight that it had brick walls and was of partly timbered construction. Outside were overgrown bushes and small trees, an ideal place to hide things. He put his spade down, and removed a tree branch from in front of the door. He picked up the spade, opened the door and disappeared inside. Daniel and Craig quickly crept closer, and peered through a broken window. In the darkness they could just make out Coombs, his torch light lit up his face and body, as he moved some boxes. Once he had moved them to one side, he started to dig. The boys watched, as after about five minutes, with sweat pouring down his face he stopped, got on his hands and knees, and started to pull at something. He pulled to one side part of an old door. Underneath was a shallow hole, inside each were six sacks. Craig and Daniel could not understand why he had been storing them there, then Daniel whispered to Craig, "This is where he's been storing his stolen goods, in the past where no one will find it!"

From the hole he pulled free a sack that clattered as though it was full of metal objects. He put it to one side, and pulled the half door back across the hole. Then put the dirt back on top of it. He put the spade against the wall, then replaced the boxes. Picking up the sack he left for the door. Daniel and Craig knew that this was their cue to leave, as they had to stay in front of him to get back to the Summerhouse first. Daniel led the way. Quickly and quietly they made their way back up the path to the road. They both looked back to see the silhouetted figure of Coombs leave the shack, placing the branch back to its original position. He turned and tossed the sack over his back, and immediately slipped on the muddy track almost falling over backwards. The boys turned and quickly walked to where the road bore to the left. They waited against a hedge to make sure that Coombs was behind them. Craig looked down the path and a shiver went down his spine when he saw a hooded figure further down the path, but he couldn't be sure. He told Daniel what he thought he saw, but Daniel had not seen anything. It played on Craig's mind for a short moment until Coombs came back into view.

Coombs was now hot on their tracks. He was certainly in a rush to get back to the Summerhouse, Craig and Daniel hastened their pace, Craig whispered, "He's in a hurry to get back. I would love to know what's in that sack of his. It sounded like metal objects, maybe silver."

They both shot through the gate, down the path and back to the Summerhouse. Once inside they jumped into the crates and pulled the lids shut, Craig murmured, "We haven't got any proof of what's happened."

Daniel put his index finger to his mouth, to signal to Craig to be quiet, even though Craig couldn't see him. From out of the dark came the sound of Coombs approaching the Summerhouse.

The door opened and he walked in. There was the sound of the sack being placed on the floor. Coombs cursed in a whisper, "Damn it, where's my notebook. I had it here. Must have dropped it on the way back"

The door shut once more, Daniel and Craig slowly opened the lids. In excited whispers, "Notebook."

Daniel looked at Craig as he realized what this meant. "Craig, he's got a notebook. He brought it with him. If it's so precious that he carries it with him all the time, then it must be full of his secrets and evidence of what he has been doing. This could be our proof. . . . We must get it before he does. You stay here just in case it goes wrong. Then get back and tell the others what happened."

"Watch yourself Daniel."

"Will do mate."

With that Daniel was out the door after Coombs. Daniel got to the gate and looked up the road to see Coombs with his head down shining his torch back and forth looking for his notebook. Daniel knew he had to get ahead of Coombs. Daniel thought, in this light he won't know who I am: let's go for it! He started to run faster and faster. As he got close to Coombs he passed brushing him slightly, "Sorry Mister! But if I don't get home quick my mum will kill me."

He kept running and Coombs mumbled, "Hope she does kill you. Damn kids, just as cheeky then, as they are now."

He carried on frantically searching for the book. Meanwhile Daniel had got to the path leading to the shack. He slowed down to where he thought he saw Coombs take a tumble on a muddy patch near the door entrance. In the moonlight Coombs fumbled and slipped about as Daniel searched for the notebook. Coombs got to his feet and brushed himself down and started to get closer once more. Daniel still searching for the notebook saw Coombs coming, the moonlight catching Coombs determined face. Daniel grovelled around on the floor using his hands to feel in the shadows for the book. Then he spotted in a clump of grass, a dark shape of a small notebook. He picked it up, and put in his pocket as Coombs approached with only metres to go.

He quickly hid in some bushes, and watched as Coombs paced up and down the path, looking for the book. Coombs quietly cursed again, "Damn, that's messed things up. I am sure I had it with me. I'll have to come back again."

Daniel headed off back up the path, powering down the street as fast as his legs could go. He raced across the road, he couldn't risk Coombs seeing him again. As Daniel neared the house, he bolted back across the last road, and jumped the gate. He only just made it, down the path to the Summerhouse. He quietly opened the door. Craig inside, prayed it was him.

Daniel opened the crate and jumped in. Moments later the door opened, closed, and Coombs stomping around as if in a rage set the Summerhouse in motion,

A glow of green light seeped through the crate. Daniel and Craig knew that they were back to present day. The door opened and Coombs stepped out into his garden. He turned and locked the Summerhouse door. The boys slowly opened the crate lids, peered out, and slowly climbed out of them, "He's locked the door", whispered Craig,

"I guessed he would," replied Daniel going to the window.

"Don't worry. The windows open like Mrs Bennett's. We will be out and back with them all, having a cuppa in a minute, soon as I . . . " Daniel stopped, "Oh! Great! he's only nailed them shut from the outside. We can't break out without him hearing us."

They looked at each other, and Daniel pulled out the notebook, "Well, we have till the morning to get out of here, unless Harry comes and gets us out. At least we have this."

He put it back, in his pocket, and the two sat on the floor to think of a plan of how to escape.

All was very quiet outside as they sat on the cold floor. Craig chuckled, "You must admit it is a bit funny. We have been going back and forth time travelling, and here we are now, stuck in an old wooden shed."

Then Daniel raised his index finger to his mouth, to signal 'quiet',

Daniel pointed to the crates, "Back in the boxes, Coombs is coming back,"

As footsteps approached Daniel whispered, "If it comes to it, you run and take this book to Harry, I will take on Coombs."

Craig quietly said, "You are a true friend, and thanks, but we go together,"

Daniel put the book down his shirt, and said, "You're alright Craig . . . for a city kid."

Then they both got back in their boxes.

The footsteps stopped, there was the sound of the door handle rattling and the lock opening, both froze and clenched their fists, ready to fight their way out. Hands took hold of the lid's, and opened them both at the same time, both boys jumped up, "Steady on you two, I've come to get you out, I thought this might happen." said a familiar voice.

Harry smiled at the two petrified faces, "Now follow me back, and be as quiet as church mice, Coombs is in his cellar."

The two got out of the crates, closed the lids and followed the policeman, now out of uniform and in dark civilian clothes. Within minutes they were back at the house. As soon as they got through the doors Hollie gave her brother a big hug. Daniel said with a big smile, "Do we all get one?"

Hollie stood in front of him, and gave him a bear hug, "That's for bringing my brother home safe."

Daniel unsure what to say or do, replied, "He looked after himself really well. We made a good team, hey! Craig?"

"Yes we did,"

After a few pleasantries, Harry asked them what they all wanted to know, "Well Daniel, Craig, what did you find out, what can you tell us and did you manage to find evidence on our Mr. Coombs?"

Daniel started to tell Harry how they went back to 1948, and followed Coombs and witnessed him bring back a sack full of what they thought may be silver goods, with more hidden in a hole in a shack. Harry listened intently, occasionally rubbing his chin, as his mind analysed all the information. Then all fell quiet, as Daniel finished his detailed report. He stood there feeling like James Bond crossed with Sherlock Holmes. Had he forgotten anything? Yes he had.

"Ah yes, one other thing, I nearly forgot . . . The evidence."

He pulled out the notebook, Harry's eyes lit up, he leafed through it, then shook the hands of both Daniel and Craig, "Boys you are heroes! I had my doubts about the whole thing, but you proved me wrong. Well done, in fact Daniel your report was so well done have you ever thought of being a policeman?"

"No!"

"You should!"

Daniel and Craig stood like grinning Cheshire Cats, while Mrs Bennett and Harry studied the book and discussed Daniel and Craig's report. After about ten minutes, Harry turned to the group,

"Mrs B and I have been going through what we have so far, and it seems to me in my professional opinion, that what we have is damning evidence alright . . . but . . . "

Everyone hung on that 'but', Harry's eyes scanned the faces of the group, he continued,

"But what we need is a little more. You see it's like this . . . How would it look in court, if I were to say that the only evidence that we have found, was by using a Time Machine, made out of an old Summerhouse, at the bottom of Mrs B's garden? And the note book only has a list of items, it does not necessarily mean that they are the stolen ones. I am quite close to retirement, but I don't wish to be forced out because I believe in Time Machines and Fairies at the bottom of the garden." he paused once more, "Daniel, Craig, can you go through what you saw again . . . in fine detail. Maybe I missed something."

Hollie approached Mrs Bennett, "I know this is important to you and Harry, and we all think you are wonderful, but we have parents who are going to panic if we don't get home soon."

Mrs Bennett ran her hand through Hollies' hair, like a mother would do and replied, "Don't worry Hollie, Harry and I can get you home at any time, your parents will never know that you were gone."

Hollie smiled, as she was reassured that it would be alright, she looked to Daniel and Craig, "Come on you, rattle those heads . . . We have a problem to solve."

Both Daniel and Craig sat with Harry at the kitchen table, and step by step went through the events as they had happened. Harry sat there soaking up all that the boys had seen, nodding his head ever so often, and making hmm, hmm, noises. Daniel finished his report again, and Harry sat back in his chair, "So you say that Coombs dug up the sack, put everything back and left the shack. Did he have the spade with him, or did he leave it behind?"

Daniel's face filled with excitement and replied, "He left it, fingerprints maybe". "Calm down Daniel." said Harry shaking his head.

"Even if it's still there, the prints will be no good if we can't connect him with the loot that is buried in a hole that is long in the past. Like I said before, evidence such as this will not stand up in court. We have to catch him with evidence here and now, and not in the past".

He looked at the boys and rubbed his handlebar moustache, "What we need is good rock hard, solid evidence that he is handling stolen goods, minus the bit about the time travel. If we could plant something in the past that is actually from the present, and have him steal it . . . and bring it back, we could nick him for theft without having to mention anything regarding time travel."

"Better still" asked Daniel

"Harry, would it be possible for you to check reported thefts over the past five years, so we could target Coombs on the job, follow him back to wherever he stashes it? Then you Harry, can say that you have had a tip off and give Daniel Coombs a visit."

Harry grinned, "That's very true, but, also very much against regulations . . . however on this occasion it might be just the thing."

Craig patted Daniel's arm saying, "We could then investigate his shop which is probably full of stolen antiques from years ago. I will see if we have any records of the thefts in the archives, and who knows we might be able to pin even more crimes on him."

Mrs Bennett clapped her hands and applauded him. "Bravo, Bravo, you could put the great Sherlock Holmes to shame."

Harry blushed slightly and replied, "Well Mrs. B, a Bobby's lot can sometimes be a happy one."

They both laughed, Daniel stood quietly thinking and Hollie came across the room to him, taking his hand in hers and asked, "What's the matter Daniel?"

He looked at her and squeezed her hand, "Just thinking about following this guy, it's all getting complicated trying to catch him red handed because we can't connect him with the past because no one would believe in time travel."

Chapter 6

The next morning all woke early and Mrs B cooked porridge. The conversation of the morning was full of the forthcoming time trip. Craig went up to her, stood at her side and asked, "When we were back in the past yesterday I thought I saw a hooded figure following us and yet Daniel saw nothing. Did time travel ever play tricks on you?"

"A hooded figure you say? . . . Like a monk?"

"Yes that's right"

Mrs B had an expression of recollection her face, looked towards the stairs behind him,

"Here are the others . . . Good morning, porridge everyone."

They all sat at the kitchen table and stuck into the steaming porridge, not a breakfast they were used to, but enjoyed. Craig did not mention the hooded figure again. Mrs B seemed to know more than she was letting on and her mind seemed to be on other things.

As the clock struck nine Harry knocked on the door. Mrs B let him in. He held a piece of paper in his hand and raised it in the air.

"This is the date I think he last struck locally, it means going back four years. The antiques stolen were very valuable and I have a good description. One item also has an inscription on it, making it ideal for identification."

He paused and then continued with a smile. "The notebook you gave me held a great deal of information, once I had unravelled what it was. It's a detailed list of what he has stolen. Which is probably in that hole you saw. Also a name and address of a dealer who he might be supplying the goods to. It also had a name of an accomplice who was stealing items to order then burying them in that building where you saw Coombs retrieve the stolen goods."

Daniel and Craig felt now that all they needed was one piece of hard evidence. Mrs B smiled and walked to her mantle shelf and took a clock down off it,

"Hold on everyone, I have been thinking that this is all too complicated, however I do believe that I have the answer. You need to find solid evidence on Mr Coombs so use this clock. Put it with his other stolen goods. It is inscribed to my parents and was a wedding gift so I can identify it!"

Harry drew breath, "Mrs B! That's planting evidence."

"Yes! But could you prove it?"

"No, that's why I like it." He gave a broad smile. Everyone loved its simplicity.

They grabbed their bags and the clock and once again everyone wished Daniel and Craig good luck as they made their way down the garden to the house. Mrs Bennett warned Daniel, "Be careful to set the dials right for the year, month and date."

Daniel acknowledged her advice with the thumbs up, much to Mrs Bennett's amusement. They entered the Summerhouse and closed the shutters. Daniel stood in front of the large copper dials. He set each dial to the date given to him by Harry, then he put the notepaper into his pocket.

Craig nudged Daniel and said with an almost grown up voice, "Once more into the Great Unknown dear friend."

"Who said that quote then," asked Daniel,

"I did . . . just!" Craig grinned.

Both crossed their fingers as Daniel pushed in the Green man's eye. A green glow lit the room. The Summerhouse moaned and creaked as the years flashed by. Then all was quiet as they arrived in the year 1949. Daniel turned to Craig,

"Let's call by that local shop again, to check out that we have come to the correct date."

"OK, good thinking, let's hope we are not too far out".

"Even if we are a little, according to Mrs Bennett and Harry we could spend days here and when we return back, no time will have gone by. I suppose we won't age either."

Craig looked at him with a broad smile, "Pity we can't bottle it, it would makes tons of money back home. Mum's forever trying to look younger."

They both laughed and cautiously opened the door. It was broad daylight.

"Oops" said Daniel,

"Our first problem . . . sneaking out without been seen. Can't see anyone. Come on, heads low."

They quickly ran, stooping up to the house, and pressed themselves against the house wall. Daniel listened to see if he could hear voices. He could, only the sound of the bird's morning song. He looked at Craig and whispered,

"I've got a feeling that it's really early morning, can't hear anything. Let's go round the front of the house." Craig agreed.

Out the front they found that all was quiet except for a milkman with his horse and cart.

"Let's go and ask him the time" suggested Craig.

The two crossed the road towards him. He looked at them with surprised eyes, not being used to seeing people up so early on a Sunday morning! "Good morning"

"You two lads are up early or have you been out all night and trying to think of a good excuse to give your parents. You can't use the excuse of being down an air raid shelter all night," he chuckled.

Daniel replied, "No we're are just out for an early morning walk."

The milkman looked at them with disbelief, "Can't say that I know your faces. You don't live round here do you? Looking at your clothes, I would think you are from America, but your accents are English.

"No we're not from here. We are visiting relatives. Do you have the time on you?"

"Yes it's 7.30."

"Thank you, we had best get on and leave you to deliver your milk."

"Yes, must press on. Have a nice walk."

They in the direction of the shop, and Craig said,

"That was close. He was getting suspicious."

"He might have Craig, but remember, we have done nothing wrong. Don't get so uptight! The only time we could be in trouble is if anyone sees us go back into the Summerhouse. That would be trespassing. Come on let's go and wait 'til the shop opens and look at a paper and find out the date. It's a pity we can't set the time of day we arrive at, but one can't have everything . . . as long as the day is close enough."

A while later when they arrived at the shop, a man opposite came out of his front gate with a dog on a lead. He closed the gate and smiled. Then they headed off towards the common further down the road. Daniel watched the man as he let the dog off the lead. It ran to the first tree and cocked its leg, the man lit his pipe. Daniel smiled to himself, "Is it me Craig, or is life in 1949 quiet and nice? Look over there where that guy is. Back in our time it's full of houses, this common has gone. People walk their dogs in a street full of cars." Craig nodded,

"That milkman could not get over our clothes. He thought we were American." Daniel replied in cowboy voice "Yep, he sure did partner!"

"But remember" he continued, "Its 1949, the war's not long finished, I suppose clothes and stuff are still in short supply."

"Guess so," replied Craig.

Then a voice from behind made them both jump, "What's this then?"

They both stood up quickly and turned. In front of them was a little man with half-moon reading glasses perched on the end of his nose. His hair was thinning on top, and he wore a white apron around his waist. Craig stared at his hand-knitted tank top, and Daniel could see his own face in the man's highly polished shoes.

"You're my first customers of the day. You two boys are up with the lark. What can I do for you?"

Craig nudged Daniel to reply, "Ah! Could we have today's paper please?"

The boys followed the shop-keeper in, the shelves looked quite bare compared with modern times, it was all simple wood selves but very clean.

"Here you are" the shopkeeper said, handing Daniel the Sunday paper.

Daniel instinctively gave him a pound coin. The shopkeeper smiled, "Sorry son, can't take foreign money,"

Daniel, for a second, looked confused, "Sorry my mistake."

Craig quickly rummaged for his dad's old wallet and held out his hand for the shopkeeper to take the money. The date was 4th November 1949, Daniel feeling disappointed, "I must have miscalculated the one dial,"

"Well not too bad. Only two days out." Daniel half smiled,

"But it means we have to survive two days." Craig's mouth dropped, "That's a long time, what are we going to do?"

"I don't know Craig, I set the Green Man as close to the day as I could, those dials are a bit stiff to get so accurate and Mrs Bennett did say that it could easily be a few days out, if we try going back a couple of days we could overshoot, and be worse off than we are now, we just will have to cope, and wait for two days."

Craig started to panic a little, "Where will we sleep? It will get very cold tonight, it is November after all . . . FOOD? What about food? We don't have a great deal of money?"

"A little"

Both now started to feel hunger set in, and there was a morning chill in the air, which reminded them of the end of the day, and a very cold night. They walked along the cobbled footpath deep in thought, Craig suggested, "I know, let's get ourselves arrested by the police . . . then they will put us in warm cells for the night and breakfast in the morning,"

"Don't be daft. We may . . . miss the meeting with Coombs,"

"I see your point, it wouldn't work."

They kept walking, heading towards the small town, although to the boys it looked more like a village. Craig sorted through the money they did have, "These are pennies . . . this is a half-penny . . . and this is a shilling . . . I think . . . We will just have to rely on other people being trustworthy and a bit of common sense from us both to get through this."

The boys headed off to the shops in search of food, all the time worrying about what they would do tonight, where to sleep, and how to keep warm.

They walked along the empty cobbled streets. Craig kept thinking how it looks back in his own time, black tarmac and parked cars, with the occasional big lorry thundering through. But here it was open, quiet, with the sound of sheep bleating in the fields in the distance. Daniel suddenly stopped, and stared at the grocery shop door, "It's shut, I should have remembered, back in these days most shops were shut on a Sunday, I remember my Dad telling me."

Daniel, with his head staring at the path moaned, "I thought we had it so well planned, but so much can go wrong."

Craig shrugged his shoulders and agreed, "Well, we weren't to know that being a few days out would cause so much hassle, and money was never thought of, as was our clothes. Let's face it, Danial, we look ridiculous dressed like this."

They both burst out laughing, and in unison said, "We sound like our parents again!"

The two lightly punched each other's shoulders, as mates do, walked back up the road. As they got closer to the pathway where Coombs had hidden the sack in the shack, and Daniel pointed out to Craig, "There's that pathway, I wish Coombes would hurry up so we can go home."

Craig agreed, "Oh yes! If it wasn't for him we wouldn't be here, I dislike him even more now."

Just then, Daniel heard a whistle and the sound of heavy feet running, "What on earth is that"

Then both Daniel and Craig were shoved in different directions as a man rushed through them, as if being chased by the devil himself. Daniel caught sight of him as he dashed down the pathway. 'It was Coombs!'

Daniel called to Craig, who had his head stuck in a hedge, "Craig it's Coombs! . . . He must have come here on this day too . . . come on let's go after him . . . this may be the day he actually nicked the stuff."

Then the sound of hobnail boots came thundering towards them. It was a policeman, with truncheon drawn and a whistle in his mouth, coming to a halt he looked at the boys.

"You two seen a man with a sack come through here?"

"Yes" said Craig, and pointed.

The policeman started running again blowing his whistle, a signal a policeman would give for assistance, however there were no other policeman near enough to hear him. The boys shot to their feet and followed in hot pursuit of Coombs and the policeman. Coombs darted into the old shack. In the distance the Policeman saw Coombs come out of the shack, he shouted, "No good hiding in there . . . Stop."

Coombes took off again and so did the Policeman. The boys stopped at the shack, dived into it and quickly moved a box, then dug with their hands at the loose dirt. Daniel had an eye on the door and ears listening out for trouble, "We may have stumbled on the time he actually stashed it here. All we have to do is put Mrs B's carriage clock in with his stolen stuff, put it back, and get the hell out of here."

The boys did just that, as they put the box back and were about to leave they heard voices getting closer. Daniel and Craig hid in the shadows of the shack, Daniel peered out of a crack and saw a man and woman, hand in hand walking by. He didn't listen to what was being said, but he did notice that their faces looked familiar. The couple passed, and the two boys crept out, Daniel whispered, "Come on Craig let's get back to the Summerhouse."

Craig looked back at the couple who had passed who were walking away from them, "That guy looked like my Dad, but younger."

"You are seeing things, come on we've done we came to do, now let's get out of here!"

They ran back up the path to the road, then quickly walked back to the house. When they arrived, they paused to check that the coast was clear, and darted through the front gate and down the path to the Summerhouse. Once inside they closed the shutters, and set the dials to take them back. Again the green glow filled the room, all was quiet as they arrived back.

They opened the door and went back to the house. They entered the kitchen to surprised looks from all, Harry said, "That was quick. We have only just got back in from seeing you two off."

"It felt as though we've been ages, and I thought I saw our Dad" Craig said looking confused.

Mrs Bennett smiled, "Yes you probably have, but you have come back right on the button. Well done. Did you manage to do the deed?"

The boy's told them all of what had happened. Harry said with a huge smile, "All we have to do now is catch him with that carriage clock and we have got him!"

Hollie touched Daniel's cheek, "You look tired."

Harry stood up, "It's getting late. In the morning I will see a colleague of mine and we will give Mr Coombs a visit. He has had his doubts about our Mr Coombs dealings, as I have, so would welcome a chance of catching him with stolen property. Well Mrs B, I will be off now but will return with news tomorrow."

They all wished him good luck, as he left, collecting his bike from the porch. Mrs Bennett turned to the others, "Well we shall have to sort out some sleeping arrangements for you all. There are two rooms upstairs, Daniel, Craig and Alex in one and Hollie you can have the other."

Chapter 7

That night all slept lightly, thinking of the outcome of tomorrow. Hollie thought of Daniel, Craig thought of his adventure, Daniel thought of more adventures possible and Alex thought of his Teddy Bear, home alone and Ben the dog dreamed of rabbits.

The next morning they were woken by Mrs. Bennett calling that breakfast was ready. They all came down the stairs to the smell of a full English breakfast. Mrs Bennett stood in the kitchen looking proud as the youngsters sat at the table. She served up for each, a rasher of bacon, an egg, a few mushrooms and toast saying, "I don't know what you are used to, but food is still rationed at the moment."

Everyone proceeded to tuck into the tastiest breakfast they had eaten in a very long time. Daniel commented that the bacon tasted better than back home. Craig was fascinated as he watched Mrs Bennett make a pot of tea, it was the first time he had ever seen someone make it with loose tea and a teapot. He had been so used to teabags that he had never thought of it being a great invention.

After a short while they sat back with cups of tea and full stomachs. Mrs Bennett and Hollie were washing up the dishes as Daniel and Craig discussed the previous day. Alex studied a porcelain vase on a shelf. He then peered out of the window to see Mr Coombs, he walking down the road to his car, carrying a large bag. He got in, and drove away. It was now nine o'clock, the morning sunshine through the kitchen window, made Alex rubbed his eyes as it was quite blinding. He turned back to look at the vase as Mrs Bennett came up behind him and placed her hands on his shoulders saying, "Do you like my vase?",

"Yes . . . very much . . . It's the sort of thing she likes my Mum likes, and I'd looking for, for her birthday."

Mrs Bennett smiled remembering, "My son, William, bought it for me, the Christmas before he went to war. It cost him his last wage as a civilian . . . then he was a soldier,"

She drew a deep breath, changing the subject, "Well, Harry should be here soon."

The others had left the room, to fetch their backpacks.

Alex turned to Mrs Bennett, "You must miss them a lot, and Mr Bennett . . . My mum said to me when Scott my pet dog died, that he would always be around as a friendly ghost. . . . "

He felt awkward because he didn't know how to say what he felt but continued, "Maybe Mr Bennett and your boys are here with you as friendly ghosts too, like my Scotty."

Mrs Bennett gave him a big hug, "Yes . . . you're quite right . . . In my heart they will always be."

Then the other three came in laughing. After Daniel and Craig described to Hollie how Coombes tripped, and landed on his backside, the room filled with laughter.

Alex looked at the clock, it was now ten o'clock, there was a loud knock at the door, and Mrs Bennett turned, "That's Harry . . . I know his knock."

Sure enough, it was, "Good morning all." he said with a large smile.

He went to the kitchen table and sat down, as all eyes fell on him, "Well . . . well . . . what happened? . . . have you got him?" Mrs B asked.

All went quiet then Harry replied, "Well I do have good news . . . and some not so good."

An air of disbelief filled the kitchen, Daniel and Craig sat down, as they saw their efforts being dashed in front of them, "Now don't get too upset . . . let me explain."

Harry pulled up a chair and sat down, as did Mrs Bennett and Hollie, with Alex standing next to her leaning on a chest of kitchen drawers, "I went to Mr Coombs shop at 9 this morning. I was hoping to find the carriage clock in his shop . . . up for sale, but I'm afraid it's not there, it must still be in the house."

"No it's not." called out Alex.

"I saw him this morning through that window leaving the house, he had a big bag with him.

"This means it must be there. Maybe at the back of the shop . . . we must find a way of getting him to bring it out front."

Daniel then stood up and suggested, "Why not let me go in and ask, I could say that I want a carriage clock for an aunt, or something."

Harry smiled, "That's a good idea, however . . . it's an expensive item and a lad of your age isn't unlikely to have such money to spend."

Daniel saw Harry's point, then Mrs Bennett had an idea, and suggested, "But if Daniel had a smartened appearance and spoke with a little more refinement, he could be mistaken for an older, public schoolboys, from up the road. They do tend to spend a lot at the shops. It's well known."

Harry agreed, "That's a very good idea Mrs B, but Daniel only has what he is wearing, which might cost a lot of money where he comes from, but here they only pass off as work clothes."

Daniel stood back smiling, "I'll have you know these are Levi jeans and a Ben Sherman shirt."

"Well give Mr Sherman his shirt back, and get a proper one, besides who wants to wear a shirt named after a military tank."

Mrs Bennett stood between Harry and Daniel, and put her arms round them both. She looked at Daniel, "Upstairs I still have Andrew's best suit. You are his size, you can wear it, as long as you pretend that you are Royalty . . . A young man from a posh school!"

The three agreed, and all of them waited as Mrs Bennett and Daniel went upstairs to try the suit on. All sat quietly. Hollie was very interested to see Daniel dressed in a suit, and Craig couldn't wait to have a laugh. Alex smirked, "My brother, posh! Never!"

After a while they heard them coming. The door opened and Mrs Bennett walked in, "It fits like a glove."

When she saw Daniel Hollie wasn't disappointed, and the others all agreed that the tweed suit made him look very aristocratic. Mrs Bennett asked Hollie, the only other lady in the room, as to her impressions of his new image. Hollie just grinned, "He looks yummy . . . I mean great . . . just great . . . looks the part."

Alex shrugged his shoulders and folded his arms, "Yes he looks the part . . . a spare part,"

"Take no notice" said Craig,

"I have to admit Mrs Bennett is right, it actually looks really cool."

Mrs Bennett frowned, "It's not too cold in that suit is it dear?"

The four laughed and explained to her that 'Cool' didn't just mean cold anymore. She took on board what they said with surprise. Mrs Bennett then went on to give Daniel a crash course on how to talk like a public schoolboy. He decided to base it on a typical Oxbridge type to help, if he let his accent slip Mr Coombes may get very suspicious. Daniel felt nervous and yet excited at the thought of tricking Mr Coombes into bringing out the carriage clock. He looked at Craig and admitted, "You know Craig, this is the first suit I have ever worn, makes me feel taller somehow."

Craig laughed and looked him up and down, "Don't get any taller or you won't get out the front door."

Hollie reached out and touched his hand, smiling, "You look like James Bond . . . Take care and Good Luck."

Daniel left for the shop shadowed by Harry and Mrs Bennett, who in turn were shadowed by Craig, Hollie and Alex. Harry had asked them all to stay at the house, but no one wanted to miss the action. As Daniel walked to the shop he looked into the passing shop windows, saw his reflection and thought Hollie was right. I look so 'Cool.' In his mind he practised his posh accent until he arrived outside the shop. He could see Coombs inside talking to another man, possibly a customer. He drew a deep breath and went in. He held his head high, nose in the air, and tried to look as though money flowed from his wallet. He browsed round the shop, picking up items, looking at them, then putting them back down, in a slightly arrogant manner, he was actually enjoying it.

Mrs Bennett, Craig, Hollie and Alex watched the shop from a distance. Only Harry ventured closer, until he stood on the opposite side of the street, and leaned against a lamppost, proceeding to light his pipe, which he had casually taken from his pocket.

In the shop Daniel grew impatient, as the man talking to Coombes could not make up his mind whether to buy a lamp which he had been looking at for some time.

Daniel thought he would never go when the man said, "It's no good, Mr Coombs, I will have to bring my wife in to see it, I just cannot make up my mind."

Coombs gritted his teeth and replied, "Not a problem sir, do come again and bring your wife."

The man left and Coombs muttered, "Bring your wife, and I'll shoot both of you . . . Wasting my time. . . . "

He rubbed his hands together and approached Daniel, hoping for better luck, "Yes Sir, can I be of assistance?"

"Yes please" replied Daniel, with his newly acquired voice.

"It's my Mother's birthday very soon, and I wish to buy her a present. But alas you do not seem to have what I had in mind, something for the mantelpiece . . . a small clock would be nice."

"Oh! . . . My word, it is your lucky day young Sir, it just so happens I took delivery this very morning of a beautiful Champlevé enamel cased carriage clock."

He quickly rushed to the back of the shop, and returned with Mrs Bennett's clock, "Here it is. Quite exquisite. An elderly lady died and I bought it along with other antiques from her estate."

Daniel looked at it and with a beaming smile replied, "You are so right, it is very beautiful . . . just what I have been looking for. Look on the bottom . . . 1880–William & Mary."

"Like I said Sir, only the very best from this shop, reasonably priced at only £85."

Daniel nodded and Coombs continued with glee, "I will just take it to the counter and wrap it up for you."

He turned and went to the counter. Daniel signalled to Harry. Harry knocked out his pipe on the lamppost and crossed the road. He signalled to Mrs Bennett and the group to follow. Coombs had just finished wrapping the clock, as they all entered. Coombs thought it was Christmas, as he does not normally get so many customers all at once. He smiled looking at them, "I will be with you all in a moment. I'm just serving this young gentleman. There you go Sir, and I hope your mother loves it as much as that dear old lady did."

Daniel smiled back and said in his normal voice, "Why don't you ask the old gal?"

He turned to Mrs Bennett, as Coombs mouth fell open, "Did you love this carriage clock, Mrs B?" and winked at her.

"Yes I did . . . Now Officer . . . Arrest this man he stole my carriage clock."

Harry stepped forward from the back, "Are you sure this is yours madam"

"Yes . . . next to the date 1880 my parents wedding date–William & Mary are their names I also have a photograph at home with my late husband standing next to the marble mantelpiece with this on it."

Coombs looked as though the world had just caved in around him as Harry asked him to accompany him to the police station. Mrs Bennett and the others all made their way back to the house, full of pride.

"We are so glad it worked, Mrs Bennett" said Hollie.

Mrs Bennett stopped walking, turning to them all, "Please I want you all to call me Mrs B from now on. Only my closest . . . handful of friends, call me that, and you all have, in a very short space of time become very dear to me."

They all were stuck for words, and also realised it was almost time for them to journey back to their own homes, families & time. Craig looked back to see Coombs being taken away in a police car with its bell ringing. On the pavement across the road standing under a tree, Craig could just make out the hooded figure again. He rubbed his eyes, but as quick as it appeared, it disappeared. Craig just shrugged his shoulders, "Me seeing guys in hoodies again."

Mrs B listened and paused, "He is not a figment of your imagination. I also have seen him. He has often been there in the background looking on, and I named him The Time Keeper. He seemed to pop up in our travels very often."

"Who and what is he?" asked Craig

"We never could find out. He never even got close, as though he would just keep an eye on what we were doing. Maybe you might get to find out more someday."

Once they had returned to the house Mrs Bennett insisted that she made them lunch before they returned home . . . Sausages with potatoes and broad beans with melted butter. It was delicious. She watched them finish every last bit of food, "I wish you could stay. It has been so long since I could fuss over young people in this house. Now it's time to get you all home as close to the day you left as possible."

Daniel and Craig sat and wrote down the years, months and weeks that they had travelled back in time for their journal. They all gathered their bits and pieces, then Mrs Bennett said,

"Before you go I have a little something for each of you as a memento of your stay here."

She looked at Alex, "For you my lad, you may have this vase which you liked so much, put it in your bag so it's safe, you can give it to your Mother on her birthday as my son did for me."

Then she looked at Hollie, "Hollie I would like you to have this," and she pulled open a drawer and took out a small box containing a beautiful pink broach, in the shape of a heart, "It belonged to my grandmother . . . She gave it to me . . . I do not have a daughter, so I wish for you to have it. A pretty brooch on a pretty girl . . . cherish it as I have, it's rather valuable I do believe. My grandma said it once belonged to a princess."

Hollie smiled and hugged her. Then Mrs Bennett turned to Craig, took his hand and led him to another chest of drawers, at the other side of the kitchen. She opened the top drawer, and pulled out a box. She opened it to reveal a silver watch. Craig was shocked. He did not expect a gift like this. Mrs Bennett picked the watch up and handed to Craig saying, "This belonged to Grandfather. My sons will not be wearing it and I want for you to have it."

Then she turned to Daniel. She handed him an envelope, and told him to put it in his inside pocket of the suit he was still wearing, "This is your gift as well as the suit. Please take it. It also is a quality suit and the envelope holds a secret that now only you will know. But I want you to have this also. It belonged to my father."

She handed him a pocket watch and chain. The back opened and inscribed inside was the name E. A. Bennett. Daniel felt lost for words.

As Daniel said thank you there was a knock at the door. It was Harry, he came in all smiles and announced, "That's that. We have him good and proper. After we raided the shop he confessed to theft . . . Well done. Without you four we would not have achieved this"

He reached into his pocket and pulled out some coins, "It's not much, but I want you to have these new shilling coins as a thank you from me."

He gave each a shiny new shilling coin, and each said they would treasure it, along with the memory of the adventure. Daniel asked Harry, "Why did he bury the stuff there under the door Harry?"

"His reasoning was actually simple, he left it there until he had a possible buyer. Then he would bring it back in the night. After all, he can't be done for possession if it's not on his property let alone his own time!" He paused, "Also . . . this is to be kept secret between us all. He has agreed, in exchange for leniency, to help set up the man who took on a lot of his stolen goods. The gentleman in question is the head of a big ring, dealing in stolen antique furniture and goods."

Daniel and Craig weren't so sure about that, "But Harry does this mean he's going to get off lightly?"

"No not quite, you see no one would believe him how he got the goods, until I told him I knew his secret, I had a quiet chat with him and said, that in exchange for organising the set up with the other crook, I wanted the Summerhouse dismantled and moved to a secret location, whilst he was doing time for theft."

Mrs B was very pleased and asked, "Harry, What's the location?"

"My back garden! I have a builder friend who will help my son and I dismantle it and move it. Except I will wall up the dials, with his copy of the book. Of course, moving it may affect its powers, or maybe not and one day someone may find it"

All agreed it was for the best, and a great result. They studied their coins as they all made their way to the Summerhouse for the final farewell. Each shook hands with Harry, and Mrs Bennett had an abundance of hugs and kisses. Mrs B took Daniel's hand and held it firmly but gently as she remarked, "You remind me of one of my son's,"

And turning to Craig, "And you are like the other."

Then she turned to Hollie, "Hollie you are like the daughter I never had."

Finally, she turned to Alex, "These are for you." She said handing him a box. He opened it and saw the most beautifully detailed lead soldiers, fifteen of them, "They were my youngest son's. I'm sure he would have liked you to have them."

Alex was speechless, and hugged her. She had tears in her eyes as the doors of the Summerhouse closed on the four. Hollie closed the shutters and Craig made sure the doors were tightly shut. Alex peeped inside his back pack, and admired the vase from Mrs Bennett. Daniel carefully set the dials and Craig placed the eye in the socket. They felt a little sad at leaving, but glad to be heading back home.

Chapter 8

The green light of the dials filled the room, as the light went off, all was quiet, they were home.

"Look, there's Dad at the same window" pointed Hollie.

They all headed off to the house, and Craig asked the group, "Anyone want a cupper,"

All grinned nodding yes, "Great . . . pity it won't be one of Mrs B's, but I'm sure Hollie picked up a few tips from her . . . eh Hollie?"

"I might have known you would say that . . . Yes OK I'll be Mother."

The four had bonded a lot through their ordeal but to Simon and Shirley they had only walked down to the Summerhouse and back.

Simon turned to Shirley, "Look at them . . . They walk one hundred yards to the old Summerhouse and back . . . and look at their faces . . . they're worn out . . . no stamina kids of today. When I was their age Samuel and I were out every day and would walk miles. Remember I told you a friend had lived in this house?"

Shirley looked at her husband and replied, "Yes you did say dear. Must bring back some memories? So what did you two get up to? No good knowing you."

"No, we behaved ourselves . . . mostly."

Then Hollie called up the stairs, "Tea all?"

"Yes please darling. See Simon, they're making us a cup of tea, isn't that sweet?"

"Since when have they been in the habit of making tea? OK you're right they're still kids . . . growing up . . . What they need, Shirley, is an active holiday, doing things, adventure . . . better still, stripping this wallpaper off for me!"

Hollie made tea, and the four sat at the kitchen table, for what Daniel called the team debrief. Simon and Shirley sat upstairs discussing the décor.

Daniel started the brief, "I think we all appreciate what has happened, and what we achieved for Mrs B. but it was not without a lot of risk. What would happen if one of us had been injured or even killed? We are delving into a dangerous world. We really should think hard about we are doing, I mean to say, what would your Mum and Dad say if they knew? And the fact it's all happening in their back garden!'

Craig and Hollie looked at each other, knowing full well that their parents indeed would be angry to say the least. Daniel ran his fingers through his hair, sighed and continued, 'What we need to discuss now is . . . If we do it again . . . we must go properly prepared with provisions, and a plan. Let's research the time we are going back to first . . . Well what do you all think?"

Hollie was still thinking of her parents and what they might say if they found out about their exploits, but with mixed emotions she also thought of the excitement they had encountered and replied, "I say yes, Alex and I were left out a bit on the last adventure. We should play a bigger role this time . . . What do you think, Alex?"

"I agree with Hollie. I may be smaller and Hollies' a girl, but that doesn't mean we can't do as much . . . "

"I may be a girl but I can run just as fast as you boys . . . "

Craig smiled at his sister's boast, but in the back of his mind flowed the thoughts of confused loyalties, part of him wanted to be true to his parents and tell the truth and the other part wanted to keep all a secret, just for the four of them to know and experience, "That's my Hollie . . . Yes Daniel let's all plan this one and all play a part . . . Hollie is a wiz in the Library, so she could do the research. Alex and Daniel know a little about the local people and gossip, so you two will be useful that way. As for me, I will go to the local Museum for information. Before we do all this we need to pick a year, and reason for going."

Daniel admired how Craig took control then added, "We'll put Craig in charge? You sure can organise. Our target could be to find

Mr and Mrs Crosby who went missing. I remember Mr Crosby telling me about the couple who had the house just before them. Their son went missing, without a trace. The police believed he was abducted, not for ransom though . . . the parents waited a long time before selling up. It was all very sad, and Mr Crosby said he was my age at the time . . . and his name was George."

Hollie replied softly, "How very sad, poor parents. Imagine never knowing what happened to your child."

To change the mood Craig clapped his hands together once and announced, "Right those are our targets. Let's split up and go and see what we can find out today. Meet back here tomorrow morning at ten."

"Why ten" asked Daniel,

"Don't you want a lie in after what we've been up to, over the past fifty odd years!"

They both laughed, and Daniel and Alex left to find out as much as they could about George and the Crosby's. Craig and Hollie told their parents that they were off out. Simon looked quite shocked when Craig said he was going to the museum to do research. He told Shirley,

"Craig's going to do research at a museum? . . . Well, who would have thought?"

Craig and Hollie left, eager to explore the past, this was turning into the best school holiday ever.

Craig walked into the museum and started to digest all that was there, jotting down notes in his notebook. Hollie meanwhile sat at a computer in the library looking through the local history archives. Daniel and Alex visited everyone that they knew in the neighbourhood, and asked about George, and what they knew about the Crosby's

When they all got to their homes they got out their gifts from Mrs B and put them away safely. Alex unpacked his vase and hid it in his wardrobe, ready for his mother's birthday. Daniel hung the suit in his wardrobe. Hollie put her pink broach in her jewellery box which was full of costume jewellery once owned by her Gran. Craig proudly wrapped his watch in some tissue paper and put it in his top drawer. That night each dreamed of yet another trip in the Summerhouse.

The next morning they sat at Craig and Hollies' kitchen table, mugs of tea that Hollie had just made were placed in front of them. Simon and Shirley were in the same room as the day before, painting the walls and woodwork. Craig addressed his mates, "Well, who's going first? Daniel let's hear from you, what did you manage to find out about the young boy George and the Crosby's."

Daniel pulled out a piece of paper with the notes he had made, and started to read them out. He paused for a second, "Well as for George, no one can seem to remember exactly when he disappeared other than it was around June, 18 years ago. He was 7 years old. As for the Crosby's they vanished 10 years ago when I was 7 or 8. They were in their early sixties."

"Well that's a start. What about you Alex?" asked Craig.

"I talked to lots of people but I came up with the same info as Daniel. Nothing more . . . sorry,"

"Not to worry, Alex, you can't expect people to remember all the facts from so long ago. Hollie, I didn't get a chance to speak to you last night, what did you find out at the library?"

"Well, I found a news clipping about George with his photo. He disappeared on 8th June 1991. His parents were devastated, and he was never found. The Crosby's disappeared on 14 July 1994. They haven't been seen since. They had a son who died in the Falklands war."

All minds were ablaze with ideas, then Daniel said, "That's it then, let's go back to 8th June 1991 and try to find little George. He probably got lost in the Summerhouse and is stuck in time . . . somewhere. Let's get to him before he disappeared. Then again, it could be a wild-goose-chase. He may have been abducted. We can only try, and we have to start somewhere."

All agreed. Daniel and Alex went home to pack their backpacks. Craig and Hollie did the same. Daniel took an old werewolf rubber mask and put it in his sack. He thought it might just be fun to scare the life out of Hollie.

An hour later they all met up again. This time they had sleeping bags and warm clothing, even though June should be warm, they weren't taking any chances. They all made their way to the Summerhouse, making sure that Simon and Shirley did not see them.

Craig looked back to check, "Thank goodness the garden's so overgrown . . . saying that I'm off to the museum is one thing, but to say I'm off in the Summerhouse to another time would be another!"

They all stood in the Summerhouse as before and Daniel smirked, "I'm beginning to feel like Dr Who!"

He started to set the dials for the year and time, Craig slotted the eye into place. The pale green light filled the room. Shaking took over for a few seconds when it stopped Hollie opened a shutter and peered out. Craig suggested that Hollie and Alex should go to the shop, to check the day's newspaper. They had to sneak out making sure they were not seen by the house occupants. As they got closer they realised that no one was home, this was a bit of luck. When they reached the shop Hollie went in leaving Alex outside stroking a cat on the pavement. After a few minutes she came out and tapped Alex on the shoulder, "Come on, let's go."

They started walking back to the house and Alex asked, "Well Hollie are we in the right time?"

"Yes, nearly, it's the 7th, let's get back to tell the others."

They started to jog back. When they had jogged back to the Summerhouse and told Craig and Daniel that it was the 7th June, Hollie suggested, "As soon as we see little George we tell him somehow not to play in here and then get out of here ourselves . . . I have a bad feeling about all this because maybe changing things that have already happened, or something!" She looked to the ceiling confused, wondering if what she had just said made sense.

Craig and Daniel agreed that it could get out of hand and that they should leave as soon as possible. For the next five hours they stayed in the Summerhouse, waiting for little George and his parents to come back.

They all sat cross legged on the floor and chatted the hours away. Hollie and Craig told of life in the city and Daniel of his past school years. Alex admitted to being bullied at school by a gang of boys.

Hollie was very concerned and angry and moved across the floor to give him a hug. Craig and Daniel agreed that it was something they would have to put right. Daniel asked, "Why haven't you told me before?"

Alex looked sheepishly at him and replied. "I didn't want to seem weak. I want to be like you."

Daniel felt honoured and yet guilty that he hadn't noticed the signs of bullying. The time passed quite quickly as secrets and anecdotes were discussed. A few minutes before six o'clock Hollie saw movement at the house. They were back. Craig had been thinking for a long time. He put his hands over his face and moaned. "What's wrong Craig." asked Daniel.

"I have just had the most awful thought. We could just make things worse."

Hollie, Alex and Daniel looked confused, "How? . . . Why?"

Craig gathered himself and started to explain his theory, "If we stop little George and he never goes missing, his parents will probably never move away. If they don't move away, when we go back to our time, Mr and Mrs Crosby wouldn't have lived here, and we won't have a home because this house may still be occupied by George and his parents."

Hollies' face dropped at the thought of not living near Daniel. Daniel had an idea, "Hold on, all we have to do is stop him from using the Summerhouse, and somehow give them a reason to move."

All nodded in agreement, and Daniel continued, "If we scare him enough so he wouldn't come to the Summerhouse again, then just, maybe, the thought of goblins and goolies at the bottom of the garden might just be enough for them to want to move. We are taking a great leap of faith here. We may even have to come back months ahead of now to make sure that that Mr and Mrs Crosby do move in."

Hollie understood but replied, "Well, let's not get ahead of ourselves."

"No, let's not." replied Craig. "One step at a time."

Daniel pulled out the rubber mask and put it on, he looked at Hollie, she jumped, "Big improvement, Daniel. It suits you."

As they were discussing the possibilities of it working, the Summerhouse was filled with the green glow and all looked at each other to see if either had touched the Green Man. Then all eyes fell on Alex, he held his hands in the air and said, "Don't look at me, I didn't do anything." Indeed no one had.

Then two strangers appeared in the corner of the Summerhouse, Daniel stood amazed,

"Beam me up Scottie, it's the Crosby's."

Mr Crosby looked at them and smiled, "Hello . . . let me guess you have used the Summerhouse too! How you have grown Daniel!"

They all introduced themselves. The couple told the four how they had returned to pick up something from the house. They were shocked to find that they had undershot the point in time they needed. Daniel then realised that this could be how little George disappeared. He explained,

"If you came back, thinking that this was the day you left, it's possible that George may have come in here whilst you went to the house. So when you saw that other people were there, you would have returned to the Summerhouse, to go back to the right time and see your son. But you would have been unaware of George being in the Summerhouse, then taken him with you by accident. Is that possible, Mr Crosby?"

"Yes, very confusing, but I do . . . sort of," replied Mr Crosby.

Daniel went onto explain, "That could explain how George went missing, and why you disappeared."

They then went on to explain their plan to scare George into not playing at the Summerhouse. Giving his parents the reason to move, so Craig and Hollie would return to the house with their parents still in it. Mr and Mrs Crosby went on to tell them that their quest to alter the past, to save their son had failed. Mrs Crosby explained, "Some things in life are just meant to be. If we assume that George was taken accidentally then scaring him might just work, put things back to how they should be. George with his parents, and you two back with yours at this house, in your own time. But you must remember there are no guarantees."

The sun had by now cast long shadows over the garden and the Summerhouse. Noises could be heard coming down the path towards them.

It was George holding a plastic sword, "I am St. George, and I have come to fight the dragon of the night."

Daniel whispered to the group, "Right that's my cue to be one hell of scary dragon."

He put on the mask, which nearly scared the life out of Mrs Crosby. He went on all fours in front of the door, the handle turned and George appeared. Daniel roared loudly, George with eyes wide open, screamed and dropped his sword. With hands and arms flailing around, he ran back up the path to the house.

Daniel closed the door quickly, "Right let's get out of here before his dad comes."

Then he set the dials to take them all back home. Mr and Mrs Crosby did not want to leave with them.

Daniel asked, "Why not?"

"Because we now have a life in another time, and that's where we want to return to. . . . "

He smiled and put his arm around his wife and continued, "Our time travelling is now at an end, we are too old for gallivanting around, the adventure belongs to you now. Keep the secrets to yourselves. Some would use it for selfish and evil reasons, respect the power of the Summerhouse. When we get back to our home I will destroy our copy of the key, making yours the only one left."

Craig put the eye, his key in place, sending the house back to their time, their home and parents. The Crosby's reset the dials and went to the time that they wanted.

Hollie walking up the path stopped, looked at Craig, "Mum and Dad might not be here! We are not positive that scaring George had worked, they might not be here! I am scared!"

Daniel reassured her, even though he didn't feel assured himself, "It will be alright Hollie . . . I hope!"

As they got to the kitchen window they saw two strange people in the kitchen, "Oh no! where's Mum and Dad?" asked Craig.

Without thinking they all burst into the kitchen, each panicking, filled with fright with the horrible thought that they had changed the past and their future. All stood speechless, the strange couple sat bolt upright and glared at the four.

A voice Hollie and Craig recognised, came from the corridor, "Craig, Hollie is that you two." It was their Mother.

She walked into the kitchen, oblivious of the panic in front of her, "This is Mr and Mrs Hazeldene from the local church, they have come to wish us well in our new home . . . isn't that sweet? These are our children Craig and Hollie, and these are their friends Daniel and Alex."

All four gave a forced smile and hand wave, then Mr Hazeldene spoke, "It's very nice to meet you all, I trust that we will see these nice young people in church one day soon."

They were stuck for words, but then Mrs Hazeldene nudged her husband and said, "Take no notice children, he's what they call these days winding you up."

She then turned her attention to Shirley and said, "We are so please that new people have moved into this house, because for quite some time we thought it would never sell . . . Well with the stories, and the other people leaving so quickly."

Simon replied, "I thought the price was very reasonable because of the décor and all the work that it needed, like the Amazon jungle out the back."

Mrs Hazeldene raised her hand as though to shake hands with the almighty, "That's very apt, as it was in the back garden it was seen. The whole family we were told saw it, an abomination of this earth our vicar was led to believe."

Simon and Shirley looked at each other in horror, each thinking the worst. "What happened?" asked Shirley.

"In the garden one night their son was frightened by what can only be described as an evil creature. The parents saw something from the kitchen window and went to investigate after calming their son down, and found evidence of disturbance in the garden.

"What had the boy seen?" asked Simon.

"The poor child described it to be a werewolf, and ever since that night there have been twenty or more sightings. Many of them in this road. When the Crosby's moved in the sightings seemed to stop, but when they vanished, no one knew what to think. The house was vacant for years while relatives were tracked. There were none, but that is why the poor house and garden are in such a state! I have heard that a large black cat has also been seen on the other side of the hills. All very strange, but true."

The intrepid four now felt they knew the werewolf quite well, then Mr Hazeldene continued where his wife had left off.

"It's all true, but no sightings in the last twelve months. I know it was at least twelve months, because it was around the time The Prince Of Wales public house closed down."

By now the four felt it was time to leave the kitchen. They said goodbye and moved back outside, and burst out laughing.

Daniel lightly punched Craig on the shoulder, "Well Craig, it worked!"

Craig replied with a straight face, "Do you need a shave, or is the moon coming out again!."

Hollie turned to face Daniel, squeezed his cheek and said, "He does need a little shave . . . but it does make you look hunky." Daniel blushed.

They all sat on the grass, with mixed emotions of relief, joy and a little sadness of the friends they had left behind. Ben, went up to Daniel and licked his face, he wiped it off saying, "Don't you start as well."

Chapter 9

The next day they all did various individual things and met up later, at 2 O'clock that afternoon. The sun was hot. Simon was painting the outside window frame of the kitchen at the back of the house. Shirley meanwhile was fitting curtains in the newly painted living room. The light fabric matched the cream walls rather well she thought, as she stood back to admire her handiwork. Hollie came in and remarked how much brighter the room seemed. She went to the kitchen and her mum followed. Simon waved from the other side of the window, splashing gloss paint over his nose. He carried on whilst Hollie and her mum sat with a cup of tea. Shirley sighed,

"I needed that cuppa. Your Father's thinking of fitting a new kitchen with marble effect work top, what do you think? . . . would be nice . . . new and fresh?"

Hollie could only think of Mrs B and how they both chatted whilst waiting for the boys to return. She remembered how the kitchen looked, although old, it was warm and comforting. Shirley could see that Hollie was dreaming and repeated,

"Well. Hollie wake up. You're on another planet."

"Sorry Mum, no I'm on this planet just in another time."

They both laughed and Hollie answered, "I think the kitchen should stay as it is. It's got character, warmth and memories."

"Memories?" Shirley questioned,

Hollie looked to the cupboards and could see in her mind eye? Mrs B reaching for tea cups.

"I mean it holds a lot of history. We shouldn't change that! Maybe just fresh paint in the original old colours?"

Her mum's face filled with glee as she went to the window, tapped on it, and called to Simon,

"Your daughter agrees with me . . . the kitchen stays as it is, old fashioned it may be but it's got character . . . like you dear." Simon's eyebrows lifted to the heavens and voiced, 'girls win again.'

Daniel and Alex arrived at the front door, Daniel rang the bell. The door opened, and they were greeted by the beaming smile of Hollie. Alex looked at her face gazing into Daniel's eye's and he walked past Hollie into the hall, saying

"Hi, Hollie, don't forget to breathe!" Hollie was oblivious to the comment

Daniel strode into the kitchen. Joining the others at the table closely followed by Hollie who was not doing a very good job of hiding her feelings for him. Hollie poured four mugs of tea. She quickly gave Craig and Alex theirs but took her time giving Daniel his, much to the amusement of Craig. Shirley had joined her husband out the back with cuppa and they sat on the garden wall enjoying the sun.

Daniel looked at the others in turn and said,

"We need to discuss what plan of action we take next."

They all sat in silence for a moment, then Craig replied,

"I say we use our knowledge to do some good. What do you think Hollie?"

"OK, but let's be careful with what we do. We don't want to come back to a right mess. I say we go prepared and equipped for any problems. Approach all things in a adult grown up manner. As Mrs B said, with the house comes great responsibility?"

Craig shook his head,

'Easier said than done, we should not be blasé about it.'

Daniel nodded in agreement,

"We should all agree on what time we go back to too! . . . and do a little research on the time we head for. As Hollie pointed out . . . go prepared"

Then Alex added

"Let's go back much, much further, maybe as far as the house will let us . . . We don't have to stay there after all. Hollie you're the History buff, what would be a good year?"

She could not answer. All sat silent. With so many eras to choose from, they had no idea how far they could go, only that they had the power to change history.

Daniel was the first to break the silence with,

"The legend of the Green Man goes far back but how far no one knows. It would be a gamble but maybe we can go back hundreds of years!"

They thought of various dates and events, but could not decide. However Simon was about to solve the issue as he entered the kitchen,

"Sorry guys but could I ask if Craig and Hollie could give a hand today?"

Craig and Hollie knew what was coming,

"I could really do with you two clearing the attic room out, I have to get back to work in a few days and I really would like that done, you made such a good job of the Summerhouse that I am sure you could do the same to the attic room."

They agreed and arranged to see the boys the next day. It was quite late when Craig and Hollie finished, but the attic room looked great, and it earned them some more pocket money. That evening they both prepared for the next adventure, however neither could make their mind up what year to go to.

The next day, all four met in the kitchen. They were all dressed for adventure in hiking boots warm clothes and jackets, carrying rucksacks of various sizes. Craig asked if anybody wanted a cuppa, but all were too eager to get on. They made their way down the path to the Summerhouse. Once inside they closed the door and shutters. They faced each other and Craig said,

"We need to decide what time we are heading to . . . Hollie have you thought it through? . . . When to?"

Hollie had been thinking of her history teacher who was a member of the Sealed Knot, an organisation who re-enacted battles of the Civil War.

"Well, the time of the Civil War always interested me. One of the first battles was fought not far from here near Lower Wick in 1642. Many battles were fought around here actually. There's a field near Tewkesbury where they say lush green grass grows due to the amount of blood spilt."

She pulled out the fact sheets that she had packed the night before and gave them to Daniel to study.

Daniel looked worried and said,

"Don't you not think that going into a War Zone may be a teeny weenie bit dangerous!?"

"Cool!" called out Alex, bursting with enthusiasm.

Craig explained to Daniel,

"She spent hours after school in the library working on it."

Hollie blushed saying,

"Yes, alright I'm a history nerd, but right now I'm sure you are all glad of it."

Craig added,

"Well we'll have to see about that! It should be OK . . . besides we have the ability to come back quickly if anything should go wrong."

"Well OK." replied Daniel.

Alex grinned at the thought of blood and guts, with adventure by the bucket full. He had a vivid memory of a film he once saw of the Civil War with cannons firing, sword fights and cavalry charges. Soon he may see it for real!

Craig went to the dials and set the date to 23rd. September.1642. According to Hollies' fact sheet that she had downloaded off the internet, this was the day of the battle at Powick Bridge. It was described as a skirmish involving cavalry, and this was an event that the four wanted to witness first hand. Alex was full of excitement, but the others felt a little apprehensive, although inquisitive. Craig set the house in motion by slotting in the Green Man's eye. The green stones glowed, a strong breeze filled the room. Dust seemed to rise into the air, as this time going back took much longer. The dials almost seemed to hypnotise as they gazed upon them. They stood transfixed. Then as the house calmed to silence, they looked at each other in apprehension.

Daniel and Craig slowly opened the one shutter and looked outside, their mouths fell open and eyes widened in disbelief.

The house had gone, the garden had gone and was replaced by an old cart, trees and grassland. Where the road had been was a dirt track, and in the distance deer could be seen grazing. Down the track they could just make out a few very small black and white cottages but no people. They slowly opened the door. Craig, Daniel, Hollie and Alex looked out in amazement. Craig removed the eye from the Green Man, placing it in the pocket of his backpack. They all took off their thick coats and put them in a pile on the floor; it was summer after all! There were trees everywhere and the bare hills reached for the sky from a thick forest and woodland. The Abbey could just be seen coming out of the treetops that sang with the sound of crows, bickering in the branches.

They stepped out and Daniel pulled out his compass and map and said,

"Well this map is a copy of one made in the early 1800s. The lay of the land is the same, I reckon we could walk to our destination in under two hours . . . everyone fit?"

All replied yes except Alex, who asked,

"How far is two hours then . . . I've only got short legs."

"Not to worry Alex, only half way to Worcester."

"That's miles." whinged Alex, then Craig addressed the group as they walked,

"We had better make sure that we don't get spotted, because—let's face it guys—we will stick out like sore thumbs, won't we."

They walked at a steady pace taking in their surroundings. The air seemed fresher and the sound of sheep bleating replaced the sound of cars. The road was a simple dirt track trampled and worn by horse and cart. Hollie pulled out a sheet of paper from the inside of her coat pocket. It was a printout of history details of the battle at Powick Bridge. She started to read from it.

"On this day, sometime after four in the afternoon, a skirmish was fought between Royalist and Parliamentarian Calvary . . . around two thousand in number . . . one hundred wounded and forty dead." Alex's face went pale as he asked,

"Dead . . . are we going to be safe? . . . I'm not sure about this now."

Daniel replied,

"Don't worry Alex, we won't be taking any risks . . . well hopefully not."

Craig slapped Alex on the back and joked,

"If it gets rough we'll just have to leg it back to the Summerhouse and go back to the good old twenty first century."

Although they seemed to be going in the right direction Daniel was a little apprehensive as there were no road signs or landmarks that he knew. They made sure that they kept close to the edge of the road, so that they could hide quickly if they should need to. Not knowing how they would be received by the local people was a big question on their minds. Hollie turned to see the Summerhouse disappear into the distance as they turned a bend. Daniel's compass showed that they were heading in a northerly direction. The only thing he could recognised as a point of reference was the tower of the Abbey at the foot of the hills.

Still not a soul in sight, only the sound of a flock of crows screeching menacingly in a nearby coppice. Cattle and sheep roamed free whilst rabbits scampered around. Window shutters on a cottage close by creaked in the strong gusts of wind that blew repeatedly. Unbeknown to the group, the local population was actually very small as most of the area was dense woodland until you reached Worcester which was also smaller than it is today.

Craig felt quite uneasy, as did Alex. The scene resembled an old horror film . . . Where were all the people? They came to another bend and as they turned came face to face with a young boy. Alex stared, eyes wide, the boy stared opened mouthed. He looked them up and down,

"You're not from here, are you? . . . what funny clothes."

Hollie stepped forward to answer him.

"Hi!"

The boy looked up to the sky, then back to Hollie who explained,

"No we're not from here, we have come from far away, that's why we are dressed . . . funny".

She smiled thinking she had been quick witted. He looked at them questioningly and asked,

"Are you looking for work? . . . Because if you are, there isn't much. Most of the men have become pike men . . . soldiers. There's a rumour that there could be a war . . . ask my father, he's in the fields with my mother working, but they can't afford to pay for help . . . the taxes are too high, so my father says."

Daniel grinned, "Same where we come from, not much work."

The boy felt at ease knowing that these people agreed with his father's views, and yet they dressed as though not poor.

"Where are you going? You have big bags, are you homeless?"

Craig laughed, then went very straight faced,

"Well we're not homeless just a very long way from home. We need to get to Powick Bridge." The boy pointed behind him and said,

"Follow this road and you will come to it by this afternoon. It leads to Worcester, beware of soldiers though . . . dressed like that might get you in trouble."

They parted company. The boy went inside the cottage with the creaking shutters and the group carried on walking at a steady pace. They now felt unsteady, keeping an eye out for soldiers. All thinking, we do look odd, we stand out like sore thumbs.

Craig looked back to where they had come from and then forward again,

"Are we in agreement to carry on with this so called history lesson? I mean, our last venture had a reason. We helped catch a crook . . . but this hasn't got that . . . has it?" They all stopped and a few seconds later Daniel replied,

"Well yes . . . this hasn't got a real goal . . . it's just pure adventure with risk."

Hollie was holding Alex's hand like a big sister,

"We could debate this all day, there is one of us that is more vulnerable and we should consider him first."

Alex looked up at Hollie and replied in a firm voice,

"I'm a big boy now, don't worry about me, I can look after myself . . . well almost."

They all looked at his short stature but admired his beaming confidence. Daniel ruffled Alex's hair,

"Alex, it's not that you are young or small, but you are my brother, so I do have a responsibility to you."

"Are you trying to say you love me?"

Daniel winced and shuddered,

"Get a grip squirt . . . it's just if anything happened to you, Mum and Dad would kill me."

Daniel rummaged through his backpack and checked that he had packed his two way radio set. He showed it to Craig, suggesting that if they should need to split up for any reason then they would still have communication.

"That's good thinking Daniel, although I hope we don't get split up, that's the last thing we need, so far away from home."

Daniel slipped his backpack back on and replied,

"Well . . . this area has changed so much over the years you wouldn't believe we're in the same place, so peaceful what could possibly go wrong?"

Craig gave a half smile, raised his eyebrows as if to say, almost anything could go wrong. They had been walking for half an hour according to Craig's watch. He turned to look back and again he saw a hooded figure standing under the large oak. The morning mist swirled around the man's feet. The hem of his habit was wet with the morning dew. Craig looked to Daniel and told him to look towards the oak. This time Daniel saw the hooded figure,

"I see him, he looks like a monk! Or is it a hoody? . . . I don't think so . . . he looks harmless enough. Well, let's just ignore him for now and crack on. We have quite a way to go."

Craig agreed and asked.

"You have a better idea than me of the area, how far is it now?"

Daniel rolled his eyes, and breathed in deeply,

"Hard to say, I don't recognise anything, but I think we're over half way . . . we must be mad! Remind us why you picked this time, Hollie?"

"I didn't pick anything."

Alex was the only one looking ahead as the others argued over who chose what. In the distance he could see men on horseback heading towards them. He stopped and pointed saying.

"Sorry to 'butt in' guys, but we may have trouble heading this way on horses." Daniel looked and pointed,

"He's not joking . . . Look . . . Head for those trees."

They quickly headed to undergrowth to hide. As they dived into the bushes they were covered by the dew falling from the branches.

The riders got closer, and Craig could make out their clothes. They wore uniforms with brown leather coats, metal helmets, breast plates and knee length boots. The horses panted as they drew closer, nostrils flared and snorting. Hollie whispered to Craig, "They're Roundheads, I've seen drawings of them. They were led by a man called Oliver Cromwell who opposed the King."

The eight horsemen circled as if looking for something, then one spoke.

"I know I saw people here, they had bags on their backs, they were not dressed like farm workers. They could well have been the King's men."

"You mean to tell me." said another "that you're not sure? You have us wasting time!"

The horseman frantically poked at the bushes with his drawn sword,

"No . . . we were told to look out for a group of the King's men . . . and I saw people just here."

Then a gust of wind blew pollen dust up Alex's nose. He sneezed. Hollie grabbed him and pulled him to her, covering his nose with her hand, but it was too late. The one soldier spotted Hollie and Alex through the bush. He ordered them out. Hollie and Alex slowly crawled out and Daniel held onto Craig, signalling to him to stay quiet. Daniel quickly reached into his pocket and took out his spare walky talky and tossed it to Hollie. She caught it and, tucked it into her pocket without the soldiers seeing.

"Sir, I have them. Come on you two, out from there . . . You're not the King's men . . . you are far too small and you are a girl."

"No . . . we're not King's men. We are just out for a walk. You scared us, so we hid." She nudged Alex to move away from the hedge to ensure that the man did not notice the others.

"Where do you live? A small boy like you should not be too far from home."

Alex searched his imagination for an answer,

"We are not from here . . . exactly, we're on holiday!"

The soldier did not believe him and was not impressed, however he paused,

"Put them on a horse they may know something, they may not. They are not from here that is for sure. We will take them back to the farmhouse for questioning."

The soldiers sat Hollie and Alex onto a horse each, in front of a soldier and they all slowly moved off.

Craig looked to Daniel "What now?"

"Craig, Hollie has a radio. All we have to do is follow them and rescue them, should be easy. Come on."

Chapter 10

They got out of the bushes and started to follow staying out of sight. Luckily the soldiers moved at a slow steady pace. Before long Daniel and Craig were running from tree to tree to keep up. Alex was not used to being on horseback: he felt quite unbalanced and scared. Hollie hindered the soldier's progress by acting as though she had never been on a horse. In the distance was a farmhouse. Craig and Daniel stopped, and studied the lay of the land. Daniel turned to Craig and suggested they aim for a wood to their left, which reached down to the left of the farmhouse. They started to make their way through the trees down towards the farm. They could just make out the soldiers taking Hollie and Alex inside. Two soldiers stayed outside the door and five went inside, and one stayed with the horses which he was tying to a wooden fence.

Daniel and Craig got closer. Daniel pulled out his small pair of binoculars. Craig kept watch and looked around. In between some trees he spotted the hooded figure yet again. Craig nudged Daniel.

"I see him, he could be one of the monks from that priory. I wonder why he seems to be following us? . . . if it's the same man."

"Never mind now . . . Look, if we move down to those bushes and fence, we can get within a stones-throw of the house."

Craig looked back again and the monk was gone. They moved closer to the farmhouse, keeping their eyes firmly fixed on the soldiers keeping guard outside. They got within distance so that with the binoculars, Daniel could see through the window. He saw the five soldiers but no Hollie or Alex. Then a familiar voice came over the radio, in a whisper,

"Craig, Daniel . . . We've been put into a room with a window but it's boarded up on the outside . . . Can you hear me?"

"Hollie I hear you, where in the farmhouse are you?" Daniel answered

"We are locked in the first room to the left of the front door."

"Hollie. Craig and I are just outside. We're going to get you out. We'll call you when we have a plan worked out."

Craig nodded at Daniel signalling that the soldier who had tied the horses was on the move. He made his way to a barn and lay down on some straw, and pulled his hat over his eyes as though he was about to go to sleep.

"Right Craig, got any bright ideas how to move those sentries away from that door, and get in there?"

"Well, some sort of diversion . . . there are two of us. One creates a diversion, drawing them all out of there. The other runs in and gets them out. Then we use two of those horses to get out of here . . . Can you ride? Hollie can manage well, and I can. Alex can hold onto Hollie on one horse." Craig didn't want to blow Hollies' trumpet too much.

"Me ride? . . . I'm the original cowboy! . . . How are you going to create a diversion?"

"Give me the radio, and when I've got them away I will let Hollie know to be ready to leg it."

Craig pulled out the two bangers from his backpack, and with a broad smile said, "Let's party with a bang."

Daniel smiled back replying, "Wish I had thought of bringing something like that. But I didn't reckon on us having a party!"

Craig moved to their left, Daniel could just see him, and waited for the soldiers to move. The two sentries stood either side of the door and through the window Daniel could see the other five, drinking ale in front of an open fire in a room opposite the door where Hollie and Alex were being held, even though it was summertime there was a chill in the air of the farm house making the fire much welcome. The eighth man was in a deep sleep in the barn, now snoring. In one corner of the roof was a barn owl, quietly scanning the floor for small rodent it was irritated by the man's heavy snoring.

Minutes later there was a loud bang. The soldier in the barn jumped up so fast that he banged his head on the stable door and the annoyed owl flew out through the trees.

The two sentries looked at each other, then ran towards the sound. The remaining five in the house reacted by spilling their drinks, two falling off their stools and onto the flagstone floor with a thud. They groped around on their hands and knees for their helmets and swords.

When the sentries were about sixty feet from the door, Daniel dashed towards it. Craig called Hollie on the radio to be ready. Daniel ran through the door and lifted off the latch, unlocking the door to Hollie and Alex's room. He ran back across the hall and bolted the door to the room where the soldiers were, locking them in. Hollie ran into Daniel's arms, Alex ran to the front door and looked out to see Craig across the farmyard. The other two soldiers were running towards the tree line, with muskets in hand.

Craig ran for the horses, lighting the other banger and throwing it behind him. It landed in amongst the trees and exploded. This made the soldiers fire their muskets into the trees. Then drew their swords and charge towards the sounds, thinking they were under attack. Craig untied all the horses but held onto three, smacked the others and chased them off. Daniel, Hollie and Alex came running out of the farm house. Hollie leapt onto one horse and Daniel lifted Alex onto the back of another with Craig. Then Daniel mounted as the two sentries turned round and shouted,

"Halt!"

The four rode off as fast as they could, with one soldier running back to the house, and the other chasing the runaway horses. Daniel did indeed go at the gallop like a cowboy, which Hollie couldn't help noticing. Craig kept looking back to make sure that the soldiers were not following. One soldier had caught one horse, and the others were now out of the house, all trying to recapture the horses. Alex was holding on for dear life with his arms round Craig as they got further away.

Daniel rode over the rise closely followed by the others. Craig looked back and could just see the soldiers mount and galloping in pursuit.

Craig and Hollie were now catching up to Daniel and in front of them was the wood. To the left was the track to Powick Bridge, and to the right, over two miles away, was the Summerhouse.

Standing in front of the tree line was the hooded man again. This time he seemed to be signalling to them. He pointed to the right in the direction of the Summerhouse and a group of trees. Daniel steered his horse in that direction and the others followed. Craig looked at the monk, who seemed to be smiling.

After a few moments they pulled their horses into the trees, dismounted and waited holding tightly onto the horses. Shortly the sound of thundering hooves could be heard. As the soldiers came over the rise they paused . . . One soldier pointed left, they all galloped off and followed him.

Daniel sighed heavily, and Craig hugged Hollie while Alex watched as the soldiers disappeared out of sight. Then a voice from behind them called to them,

"They will be back . . . You must leave now . . . or face recapture."

They turned, and facing them, was the hooded man, with his head lowered. All four stared at the stranger. He raised his head slightly, so they could see only his mouth. His voice was soft, yet very clear. He was slight in build yet had the presence of authority, which captivated them.

"Who are you and why have you been following us?" asked Daniel

"I follow, to protect you and whoever you come into contact with . . . to ensure The Futures plan is respected" he answered.

"Protect us and them? We were the ones captured!" proclaimed Hollie.

"This is true, and yet you could have altered the course of their lives . . . or they could have ended yours. To travel in time takes Care and Respect for all living things, we are all part of The Future's plan."

He gave a little smile, then Craig asked.

"So are you here to stop anyone messing up The Future's plan as you put it. Who are you?"

For the first time he smiled, and answered,

"Yes, your quest here is full of folly. You must take greater care or refrain from using the Summerhouse. There is a delicate balance binding The Past to The Future, You have already used it to some advantage and had a man arrested for crimes. This I overlooked as it was for The Greater Good."

"I thought it may have been you I saw." said Craig.

"So you travel in time making sure everyone behaves . . . so to speak."

"In a manner of speaking. Yes." With that Craig started to rummage through his backpack.

Daniel addressed his colleagues,

"I think we should leave before those guys find out that they have gone in the wrong direction. All those in favour of getting back to modern times raise their hands.

Both Hollie and Alex quickly raised their hands. Being held prisoner even for a brief time, was enough adventure for one day. Craig still rummaging through his backpack, started to panic saying,

"Oh no, please no."

"What is it?" asked Daniel.

"The one eyed key for the Green Man is gone. I had it in my backpack for safe keeping. It must have fallen out when I pulled out the fireworks."

"We'll have to go back." replied Daniel.

The hooded man sighed and added.

"You must find the stone quickly or be stranded."

Chapter 11

After some contemplation Craig looked to Hollie and Alex and said. "You two must stay here, out of sight. Daniel and I will take a horse each and go and find it . . . Agreed?"

The hooded man nodded in agreement, and said he would take Hollie and Alex back to the Summerhouse.

Daniel and Craig mounted the horses and turned to the hooded man, to find that he had vanished. They looked at each other and Craig said,

"That guy gives me the creeps."

Craig and Daniel moved slowly, out of the trees to check that the coast was clear. It was.

They put the horses into a fast gallop, up the long sloping hill and over the rise and towards the farm. At the farm was the soldier with the sore head, recovering from head butting the stable door. Outside was his horse, tied to some fencing. As the two got closer they spied the soldier's horse, so they knew he was still there. Craig pointed to the horse,

"One soldier is still here." They pulled up their horses into some trees.

Their horses snorted and stamped the ground as they watched from shadows of the overhanging trees. The soldier fumbled for his helmet and sword belt, putting them on, then mounted his horse and made off in the same direction as his comrades.

Daniel signalled to Craig and they moved off carefully towards the farm buildings. They knew if they retraced their steps that they may hopefully come across the key. The soldier was now out of sight as Daniel and Craig pulled up on their horses in the farmyard. They tied them up, dismounted and started looking. Craig took one area and Daniel another. The grey clouds which had been building up for the past half hour, hindered their search by periodically blocking out the sun. The trees leaves rustled in the stiff breeze. Craig picked up a stick and probed under surrounding bushes. Daniel kicked at the ground in frustration. The horses shuffled in a restlessly.

Daniel took his eyes off the ground and looked around, all was still clear. In the back of his mind he was concerned that the soldiers would return. Both thought of life stuck in the 1600s as they searched the undergrowth. Not a pleasant thought! Craig looked up again and in the distance he could see riders heading their way. He shouted to Daniel. Daniel looked round and beckoned to Craig to run to the horses. Craig started to run and tripped, falling flat on his face. He felt like an idiot as he got up wiping dirt from his mouth. Daniel called.

"Craig hurry . . . I don't like the look of this."

Craig picked up the stick which tripped him up and threw it to one side. On doing so he spotted the key. He quickly picked it up, and sprinted towards the horses. Daniel had mounted as Craig grabbed his own horse, jumping on, shouting,

"I've got the key!"

"Excellent! Come on, we must get out of here."

They galloped up to the rise and over. Daniel signalled to Craig and yanked at the bridle steering the horse sharp right into some trees. Craig looked back, no sign of the other riders. Even so they kept the horses at a gallop, dodging in and out of the trees. They panted heavily and kicked up dirt as they raced back to the Summerhouse, pulled up and tied the horses to a tree. Entered through the doors, quickly shutting them behind them. Inside, Hollie, Alex and the hooded man were waiting.

Hollie asked.

"You two OK? you both look flustered!"

"Yes . . . why" replied Craig, panting, "We nearly got caught again . . . but managed to find the key, just in time. Luckily they didn't see us, I think . . . they were headed in the direction of the Priory . . . "

Daniel pointed North with his finger.

The hooded man looked concerned, "Could you see who these riders were? . . . How were they dressed?

Daniel thought for a moment,

"No sorry . . . we really weren't close enough, they had helmets on . . . I think."

The hooded man paced up and down. Alex looked to Hollie,

"I am starving, can we find something to eat?"

Hollie smiled,

"Well fast food café's, are out of the question."

The hooded man offered, "You could all come with me to the Priory, there is food there". Alex then asked

"Why don't we just go home?" Alex asked hopefully,

"Come on Bro, we've been in the Priory in the 21st century, let's see what its like now, might be fun, they might have roast pork on a spit, like in the movies.!"

The thought of this made them all salivate, although Hollie had reservations about not returning straight home.

The hooded man smiled and put his hand out to Daniel and said, "I am named Samuel".

He shook hands with each of them, when it was Hollies' turn, he lifted his hood revealing bright green eyes. The others got their bags together as Hollie exchanged pleasantries with Samuel. He had olive coloured skin, high cheek bones and long hair with trimmed beard. She picked up her backpack and they left the Summerhouse. Craig put the key into the side pocket of his combat trousers which he zipped closed. Daniel and Craig shared one horse, Hollie and Alex shared the other with Samuel. Alex was sandwiched between them with Hollie in charge of the reins.

They rode slowly towards the Priory, horses heads hung slightly low and hooves plodding along the dirt track. Everyone was tired, as were their mounts. It was a long uncomfortable way. Flocks of sheep roamed the open pastures, sharing with cattle who grazed without a care in the world. The clouds had cleared, the sunshine making the ride enjoyable despite the discomfort. Samuel was the only one looking out for danger, the others simply enjoyed the peace and quiet, just listening to the sound of the surrounding wild life.

In front of them no town or tarmac roads, just the Priory standing alone majestically at the foot of the hills. It had more outbuildings than in the twenty first century. They would later be replaced with a large hotel and shops, period buildings in their own time, but not like these.

They could see horses tied up outside. Daniel gave the order to stop.

"Those look like the horses we saw."

Craig agreed. Samuel suggested they go to the back, out of sight, until they knew who they were. They dismounted and waited as Samuel went inside the Priory to investigate. Daniel peered through the slightly open door and saw Samuel speaking with parishioners inside, between the towering pillars. The whispers seemed to echo around the stone walls. Daniel could see men near the large entrance door. They wore uniforms like the others and seemed to be searching for something. Their large boots echoed like thunder around on the flagstone floor in an intimidating manner. They approached the monk near the door, exchanged words in raised voices, and then stomped out and left on their horses. Samuel came back outside.

"It's alright the soldiers were looking for Royalist troops, not you . . . You hardly look like soldiers."

As they entered the Priory, both Daniel and Alex could not help but notice how different it looked, and smelled. Craig and Hollie were in awe of stepping into Living History, on their return they would visit this place again to see what changes had occurred in 400 years. The aroma of food came wafting through the air. The delicious smells made their mouths water. Samuel took them into a room and sat them at a large, dark, heavy oak table. The table was plain and simple in style and craftsmanship. The benches were well worn. Thick clay bowls were laid before them with wooden spoons. A wooden candle holder was positioned in the middle of the table with a candle burning with a bowl of apples, fresh from a tree in the garden. The flames danced and filled the room with a dim light as they all sat and a man entered with a large bowl of steaming food. He had grey hair and a haggard face. He slowly lifted his head to each as he ladled their food into the wooden bowls, greeting them with a warm smile.

"Hope you enjoy your stew. You are most welcome here."

He came to Hollie and his eye's sparkled as he said,

"You are very pretty My Dear. You remind me of my daughter."

Hollie returned the warm smile and asked after her.

"She died some years ago in childbirth, her first and last."

Hollie tried to brighten the conversation,

"Do you and your wife have any other children?"

"Sadly no, my wife died the very next winter. I do what I can here now."

Hollie didn't know what to say next, then Samuel said,

"Thank you David, that will be all. Let's leave our guests to eat in peace."

Craig whispered to Hollie,

"Way to go Sis!"

Alex was just about to start eating when he felt a kick under the table from Daniel, who signalled with his eyes towards Samuel who put his hands together in prayer.

"Let us say Grace."

They all lowered their heads.

Samuel then said a short prayer which they couldn't understand as it was in Latin, Samuel looked up and they began to eat. The stew had large chunks of vegetables and a little meat in it and tasted wonderful. They also had some bread which they dipped into the stew. It had quite a rough texture to it. Samuel slowly stood up and spoke,

"I hope you enjoy what little we have to offer. Some years ago we, as an Order of Monks, were forced to leave. Some of us returned later after the soldiers plundered the Priory. We had made many friends here, it was our home. When things had calmed down a little we returned, however it will never be the same again. No other monks will return. We just want to help restore what damage was done and maintain this wonderful place."

They all listened to what Samuel had to say whilst stomachs digested the much welcome food. Once finished, they thanked the man who had served them as he proceeded to clear the table. Hollie asked if she could help, but the man said,

"You are our guests . . . please sit and rest."

Hollie sat, and Samuel walked round to Hollies' side,

"I am pleased you enjoyed the meal. My brothers here are aware of who you are, however this knowledge stays within these walls. This leads me to a favour I want to ask of you in return."

Their faces changed, as they thought the worst.

Don't look so worried. I will endeavour to make sure you are not put in any danger."

They felt slightly more at ease until he said,

"I actually have two favours to ask of you. A task for Hollie and Alex, and a task for Daniel and Craig. Hollie and Alex, we have a man who is ill. I realise you are not medical people, but you could have access to such people . . . I leave that in your capable hands."

Hollie replied with relief,

"Well, we'll see what we can do. Is he an elderly man?"

"No he is only 27 years old, but has a weak chest and has been plagued with illness and fever for the past two months. We fear for his life. Daniel and Craig, your task is to help a farming family that has served us well over the years. The country is on the verge of Civil War, and the young men are being herded like livestock to the slaughter. They are being pressed into joining the Modern Parliamentarian Army or the Cavalier Kings army. This is a royalist area with many supporters for the King, especially in Worcester, so naturally everyone is very worried about Roundheads being here in numbers. We cannot help all, or even avert this war. Hopefully we can save a few lives and a way of life for this farming family."

Craig looked to Daniel and asked Samuel.

"How can we save this family?"

"There is a farm owned by the Foley family near Hereford. The family are expected there and there they will be safe. The Foley family are very well connected. But it is a long way from here, much could happen on the way, but I feel, after seeing how you performed today that they would stand a good chance of reaching safety."

They thought for a moment, then Daniel asked,

"How big is the family?"

"Four . . . Mother and Father, two sons aged 14 and 16. After you have escorted them to the farm, a brother monk will meet you there. You will give him this box. He has the key. It is important that he receives it. His name is Brother David. He is due at the farm tomorrow for supplies."

Then totally out of the blue, Samuel asked.

"How is your father, Craig?"

"He's fine, working on our new home, he's . . . you asked that as though you knew him?"

"Yes we have met . . . many years ago. He too used the Summerhouse with a friend, and he too helped us. He saved a life. For that he will never be forgotten."

Craig stood amazed.

"My dad did this too! . . . the dark horse!, he never told us. In that case that would mean that he had lived in that house before."

Samuel smiled.

"No he did not, but his friend did. They were both young and adventurous, and now I expect he is older and wiser."

"Yes he is." replied Hollie.

Still adjusting to the fact that their father had suddenly become quite cool, they agreed to help, if their Dad could do it, so could they. Daniel and Alex felt the same.

Craig held the wooden box with its iron hinges & padlock,

"Samuel, what's in this box, it's quite heavy?"

"Rocks and some papers."

Craig and Daniel were bemused it had a very large padlock on it. They knew not to ask any more questions about it.

It was getting late and the sun was going down. Samuel offered them a bed for the night, which turned out to be made of straw. They were so tired that they slept soundly.

The next morning Hollie and Alex went to see the sick monk. As they walked along the corridor they could hear the sound of morning prayer echoing around the stone walls it seemed so peaceful and yet quite spooky too. They came to the room where the ill monk lay. The stone floors kept the room cool yet on seeing the man they noticed he was in a sweat. It was evident that he needed a doctor, and possibly antibiotics. They would need her Dad's help and modern medicine. Hollie looked closely at the monk by candle light and quietly said,

"Don't worry we will bring help and you will soon be better."

Shortly afterwards they all met at the table, breakfast was served. It was a sort of thin porridge. As they ate they discussed their tasks. Hollie looked at Samuel,

"He needs a doctor's help. I suggest Alex and I go and ask for Dad's help."

Craig was a little concerned about their Dad getting involved as it had become clear that he had been trying to keep it a secret that he knew all along about the Summerhouse's secrets. Indeed he may have had many adventures in it. What else was there to find out about their Dad?

"Hollie, be sure to choose your words carefully when asking Dad to come, remember we've stumbled onto his secret!"

Craig gave Hollie the key to the Summerhouse and wished her good luck. Then Craig joined Daniel to prepare for their journey with the farming family. Daniel had thought a lot about it before falling asleep, and on waking, voiced his plan.

"Craig, if you and I act as outriders on horseback, the family could ride in a cart. Now in a car on tarmac roads, it would only take about fifty minutes. In a horse and cart along a dirt track, it may take all day . . . and another day getting back! . . . with no road signs, no real roads just a dirt track I am assuming it will be long and uncomfortable."

Craig thought it through, "No modern roads, that's true, but no traffic jams either. The length of travelling time does leave plenty of opportunity for us to get into trouble. We had better have some sort of backup plan . . . or better still a 4 x 4 armoured truck!"

Daniel grinned and agreed that this could be a trip to remember.

After collecting their backpacks, Hollie and Alex mounted their horses and set off at speed to the Summerhouse. Meanwhile Samuel introduced Craig and Daniel to the farming family. They were very grateful for a chance of help.

Samuel started by introducing them,

"Daniel, Craig, I would like to introduce you to Harold and Vera who have worked on a nearby farm for many years and have helped us enormously. These are their boys, William and Alfred."

Samuel went on to explain Harold and Vera's plight,

"With civil war imminent and the Parliamentarian and Royalist troops both ransacking the poor in the area, and persuading the young men to fight for their cause, we want to send them to a safer place. It's also a way of us saying thank you for near on twenty years of service."

Craig and Daniel helped Samuel and the family to load a cart with all their belongings, which did not take long as they had very little. There were two wooden chairs, a few cooking pots, a wooden box of clothes and blankets, and a basket of oddments. Both Craig and Daniel thought how many possessions and luxuries they had back home and felt a surge of guilt. With the cart loaded Craig and Daniel mounted their horses. Samuel put the box in a sack and on the cart and said,

"Take great care, I will stay here and wait for your return."

Daniel led the horse and cart out of the Priory gates with Craig in the rear. The wheels of the cart rumbled and clattered in the ruts of the road leading up the hills. The road was long and steep, with a drop on the left hand-side and the panoramic view which went on for miles. Once they had reached the top, it became easier going down the other side, and onto Hereford. The countryside was green and unspoiled. Daniel called to Craig.

"Craig, every ten minutes or so have a good look around and check for troops."

Craig lifted his binoculars which he had around his neck.

"Great minds think alike Daniel, I've got my binoculars ready, I've also got one firework that I found at the bottom of my bag . . . you never know."

Daniel realised that at this pace it was going to take a very long time to get there, Craig looked through his binoculars, scanning all around; it was clear. They had some food rations and water, what they did not have was that tank he had pictured in his head. It wasn't all bad though . . . the sky was blue, the sun was warm, the trees offered shade and sanctuary. The sound of bleating sheep could be heard, shepherd with a dog walking at his side waved as they passed, reminding Daniel of his Border Collie Ben. Harold and Vera sang songs and nursery rhymes with their youngest boy, the other looked round at the countryside, and the home they were leaving behind.

Harold and Vera had spent many long years building up their home, where their life was a self-sufficient style. They grew all their own food and Harold earned a little money on the organised hunts run by the local gentry. The children had been born there and now found themselves leaving for a new home. For them it was full mixed emotions, wanting to stay in familiar surroundings, and yet new ones seemed exciting. It was the excitement that made Harold and Vera very apprehensive, although they knew they were going to a safer place and people they could trust, anything could happen on route to their destination. These were uncertain times, the country on the verge of civil war, with its people torn in two. Most local people were loyal to King James, but there were those who opposed the crown and supported Parliament with its policies.

The sound of the cart wheels seemed to clatter in tune with rhymes that Vera and the children were singing. Harold was in no mood to sing as he saw their home slowly disappear in the distance, along with all the work he had done. However hopefully one day they maybe able to return.

Chapter 12

They were a long way from the Priory and hills now, Daniel thought they had covered about three miles, he was feeling more relaxed. They all started to chat, small talk mostly. Then the boys asked what the binoculars were. Daniel replied that they were magic, and he might let them look later when they had covered a safe distance.

Back at the Summerhouse Hollie and Alex, who had left the Priory a little later, had arrived safely and were setting the dials to return home. The house groaned as before. It was as though they had never left as they arrived back in their own time. Alex waited in the Summerhouse whilst Hollie went to find her Dad. Alex's eyes drifted up and scanned the wooden beams, until his eyes came to rest on two names carved into the wood. It read, Simon and Sam were here 1640.

Hollie found her Dad in the front room staring at a large crack in the ceiling, muttering to himself,

"I've had easier times with a dying patient on the operating table, there seems to be no end in sight with this house. I solve one problem, turn a corner, and there's another . . . woodworm in abundance, dry rot, wet rot and a sore back."

He held his back with his hands and stretched.

"Hi Dad. Where's Mum?"

"Upstairs, painting the bedroom, a rather odd colour. Your mother's idea of neutral colours is different to mine, by miles!"

Dad can I speak to you in confidence? I have a secret to tell you and a favour to ask."

Simon went rather pale.

"Oh good grief Hollie . . . has this got anything to do with the birds and bees, if it is that's your mother's department. I've only got woodworm and dry rot!"

"No Dad, it's the Summerhouse. Craig and I know it's secret, and that you have used it . . . You know what I mean."

'Oh! No. Hollie I remember saying to you and Craig before we moved that you were to stay away from old thing, it's dangerous. You have both really disappointed me.'

Simon sat down in shock,

"You mean to say, you two have used it! . . . It still works, after all these years?!"

Hollie put her hand on his shoulder and continued.

"We need you to come with us and help a sick man, a monk. Your friend Samuel sends his regards and waits our return. Dad please help."

He could not refuse her big pleading eyes, never could. There was also the memories in his head of two young men with dreams and ideas, called Samuel and Simon.

"Where or when is he and what symptoms does he have?"

Hollie counted on her fingers.

"High fever and he has had chest problems for some time, and we are in the year 1642 in the Malvern Priory."

I had better get some things together and tell your mother that I'm popping out: I will need to fill out a prescription, and pop to the corner chemist."

He got a bag of medical equipment together and then went to the bottom of the stairs and called up.

"Just popping out dear, to get some more filler for these cracks in the ceiling and walls."

"OK dear." came the reply.

"Going to walk it but shouldn't be too long. . . . 400 years maybe"

"Oh! Simon, you are a joker."

Then he winked at Hollie and said,

"Let's go then, it's like being young again. I'll meet you in the Summerhouse with the meds in 15 minutes."

Whilst Hollie, Alex and Simon travelled back to 1642, Craig and Daniel were making good progress on their journey.

Craig discreetly looked at his watch. He did not want them asking too many questions regarding twentieth century technology. It was two in the afternoon, they had been riding for five hours now and were well over half way to their destination. He checked his compass, then wiped sweat from his brow.

Daniel looked to Harold and was thankful that he knew where the farm was even though it had been ten years, they both exchanged smiles. Daniel looked through his binoculars as he had done countless times to survey the horizon. It was clear. The young boys were getting tired. Vera offered them some bread and a little cheese to eat. Harold nibbled on some and offered Daniel a slice, but Daniel politely declined, he was still full from the breakfast they had had. The sun had gone past its high point of the day when Craig peered through his binoculars again. He could see movement in a tree line behind them. He kept looking, there was no mistake, then called out.

"Roundheads at six o'clock."

Harold and Vera understood about the Roundheads, but were confused about the six o'clock part. Harold turned the cart off the road and moved swiftly behind tall bushes. Craig and Daniel followed, and dismounted. They all laid low and waited until the sound of thundering hooves raced by. Eight Roundheads passed them, not stopping or even slowing down. Their horses panted and there was the rattling sound of, metal on metal from swords worn by the menacing looking soldiers. The question on Craig and Daniel's minds was where were the soldiers going and who or what were they looking for this time? After a moment Daniel came out and looked down the track,

"It's OK, they're gone, now we know that they are in front and could come back. Harold, how far is it now?"

"Quite close, maybe two miles at most."

They started off again, at a quicker pace. They had to be there by sunset, visibility through the binoculars was getting difficult. They would have to be more vigilant. Craig and Daniel were starting to feel more in control now after that episode, and at home on horseback.

The next hour passed uneventfully as the sun went low in the sky. Craig checked his watch, it was seven thirty. Harold told Daniel to take the fork in the track off to the right. As they came round the bend Harold pointed at the gate to the farm. There was light from the window of the house. It had a thatched roof and a strong farmyard smell lingered in the air. Daniel and Craig dismounted, Harold and his family got off the cart and approached the oak door. Daniel knocked. Footsteps could be heard and the door opened.

A tall, well-built man stood in front of them.

"Yes can I help you young sir."

Daniel felt slightly tongue tied,

"Samuel from the Priory at Malvern asked us to escort Harold and his family here, to you. You are expecting them. . . . Yes?"

The tall man gave a broad smile and said

"Yes, I'm William, I look after this farm here for the family Foley who live up at the big house. Come in you must be tired. We have a spare room for the family, and if you young gentlemen would like to sleep in front of the fire you are most welcome. Pip and Sorrel won't mind sharing."

He pointed with his left hand to two Irish Wolf Hounds dominating the corner of the room. Craig smiled broadly as he loved dogs, Daniel was not so eager, they were enormous, smelly and extremely hairy unlike his own dog, Ben, who was shampooed regularly by his Mum and was a lot smaller. They said people resemble their pets, in this case it was very true!

Daniel put his hand out to them and the dogs soon made friends. They seemed happy to share their spot in front of the log fire.

That night Craig fell asleep quite quickly, Daniel couldn't. The dog nearest Craig was curled up in a large ball, Daniel's however liked to stretch out. This made it a little difficult for him to get comfortable, added the fact that the dog had terrible flatulence. Gradually Daniel's eyes grew heavy, and so did the air, sending him into a deep sleep.

When they woke up, each had a very hairy bedfellow giving them a face wash. Breakfast consisted of fresh eggs with a slice of oven baked bread. The family thanked both Craig and Daniel for getting

Robert Lambert

them safely there. Vera had big hugs for their and Harold shook their hands. The sons asked if they were allowed to see the binoculars now. Daniel went to his backpack to get them. Next to it was the box from Samuel, which made him forget all about the binoculars. He turned to Craig then to William.

"This box Samuel gave to us to give to Brother David . . . He said he would meet us here."

William crossed the room to Daniel and replied,

"Brother David has not been here for weeks. He does come for some provisions every three weeks, in fact he is overdue."

There was silence until Craig asked,

"We made a promise to get it to Samuel. Where can we find him?"

"That is a good question. He could be at the Cathedral in Hereford or he may have travelled to Tewksbury. He travels around a lot, buying and selling."

Craig and Daniel pondered on the problem for a few minutes, then Craig asked,

"Could we leave this box here for him to collect?"

Daniel grabbed his arm and whispered.

"We can't do that, we promised we would get it to Brother David."

"True, we did promise, but he's not here, and we don't know where he is."

Suddenly there was a loud knock at the door. Craig jumped, Daniel turned to the door sharply.

"Soldiers." whispered Craig, and they both swept up their backpacks and ran for the back door.

William peered through the window shutters and gave a sigh,

"Soldiers indeed! . . . It's Brother David! . . . You two are very jumpy this morning, why are you so concerned about soldiers?"

He opened the door, Brother David stood there and smiled.

"Sorry I'm a little late, had a spot of trouble on the way."

"Soldiers?" asked Craig.

"No, broken wheel, had to stop off at the wheelwright to have it mended . . . Why?"

"No reason . . . we just like to avoid them where possible, they seem to take great pleasure in chasing us."

Brother David looked at their clothes, and said.

"Dressed like that, no wonder!"

Daniel held out the box,

"Samuel gave us this box to give to you. He said you have the key."

"Yes I do. Could you put it on the cart for me? I just have to pick up a few other things."

Daniel and Craig put the box on the cart, saddled their horse and tied their bags on. Then Brother David came out with William and loaded his provisions. William and his family said their good-byes and Daniel, Craig and Brother David were left outside. Daniel grabbed the chance to ask Brother David about the stones in the box, he was a little surprised by Brother David being quite open and truthful with his reply,

"I cut them and send them back to Samuel. Look I will show you."

He pulled out a bunch of keys from underneath his habit, which were tied to him on a length of rope. He opened the box. Inside were a dozen green stones, a letter and a smaller box. He gave the smaller box back to Daniel saying.

"You can have this. Samuel wanted me to have it as a gift for a favour I did, but my needs are simple . . . I do not need it."

Craig took the box and nudged Daniel and with his eyes pointed to the green stones saying, "Look, they look like the ones in the dials at the Summerhouse." Daniel agreed and asked,

"What's in this box?"

"Open it, but be careful, do not let the soldiers find it on you. There are many who want it, not just because it is gold."

Both boy's eyes showed their surprise when he said it was gold, it was a gold goblet, small but beautifully decorated. He handed it to Craig to look at,

"Thank you, this is very generous, it's been a pleasure meeting you, however we must be going."

Craig looked at the goblet,

"Another reason to avoid those Roundheads."

He put it back in its box, put the box in the sack and tied it to his horse. They mounted their horses and make their long way back to the Abbey.

Chapter 13

Hollie, Alex and Simon arrived at the Priory. Samuel was there to greet them.

"Hello Simon." They hugged; something Simon thought he would never be able to do.

"It's been a long time" smiled Samuel.

"I have wondered for many years why we lost touch, now I know, you came back to live."

Simon turned to Hollie and explained to her and Alex.

"We, as young men, also explored the Summerhouse and its powers. We came back to 1620 and had what you might call a big adventure."

Samuel went on to explain that he returned to stay as he loved the simple life and felt that with his medical knowledge he could be of help to the monks, who had been so kind to them.

"Your Dad saved the life of one, even though he was only a Student Doctor, he was brilliant, even then! I have been of help in other ways. Keeping a tight rein on those who entered through the Summerhouse being one example."

Alex looked up to Simon, who he was starting to see in a different light.

"On the one beam in the Summerhouse are the names Simon and Sam, that's you two isn't it?"

"Yes, Alex . . . a long time ago." Hollie looked at Samuel,

"Do you know who built the Summerhouse then?"

"No, I don't, and I don't know of anyone who does. Unfortunately the man your Dad saved died not long after in an accident. He seemed very spiritual, intelligent, and may have known more than we know, but I never got the chance to ask him."

Hollie was about to reply, when her father intervened.

"Where is the patient Sam?"

"This way Simon . . . Never thought I would meet your kids here, they're very nice . . . you did well there. Hollie is lovely and Craig's a handsome lad, didn't follow you then!" He grinned.

"Thanks, Mate."

Samuel led them to the sick man. Simon examined him, and announced that with his help he expected him to make a full recovery. Hollie bent down to her kneeling father,

"Is it just a chest infection? . . . not plague is it?"

"No Hollie, however in these days a person with his condition would have died, but I can put him on to the road of recovery. You were right in your diagnosis, he does have a very bad infection which is set quite deep in his lungs." He paused, then continued.

"But he has developed Beriberi too."

Hollie looked up in horror,

"That sounds like a tropical disease."

"No it's simply an acute vitamin B deficiency which is why he has the leg cramps & nausea. Hand me my bag, everything I need is in it."

Then he went on to administer drugs to the monk. It was good news to the other monks that he would soon be better.

"Sam, where are all the other monks then? I saw some local people but no monks." asked Simon.

"We are the only two left, the others had to leave. When the King took over the Monasteries. He was too ill to travel so I stayed with him. Shortly after, the local people came to our aid. They were very fond of their church . . . not all agreed with the King's actions. The land is owned privately now . . . but there are plans for the people to raise the money to buy the church for the community. Have things improved in your time?"

Simon smiled then laughed and replied,

"Well the Crown doesn't have that sort of power anymore as you know, Parliament . . . Government rules . . . tries to most of the time."

They both laughed. Simon, in a serious tone then asked,

"Tell me the real reason you came back, I think there's more to this story than meets the eye." Samuel nodded, "Yes there was one more reason for coming, but I did not want to say in front of the others. When you and I were here last do you remember that young farmers daughter Jane, that I rather liked?" Simon grinned,

"Liked . . . you were besotted with her!"

"Yes OK, I admit that . . . well she was the other reason to come back. We hit it off really well, in fact we were going to marry."

"What happened?"

"She died very suddenly, of an illness that I dare say is no longer a danger in modern times. What seemed an idyllic life has its setbacks. I did not want to return to our time. I had a new life here, even though Jane had died." He paused for a moment,

"I hope the future gets better. Do you know Simon, the first recorded war started by man was nearly 5000 years ago, and in all that time we have not learned a thing."

Simon hadn't the heart to tell him that wars in the modern world still happen,

"Well there is improvement in the world . . . in some ways . . . But tell me Sam what has life been like as a monk?"

"Well it's been tough. When the dissolution of the monasteries started, life became a little stressed to say the least when we heard stories of monks being murdered and the looting, many went into hiding or disappeared."

"So why didn't you try to go back home to modern times? The Summerhouse was a gateway home, you could have returned and no one would have noticed that you had even been missing. As it was there was a huge police search with me saying nothing, after all how could I . . . it was a secret I had to keep." Samuel smiled,

"Yes it must have been difficult for you . . . sorry Simon."

"All in the past . . . pardon the pun."

Both men laughed, it was getting late and everyone was asleep as Simon and Samuel said goodnight, then he thought of one last question he felt compelled to ask,

"Simon before you go to bed can I ask you a personal question?"

"Sure, what's that?"

"Your children know of your secret of the Summerhouse, which it seems they have only just been told about, however have you told them of the other?"

"Do you mean what I think you mean?"

"Yes, the dark secret you might say."

"No. Nothing, and I don't want them to know."

Samuel thought for a moment on the subject that was a secret between the two of them.

"One day they might find out now they have the use of the Summerhouse, it would be better coming from you than finding out via someone else. Obviously your secret is safe with me, but others might tell IF they ever meet them!"

"I am a doctor I took an oath, I can't risk destroying that image with my own children."

"But Simon my friend, at the time you had no choice."

"I know Sam, but no, not yet at least."

"I understand, goodnight, Simon."

"Goodnight Sam, you're still the best friend I have ever had, apart from my wife."

Meanwhile Daniel and Craig did not have good news. They got within sight of the hills when Daniel spied troops in the distance behind them.

"Two, Roundheads at our rear . . . they really are becoming a pain in the rear! We are nearly home and dry, and now they have to turn up again!"

With that in mind they put the horses into a gallop. They could see the hills just ahead standing large and bald above the tree tops. With heads down they rode like jockeys in the Grand National horse race. Up and over a rise, the horses panting hard. The Roundheads were in hot pursuit, trying to close the gap. They could see the road over the hills, which lead to the Priory, but more troops were blocking their path.

Two of the soldiers drew their flintlock pistols, aimed at Daniel and Craig then fired. Daniel felt one shot whistle by him, calling to Craig to steer the horses off to the left. Craig shouted back to Daniel,

"Where does this road go to?"

"Further North round the hills and onto Worcester . . . we have no choice, let's see if we can lose them in the woods where the road bends."

They were just staying ahead because, as riders, they were lighter compared to the soldiers who wore breast plates, helmets & heavy boots. They reached the end of the hills and started to bear to the right in the direction of Worcester. The horses thundered along the road as they overtook a horse and cart carrying wood. The boys were starting to gain more and more ground from the pursuing Roundheads. Daniel shouted back to Craig.

"We must be close to Powick now . . . Craig, into these trees."

As they rounded the next bend they shot into the trees and waited. The horses panting heavily. The troops went galloping past like a thundering juggernaut . . . their actions had paid off. They waited for a few minutes, then dismounted and crept out of the trees,

"That was too close. These horses need rest and water." said Craig. Daniel agreed, "The River Teme should be not far from here, let's go there, then back to the Priory. Actually that's where we were heading for originally. Where Hollie said the battle was fought."

As they made their way to the small river they could hear what seemed like gunfire in the distance. What they didn't know was that mounted soldiers and foot soldiers were in full battle, pole axes being swung left and right, pikes thrusting and muskets being shot in uncontrolled panic.

It was a short while before they came upon the bridge. The sun was getting low in the sky, marking the end of another day. All the fighting soldiers had moved on, the boys could see the water, the horses could smell it, and made a bee-line straight for it. The sight that greeted them was shocking.

Craig turned to Danial, "Are those bodies at the water's edge . . . next to that bridge?"

Indeed they were. Some fifty bodies lay motionless, a mixture of buff leather coats, Parliamentarian to flamboyant Cavaliers.

"This must be the battle site Hollie spoke of." They moved to the waters edge just to let the horses drink then moved on fast. Craig put his hand to his mouth as he saw a crow pulling the eye from the socket of a body.

"I feel sick, the smell is just awful."

Daniel agreed. "What a waste of human life . . . and all for politics of the rich." Just then they heard a faint voice.

"Please help me." They spun around and saw a young drummer boy, bleeding heavily from a head wound. Daniel pulled a bandanna from his jacket pocket and stooped down and proceeded to bandage the young boy's head. Craig asked the boy.

"What's your name?

"Albert. That's my drum. There was fighting all over the place, then I heard someone say that it was Prince Rupert himself and his Cavillers. They charged us and men were running in all over the place, we are not proper soldiers like them, but one day we will be, I have heard it said that Mr Cromwell wants us to be a modern army.' His eyes were constantly looking out for the Kings men, Daniel picked him up and put him on his horse,

"Don't worry you are coming with us to the Priory at Malvern. There's a man there that can make you better."

They mounted the horses and started back, all three were exhausted. The sight of the dead soldiers they had left behind still fresh in their minds, the smell still in their nostrils. A short distance away some people with a cart were coming in their direction. They were travelling from the city to pick up the dead. Daniel and Craig still felt that taking the young boy was in his best interest.

They rode back to Malvern and the Priory. There was no sign of soldiers, only sheep, grazing without a care in the world.

Chapter 14

The sun had set as they knocked on the door of the Priory. Samuel answered the door, and they staggered in. Simon went straight to the young boy and examined him. "Head wounds always look worse than they are . . . Yes son, you were very lucky . . . Daniel did a good job of bandaging you up. If he hadn't and you had kept bleeding it would be a different story." Simon looked to Daniel,

"No doubt you saved this boy's life Daniel. He will be weak for a few days, but no permanent damage done, but he may have died if you hadn't stopped the bleeding."

Daniel felt like a hero for a moment, then Hollie started filling Craig and Daniel in on the history of Simon and Samuel, whilst Simon cleaned & dressed Albert's head.

"You kids must be so tired, to bed, all of you. Samuel and I will stay up and keep an eye on the patients, and we have a lot of catching up to do."

Daniel took the box from his backpack and signalled to Craig that they should give it to Samuel. Craig nodded.

"Samuel, Craig and I were given this, however we think you need it more. It's worth quite a lot I would imagine."

Samuel took it from Daniel, and smiled,

"That is very kind. Thank you both, very much."

That night, all slept heavily, especially Daniel and Craig. Simon and Samuel stayed up till the early hours. Simon told him of his family and his work as a surgeon, and Samuel told him of life as a monk. The hard times, long hours and yet the simple life had something that was missing in modern times, Simon asked what was it.

"It's hard to say in one word what exactly was missing. I found that the simplicity here, was more suited to me, compared to the busy modern life full of pollution and big cities. Yet out there the political forces are at work to bring war to this beautiful land. You and I know as history has shown it is the innocent who pay the biggest price."

They looked at each other in silence, then Samuel continued,

"Simon be careful of the Summerhouse, it is capable of more than any of us know. Before the monk died he told me that there is a second key . . . another eye. It is red, and has different powers. It has been lost for many years. The Monk believed it is in this area somewhere, buried. Well on that note I think I will retire to my bed and get a few hours sleep. Good night dear friend. . . . and thank you again for coming and helping these people. Sleep well Simon."

The night had passed quietly when the larks sang morning song, natures early morning wake up call. The sun started to rise over the horizon. It filtered through the windows of the Priory lighting up the stone pillars. The light moved across the stone floor where Simon had fallen asleep in a chair in the room with the injured boy. The light slowly made its way up until it shone onto his face, his eyes slowly opened, and he stretched.

The young boy was sitting up in bed,

"Thank you for what you did for me."

There was a loud knocking at the door, followed by shouting.

"Open the door, in the name of the King."

Outside were Soldiers, Cavaliers. Samuel ran from room to room waking everyone,

"Come quickly you must hide."

He took them to the Guesten Hall, inside he led them to a trap-door in the one corner, he opened it and they all quickly went down,

"This is a hiding place the brothers and I built some years ago, stay quiet in here and you should be safe."

He closed the trap door and he stacked sacks of grain on top of it.

The Cavaliers entered the hallway, and one called Captain Rich shouted,

"I have orders to search these premises for enemies of the Crown."

He addressed his men.

"Check all the rooms."

It was not long before a soldier came and found Daniel's bandanna covered in blood, he showed to the Captain Rich,

"They are here somewhere, search."

Two soldiers opened the door of the sick monk. A woman who had been nursing him, was sitting at his side on a stool, wiping his brow with a cloth. Hidden at her feet under the bed was Simon's medical bag. The woman was praying that they would not find the bag which in all the rush Simon had left there. The soldiers entered the room, the one looked behind the door and the other walked to the bed. The woman looked at the soldier, then raised her hand to signal stop. The soldier stood still and the woman said.

"I would advise you not to come closer, this man is very contagious."

Then covering her mouth she gave a convincing rasping cough.

The soldier grabbed the other by the arm,

"He has the look of death upon him. . . . There's no one here, we should leave." They left closing the door. The woman, sighed, looked to the ceiling and kissed her crucifix, and whispering,

"Sorry Lord, it was only a little white lie."

The sound of heavy boots stomping around, opening doors and checking rooms echoed down the corridor.

The air was getting tense as the sounds got closer and closer. Below all eyes were fixed on the trap door. A voice was heard,

"Odd place to store grain, you men move them." Samuel thought quickly, "Captain Rich these are stone floors, there are no cellars, your men are wasting their time. Before you mess the whole place up, I will tell you what you want to know. Yes, they have been here, but our lives were threatened if we talked. They left just moments before you arrived. I heard the one say they were heading for the Welsh border." In the cellar, all were praying that Samuel would be believed. The Captain rocked on his heels and pondered Samuel's story. Then Captain Rich gave the order to leave. He gathered his men and marched outside, they all mounted and then set off on their horses towards the border.

Samuel stood outside and watched as the Cavaliers disappeared in the distance, then rushed inside to open the trapdoor. They all came out, squinting into the daylight.

Simon shook Samuel hand,

"Thank you for saving our necks, that was too close for comfort."

"They have probably gone onto Worcester. You should be going . . . they could return."

"We will, once I have checked your sick friend."

While Simon and Samuel went to check on the sick monk, Hollie, Alex, Daniel and Craig went to feed the horses, which were kept out of sight in an old store house. Craig and Daniel had become quite fond of them. Hollie noticed how Daniel admired the horses,

"You were very good on horseback, Daniel, I was impressed."

Daniel fed the horse a handful of hay, and replied awkwardly.

"Yes . . . Good fun."

Just then the drummer boy appeared from a pile of hay,

"Have the soldiers gone? I heard the monks say soldiers were here, so I ran and hid." asked Albert.

"Yes they're gone . . . good hiding place." Simon came out followed by Samuel and saw Albert.

"Albert, thank goodness you're OK. Come here son, let me have a look at that head wound."

Simon studied the wound and told Albert, that he was on the mend, but should stay with Samuel for another day or two. Then he turned to the others,

"Right gang, we must be getting back, and no . . . we can't take the horses."

Hollie and Craig's eyes lit up with an idea,

"Dad, these horses would cost a bomb in our time. We could . . . "

"No" ordered Simon. Then Samuel added.

"Actually Simon, you would be doing us a very big favour because they do not belong to us. The soldiers did not search this store house but if they come back and find the horses, we could be in trouble."

Hollie held her Dad's hands and smiled her sweetest 'Daddy's Girl' smile.

"Please! . . . Also, we need them to get to the Summerhouse, it's big enough to fit them in."

Simon nodded feeling that he was fighting a losing battle,

"Yes I know Hollie, but sweetheart, stables and food cost a lot of money."

Daniel put his hand in the air to aid Hollies' plight,

"That's no problem Sir, my uncle has a farm with stables to spare, he wouldn't mind at all, as long as we pay for food and muck out the stables."

"OK. But your mother knows nothing of the Summerhouse, so you will have to get them out without her seeing them, not an easy task! Then I will have to explain how, and where they came from."

"Or we could keep quiet, it would be easier" Daniel replied with a wink.

Hollie mounted one horse with Alex, Daniel and Craig took another, and Simon mounted the third.

Samuel shook hands with each of them,

"I hope we will meet again. I wish you luck and a safe journey, now go quickly." They all set off through the gates and to the Summerhouse.

It was still early in the morning, the sun was bright and sparkled in the dew which covered the ground as they rode along the track. After a mile the Summerhouse was in sight. Craig held the reins tightly as Daniel looked all round. His eyes focused on riders coming from behind.

"Craig, riders coming up fast from the rear. It could be it's the same lot who came to the Priory."

Craig shouted to everyone to gallop. Simon took the lead as the others followed. Craig pulled a large firework from his backpack, and handed it to Daniel. Daniel fumbled, but managed to light it, then threw it behind himself into the path of the soldiers' horses behind them. Ten seconds later it exploded, scaring them, making two fall off, the remaining six thundering on in pursuit. The soldiers were gaining ground as Simon rode his horse straight into the Summerhouse, ducking to miss the lintel. He quickly dismounted and held the doors open, signalling to the others to ride straight in.

They did, it was a tight fit as they closed the doors. Craig rushed to the dials and set them. The soldiers thundered to a halt outside and dismounted. In the Summerhouse, Craig pulled the key from his back pack, pushed it in, the eyes lit up and the green light filled the room. The soldiers ran to the Summerhouse swords drawn. The green light embraced the time travellers as the last two soldiers also pulled up and dismounted. The soldiers rushed to the doors and crashed through them. They could not believe their eyes, it was empty!

"Where did they go . . . the Captain Rich will never believe this."

"That's why we will not say anything . . . what he doesn't know he won't worry about. Agreed? . . . Right let's get out of here, gives me the creeps, no one ever comes in here because it's haunted. I have people say they have seen strange lights and ghosts here."

"Witches on broomsticks too I suppose." came a sarcastic reply.

Simon opened the doors of the Summerhouse, and Craig led one horse, Hollie another and Daniel held onto Simons. Once outside Simon suggested they take the horses to Daniel's uncle. Simon went inside the house and kept Shirley occupied while they sneaked them out to the road. They jumped on, and road off to Daniel's uncle's farm.

Simon went upstairs to Shirley calling.

"Hi, I'm back"

"Did you get what you needed from the store?" Simon looked puzzled, then remembered.

"The filler . . . No. . . . Can you believe it they've run out, new delivery coming in Tomorrow morning."

"Typical . . . never mind, get it tomorrow." replied Shirley

"Yes I will . . . want a cup of tea, I am dying for one. It's been ages since the last one!"

"We had one just before you went out . . . but yes OK, I will have one if you're brewing up. I've been painting all this time!"

Daniel led them all into the stable yard of his uncle's farm. Daniel's Uncle approached them.

"Daniel my boy, good to see you . . . mighty fine horses you have there."

"Yes they belong to my friend's Uncle, this is Hollie and Craig."

They were all introduced to Bill who was more than willing for Daniel's new friend's horses to stay in the stables in return for helping out once a week. He put his hand on Daniel's shoulder,

"Nice new friends Daniel." He admired the horses.

"Very fine horses, they will like it here."

On the way home Hollie walked alongside Daniel, and Craig was messing about with Alex behind them. Hollie stretched her arms in the air and said,

"Daniel I just want to say thanks for all your help with the horses, I couldn't have done it without your help . . . I can't wait for us to go out riding."

"Yes, I must admit a ride around the hills not being chased by soldiers would make a nice change."

Once they reached the street where they live, they went their separate ways, but not before they had arranged to meet in town. Hollie and Craig had lunch with their parents and discussed decorating ideas for the house. Daniel and Alex were at home with their parents having lunch and discussing Daniel's future, which Alex found boring. Two hours passed and they all met in town. Hollie asked Daniel if he would show them the Priory, as she was interested in seeing the difference since 1642, and whether there was any sign of Samuel and Albert. Daniel took them to the Priory and they started to look round the now familiar building. Hollie scanned the floor inside where names decorated the stone floor, more worn since they last saw it. Craig and Daniel searched the walls for clues. Alex sighed deeply, and walked up to Hollie,

"Hollie, it was a very long time ago, there might not be any trace of Samuel or Albert now." Craig added,

"No Hollie, there is nothing here." Daniel put his arm round Hollies' shoulders,

"Hollie you have to remember that this is 2011 and you are looking for signs of people from 1642. It is very likely that we will not find anything." And Craig agreed,

"It's true . . . I don't see anything close to 1600s."

They all walked out feeling a sense of loss, they all agreed that it was pointless as they did not know their surnames. Daniel suggested that he and Craig try the local museum and Hollie and Alex try the library records. Hollie smiled,

"I've got a better idea, Craig and Alex do the museum and Daniel and I do the Library. I think Alex would enjoy the museum more than the Library." Alex jumped at the idea,

"Good thinking Hollie, Libraries are not my thing. . . . mind you . . . a museum isn't much better, but at least I get to hang out with Craig." Craig grinned and ruffled Alex's hair.

The sun was still very hot even though it had turned three. The town was buzzing with people carrying shopping bags. Craig and Alex arrived at the museum, Craig had his digital camera to record the event. The first display they came to was dealing with the right period, but hardly any real information, just wooden artefacts.

Hollie and Daniel, meanwhile, were enquiring at the library. They spent ages picking the Librarian's brain, however this proved to be fruitless too. When they got back outside, Hollie called Craig on his mobile. They arranged to meet back at the Summerhouse. Hollie and Daniel started walking and he pointed to a street sign.

"There is a road here called Albert Crescent, but the chances of that being 'our' Albert? . . . " They left the question hanging in the air.

"It's been over four hundred years what are the chances of us finding traces of their existence?" replied Hollie.

Hollie nodded grabbed his hand and they started walking back to the Summerhouse. When they arrived at Hollies' house, the front door opened, and out came Simon with the vicar, Rev. Davis. He was in his forties, slim, clean shaven with round spectacles. Simon introduced them.

Hollie announced, "We've been to the library trying to find out about Albert the drummer boy and Samuel."

Rev. Davis was bemused, and introduced himself and shook her hand.

"You must be Hollie, your Father has told me much about you. I am Rev. Davis from Holy Trinity, Gods local hang out I call it with the youngsters.'

He chuckled with Hollie who was looking bemused by his odd, yet friendly introduction.

'I called in to welcome you all to my parish, may I enquire why you are trying to trace them. Is this a history project for school?"

"Yes" replied Hollie.

"Well history is a passion of mine, let's see if I can help. Give me some details."

Hollie went on to give as much detail as she dared, then continued,

"In 1642 there was a battle at Powick Bridge. Is there any truth or record of a drummer boy who was injured, but survived? During the same period, Malvern consisted of the Priory with a wall, gate and some other buildings. Monks lived there, one was possibly called Brother Samuel. Is there any record of what became of him?"

Daniel winced at Hollies' questions, thinking they sounded too specific, too precise. Rev. Davis removed his glasses and started to polish them with his handkerchief. Simon trying to relieve the situation said,

"I don't think Rev. Davis even understands these questions, besides I think they are a bit too specific . . . that was a long time ago, I shouldn't think you will ever find out." The Rev Davis however, had other ideas.

"On the contrary, it's possible. You two would have to enquire around the various churches dating back to then. Drummer boys were used, there would have been one there at the battle. In fact, I did once read that a soldier, a pike-man to be precise by the name of Bridgewater, had a son named Albert. He may have been drummer a boy. That was common in those days. Unfortunately, they both died in the battle. Mrs Bridgewater, on finding this out was so distraught that she leapt into the river and drowned. Unfortunately she had been misinformed and the son Albert had survived. It was all very sad. Can't help you with the monk I'm afraid. Never heard of him."

Hollie was thinking, 'poor Mrs Bridgewater, if only she'd known that Albert had been saved.' Daniel was just sorry that they couldn't have saved Albert's Dad.

Rev. Davis shook hands with everyone, then left, waving as he went down the garden path and out of the gate.

Simon with worry written all over his face said.

"Well there you go, you may have altered the past by saving a person, then again it may not have made much difference . . . we will never know."

Craig and Alex had left the museum and were walking home. On the way a man wearing a political rosette approached them,

"Hello boys, take this leaflet home to your parents and ask them to vote for me, come election time."

"Why should they vote for you?" asked Craig.

Alex looked blank, and added

"Don't ask me, my dad says all politicians should all be shot."

The man replied laughing

"Well son I am sure he is only joking, although one of my ancestors was shot in the Civil War at Powick, but he survived, I was actually named after him. My name is Albert Bridgewater. Leave the past behind and vote for me and a brighter future."

The boys nodded and carried on walking until they got home and met Hollie and Daniel in the Summerhouse. Hollie asked them about everything that had happened, Craig started to explain about the political candidate they had met.

"Hollie we think we may have met one of Albert's relatives. Albert Bridgewater." "Albert Bridgewater you say? That may be Albert's surname! . . . could be a coincidence I suppose, it is a small world. Daniel and I spoke to a Rev. Davis who is a history buff. He said that Albert and his father died in the battle but we know different. WE actually changed the past and if the man you met is a descendant . . . " Then she shook her head and corrected herself,

'It must be a coincidence. It has to be, surely we can't hold so much power."

Craig thought for a moment, then agreed,

"Hollies' right. It's just a spooky coincidence. There could have been two Albert's in the battle!"

Craig picked up the big old book and said.

"The book said that with the house comes Great Power, Wow, doesn't it just!"

Changing the subject Alex said,

"My vase Daniel, I told Mrs B that I would give it to Mum for her birthday, I must get back and do that . . . it's tomorrow."

Daniel remembered that Mrs B had given him an envelope.

"I've got something too . . . yes, come on Alex let's get back. I will help you wrap the vase for Mum."

The brothers started walking back. Daniel said,

"You know, Mum will love that Alex. She has always been a keen collector of Royal Worcester and that one is in mint condition as well as being a fair old age."

They arrived home and walked into the kitchen. Their Mum and Dad were sitting at the table. They looked worried. Their Dad, Chris, was holding a letter. Their Mum, Mary greeted them.

"Hello boys"

"Hi, Ma" replied Daniel, "You two down in the dumps . . . Someone die?"

They did not smile as they normally would. She raised her eyes from her cup of tea and replied.

"We have a little problem."

"Little? . . . Big!" replied his Dad.

"What's happened?" Daniel asked.

"I've been made redundant, as from the end of this week . . . We are in a financial mess. Because I've only been with the company for four years, the redundancy package is quite small. If it was bigger then maybe, just maybe, I could have managed with the mortgage, and set up my own business, painting and decorating . . . Hell, Daniel you could work with me."

He sat there full of perfect dreams and intentions. Mary looked at him,

"We can sell my collection of porcelain, that would help, love."

He looked back at her, and said with a tear,

"You've always been there to pick up the pieces . . . as well as being a wonderful Mum."

Daniel looked down at Alex, they knew what the other was thinking.

Alex ran upstairs and brought down his backpack containing the Royal Worcester Bone China. He took it to Mary and opened it,

"Mum, Daniel and I have worked hard, and had a spot of luck to get you this present for your birthday."

Daniel picked up from there,

"Yes, we did a lot of work in exchange for this to go with your collection. I do think it's very special, and it is yours to do with as you please."

Alex pulled out the vase, Mary looked at it in amazement, and so did their Dad.

She studied it closely, and smiled at her husband,

"We have wonderful kids . . . who never fail to amaze me."

Alex and Daniel felt a strong sense of pride knowing that they may have been able to help. They went to Daniel's room,

"Good isn't it? . . . that we are able to help Mum and Dad."

"Yes it is, and through the Summerhouse we saved little Albert and the monk. A lot of good came of using it. We should ask Craig and Hollie if they would like to do it again, soon."

Daniel put his hand inside his jacket and pulled out the envelope from Mrs B.

"Still haven't opened this."

He opened it and started to read. His eyes widened, and Alex asked.

"What does it say?"

He paused reading the letter to himself,

"Never mind that now . . . I will read it out loud to all of you tomorrow. Now then you . . . it's been a long day, off to your own room. I'm going to have a bath and veg out. See you in the morning, Alex."

Next morning Alex and Daniel's parents were in a much better mood as they made plans to take Mary's vases, including the one Alex gave her, to an auction house. Staying positive, and focusing on the task of packing them, they chatted light-heartedly. The boys had breakfast then said goodbye and walked to Craig and Hollies' house, Daniel had a smile on his face all the way there. Alex asked if it was because he was about to see Hollie again, but it wasn't, it was because of the letter off Mrs Bennett that he had in his inside jacket pocket which came with a treasure map!

Chapter 15

In the Summerhouse the four sat in a circle and Daniel pulled out the letter and explained,

"Mrs B gave me this letter before we left. I opened it last night for the first time and read it. Now I'm going to read it to you."

Everyone looked on, with deep interest. Daniel started.

"Thank you for what you did. Now I want to do something for you. The Summerhouse can be a lot of fun, take you to many places in the past, as you know. Always take great care when using it, plan your journeys well. Keep these Words of Wisdom in mind."

"What else is in there?" asked Hollie,

"It's a hand drawn map . . . a map of part of the Malvern area. It's not dated but it was drawn a very long time ago that's for sure. I have put sticky back plastic on it to stop it from falling apart. It's quite faded but there's still a lot of visible detail on it. Now I need another dated old map to compare it."

Alex looked up to Daniel,

"Daniel our local shop has got loads of those."

"True bro . . . but will they have one that's old enough? Mrs B came upon the map on one of her journeys, but to cut a long story short, she and Mr B never got round to exploring it because of family matters then World War II."

"So, is there a treasure?" ask Craig.

"Well it seems that before leaving for the crusades a Mr Beauchamp buried some gold in or around the moat of his castle, Bronsil Castle, which was situated near Obelisk Hill."

"Where is that?" asked Hollie.

Daniel pulled out an OS map from his jacket pocket,

"I used my ordinance survey map and marked where the castle would have been in the fourteenth century . . . as they say, 'X marks the spot.'"

"According to the map, a moat still exists and maybe some of the wall. So last night I used my computer and that satellite mapping program and found it. The moat is still there."

There was silence until Craig said,

"Well done Mrs B. . . . everybody up for it? All keen to find some treasure?"

Within no time at all they were walking alongside the hills, past Midsummer Hill and onto Quarry Lake. Here they cut through the hills onto Obelisk Hill. Daniel, with map in hand, led the way.

To the south west the morning sun lit up Midsummer Hill and as it rose higher in the sky it gradually drove the shadows away from the castle ruins, down the hill ahead of them. Daniel kept referring to his compass, stopping and looking around,

"There it is ahead of us, mostly all overgrown."

Craig and Hollie were unsure what to look for as they were strangers to the area.

"Where?" asked Craig.

"In between those trees ahead."

They continued down the hill and followed the track through the trees. Many tracks were worn by hill walkers over the years, all seemingly headed the same way. Hollie was enjoying the views. She had heard that the composer, Edward Elgar had walked these hills. He was a favourite of her Dad's. Alex picked up a stick and occasionally whacked at the ferns growing at the side of the path, each one an opposing foe, his stick a shiny sword. Craig was daydreaming of life in the days of the Crusades, the Knights Templar and Robin Hood, all these he remembered from his history lessons, books and the movies.

Daniel saw the location opposite some more modern buildings.

"This is it . . . the castle would have been here. . . . somewhere!"

They all looked around, trees, plants and weeds now covered the once castle and moat. Some stonework remained, the moat still filled with water, but nature had taken over with trees and bushes growing in abundance. Craig gave a sigh,

"Well, folks, it will be impossible to dig here."

Alex hit at the undergrowth with his stick,

"If only those big trees weren't here, it would be no problem."

Craig and Daniel looked at each other and smiled, then together said,

"The Summerhouse."

Hollie agreed and hugged Alex,

"Clever boy Alex. We use the Summerhouse to go back to when there were no trees."

Craig studied the map and said to Daniel.

"If there's an old bookshop with old maps we could get one which will show us the position of the castle and the surrounding area . . . and compare it to this one. You never know we might get lucky! I know that we know where the castle is but the more info or maps we have, the better."

Daniel had an idea,

"As it happens, there is a bookshop which has maps in Upton. That's only a few miles away, if you like we could head back home and go there . . . have you and Hollie got bikes? We could all bike it over or if you're game, I could take you on my trail bike?"

"Motorbike, cool, Yes! I'm game." replied an excited Craig.

It took two hours to walk back across the tops of the hills, veering off to the right down the track to their homes. A different route so Daniel could show Hollie the views from the top of the hills. Daniel had been walking quietly thinking, when Hollie asked.

"Penny for your thoughts?"

"Oh it's nothing, just that this is a long walk, maybe if we go back in time in the Summerhouse we should take the horses."

"Good idea, we will need them if we actually do find a box of treasure."

Daniel smiled at Hollies' hope of high adventure, adding "Digging tools too, tents maybe, it could take a while to find it, if it exists."

On their return Daniel and Craig went on to Daniel's house to collect his bike. Craig put on a spare helmet as Daniel got the motorbike out of the garage and the two rode off to buy an old map. At the shop Craig went to the counter. He asked an elderly man with small round spectacles for a copy of the oldest map of the area the shop had to offer. He found a copy of one dating back to 1823 and handed it to Craig saying,

"This is the best I can do for you, it's a copy of one of the early 1800s."

"Nothing older? We were looking for one quite a bit older."

The man smiled, peered over his glasses at Craig and replied.

"Sorry that's the best I can do. You might find older maps in a museum or private collection but not in here I'm afraid, sorry son."

Daniel handed over money for the map and he and Craig left thanking him for his help. They put their helmets on, jumped back on the bike and made their way home. In Craig's kitchen they spread the map out on the kitchen table. Daniel pulled out from his coat another up to date ordinance survey map. Craig asked,

"What's that for?"

"To compare and get bearings, we went to the site of the castle ruin, all that's left is a little stonework, the moat and a lot of undergrowth. When we go back in time, the area will be a lot different, so we will need all the reference help we can get."

Daniel pointed to the ruin on the modern map, with his other hand he pointed to the same spot on the old copy.

"See, this is today and this is in the early 1800's, we would be going back in time further but it's as good a guide as we are going to get, and the castle is marked on the old map but not the new."

"When shall we go back to?" asked Craig.

"Let's go back two years after. By 1644 the soldiers should have given up looking for us." Both laughed, then Hollie walked in.

"Hi you two, you're back then. Did you get the map?"

Daniel filled Hollie in briefly. Hollie thought it through and replied.

"I disagree, the Civil War will still be on, soldiers everywhere. Why not go earlier by a 100 years."

Craig and Daniel pondered this, then Daniel said.

"I do see your point Hollie."

She warmed to his eyes and smiled, he continued,

"But where we have just come from we have Samuel who we know we can trust, we might need that. I thought if we go back two years later then all the action will have moved away from that area. I seem to remember that it moved North . . . or was it South." Hollie was not totally convinced. Nevertheless he was older and maybe there was sense in his suggestion.

Alex walked in listening to music on his iPod, shouted, "What's up?"

Daniel stared at his little brother, "The sky is up Alex! Switch that thing off"

"Oh! Funny, sky is up, so funny bro . . . that's so old" Alex replied with sarcasm as he was annoyed at being asked to switch his iPod off in front of Hollie.

Hollie put her arm round Alex,

"We are all going to 1644, to dig for treasure, get chased by the odd soldier, you know the usual."

"Count me out on this one, I will stay here and look after Ben."

Daniel looked at him in surprise.

"Maybe you're right, we will take the horses, the less doubled up the better."

Hollie looked annoyed at Daniel,

"Does that mean that I shouldn't go so you two can go not doubled up?"

Daniel suddenly realised his size 10 boot had done it again.

"Oh! Hollie I want you . . . to come along . . . it's just that I am bigger and heavier to double up with, it's not fair on the horse. You and Craig are lighter . . . and can double up, which leaves Alex."

Daniel's face grew crimson until Alex came to his rescue.

"I believe Hollie that my brother is just trying to be practical and look after me, he's not getting at you. . . . he fancies you."

Suddenly, Simon Templeton walked in,

"Hello all, Craig, Hollie your Mum is busy packing her quilting stuff for her meeting tonight. Go and say bye to her before you go out she won't be back 'til tomorrow. She's staying over at her friend's house. Hollie could you . . . why are you grinning like a Cheshire cat?"

She just kept on smiling at Daniel, Simon shrugged his shoulders, "Never mind, I'll put the kettle on, I am dying for a cuppa."

He patted Alex on the head, then bantered

"Alright Alex my boy . . . good . . . Daniel you feeling alright? Your face is quite red. Are you coming down with something?

Daniel left saying, "Right, best be off and get those horses for us, won't be long."

Several hours passed until Daniel returned with the horses and a large rucksack full of provisions including food for three people.

"Hi guys, I'm back, I've put the horses in the Summerhouse, so we don't need to hang around too long. Are we going to find the treasure?"

He looked round the kitchen expecting all to be present, however there was only Hollie who had just finished washing up some tea cups, she smiled broadly.

"Only me here, Craig is upstairs and Alex is in the back garden with Ben."

"Well we need to collect everyone so we can get off, it's not a good idea to leave the horses in the Summerhouse on their own. I best get back to them, could you get Craig to meet us there?"

Hollie smiled as Daniel backed out the door, she called up the stairs to Craig to come down to the kitchen.

Craig picked up a pre-packed backpack for himself and Hollie and his father's metal detector. This he thought it might help them find the treasure.

They made their way to the Summerhouse, entering as Daniel comforted the horses. Moments later they had strapped the packs to the horses and Craig set the dials. He set them to 1644, Hollie closed the shutters and Daniel checked the saddles once more. Meanwhile, away from the Summerhouse, Alex took Ben for a walk around the common. He compared what was around him to the past. Some things were comforting but it also lacked something the past had, unspoiled beauty.

The Summerhouse quivered and filled with the green light as they slipped back into 1644. All became quiet as they slowly opened the shutters. Outside they viewed a familiar site, trees and bushes fractionally taller, all else the same as in 1642. Hollie opened the doors, and the boys led the horses out onto a treasure hunt of a lifetime, however this did depend on whether the map was genuine

Chapter 16

The weather was grey and cloudy with not a soul in sight. Only the sound of familiar crows that squawked in the tops of nearby trees. They cautiously ventured out, Daniel mounted his horse, Hollie and Craig mounted theirs. With the backpacks strapped to the horses they slowly rode towards Bronsil Castle. Daniel again read Mrs. B letter,

"Well according to Mrs. B the legend says that ravens guard the treasure, waiting the rightful owner to retrieve it. I hope that metal detector works."

Craig grinned and turned to Hollie,

"Ravens guarding the treasure, sounds like something from an Alfred Hitchcock film, best hold on tight Hollie or the birds might get us."

An hour had passed and they had made good progress. They decided not to visit Samuel at The Priory as it was a little out of the way. After a few miles they turned west through a lower part of the hills. In front of them was a track leading through a dense wood, which according to the map led to the castle. Daniel peered through the trees, it seemed clear, they carried on. All three kept looking around. It was so quiet, just the sound of rustling trees blowing in the breeze. They had gone just a short distance when Suddenly Daniel pointed to his left, "Soldiers, over there!"

They were Roundheads, coming in from a side track. Daniel put his horse into a gallop, Craig and Hollie did the same. They raced through the trees, ducking the overhanging branches. The Roundheads followed in hot pursuit, Daniel looked back and saw them gaining ground and called to Craig,

"They can't have remembered us surely!"

Craig called back.

"Just ride and stop calling me Shirley!"

Daniel smiled at Craig's coolness and rode harder, he saw Roundheads in the clearing ahead, two lots of soldiers, there seemed to be no way out. They pulled up short of the Roundheads in front of them, the soldiers at their rear got closer. They were trapped. The captain of the troop came forward, looked at each of them and asked.

"Why did you run? Are you guilty of something? You are acting very suspiciously, and dressed in a fashion I am not familiar with."

Daniel replied cautiously,

"We were just out riding and your soldiers scared our horses, and us!"

"That may be so, however now you will have to come with us."

The Roundheads numbered a dozen in total. They knew they were outnumbered. The captain told one soldier to take five men and escort them to Bronsil Castle for questioning. He would join them later, as he had business at the Priory in Malvern. They parted company, the captain took five soldiers and the other six took Daniel, Craig and Hollie to the castle.

Hollie whispered to Craig,

"This is not how I expected us to get into the castle, if they look in the sack on Daniel's horse and find the metal detector, how do we explain that?"

Craig did not reply as he had no answer, he just shrugged his shoulders. It took only fifteen minutes to reach the castle, whilst Craig sweated buckets trying to think of an answer to Hollies' question. They rode over the bridge and into the castle grounds. It was an impressive sight with towers at the gate entrance and a large courtyard. They were told to dismount, and they did so, leaving the various bags and the sack with the metal detector on the horse. The soldiers ignored the bags and just took them straight in.

The soldier in front turned to another,

"Leave the horses there and put them into the room at the end of the hall and lock the door, then join us in the main room in front of the log fire for some ale. The captain can speak to them on his return."

With that, the threesome were lead to the room and locked inside. Through a small window with bars at head level in the door, Hollie watched the soldier walk away down the hall. She sighed,

"Just great . . . locked up again, how on earth are we going to get out of this one? I am really tired of been taken prisoner!"

She started to pace up and down the room, which for now was their prison cell.

Daniel tried the door saying,

"Typical . . . come back to nick someone else's gold and get locked up for our trouble. Oh! well let's face it, this is what happens to criminals."

Craig replied with a slightly annoyed tone of voice,

"Come on Daniel we're not crooks, the treasure is buried and forgotten. We are . . . archaeologists just recovering it."

"Maybe, maybe not we were told not to abuse the Summerhouse's powers, maybe this is payback?"

They all smirked and saw the irony of the situation. Hollie smiled and looked to Craig,

"I have an idea . . . Guard, guard." she shouted through the little barred window in the door,

"We are really thirsty, water please!" She turned to Daniel.

"When he comes in Daniel you knock him out with that chair over there in the corner."

Daniel and Craig looked at each other,

"It's so ridiculous it might just work."

Craig looked to his sister and added,

"Hollie, you've been watching too many movies, yet . . . it's worth a try!"

Daniel stood with the chair behind the door, Hollie shouted again. "Water, please!"

A soldier hearing the call said to another,

"They're calling for water."

"We'll go and take some, I am not leaving this ale. When the captain gets back, we will be back on our horses, charging around the countryside yet again."

He sipped his ale, then licked his lips and continued,

"So I need my rest, you are the young recruit, you go. They're only children, we can't be too hard on them."

The soldier left the warm room with a jug of water and walked across the entrance hall, down the long corridor to the room where Hollie stood calling. After a moment she saw him coming,

"It's so kind of you, I am so grateful, it's been such a long day."

His young eyes were drawn to Hollie who's blond hair and sparkling eyes did the trick, he did not bother to look where the others were. He unlocked the door and walked in, looked at Hollie with a big smile,

"Here you are!"

Daniel brought the chair down over his head. Hollie winced, "Ouch! I am so sorry but . . . Oh! Look he's only our age, so young. He's not too hurt is he?"

Craig jumped up and Daniel grabbed Hollies' arm,

"Come on no time for sentiment and saying sorry, we have to get out of here."

Hollie looked at Daniel with piercing eyes,

"Did you have to hit him so hard?"

"That was the whole idea, Hollie, your idea in fact!"

Hollie felt so guilty now that the young soldier was lying on the stone floor, out cold. They lightly tip-toed down the hall as quickly as they could. They could see the light across the entrance hall from the other room where the other soldiers were. Loud laughter from the soldiers echoed around the building. They crossed the entrance hall like church mice and out into the daylight to the horses. Mounting quickly and rode out of the gates, Daniel leading them back into the thick woods. He motioned to them to dismount and hide amongst the bushes. He grabbed his pack off his horse and pulled out a large camouflaged net and said to Craig,

"Grab this and cover the horses and us . . . quick they won't be long."

In the castle the young soldier staggered back to his colleagues in the hall and told them what had happened. The Sergeant who was about to put another log on the fire, threw it at the fire dislodging the burning logs, which rolled out onto the floor. He shouted to the others to mount up. They ran out not noticing the burning logs. The soldiers mounted, the order to break up into two groups was given. One group went south, the other north. Back inside the hall the burning logs on the floor set fire to the long tapestries hanging on the walls, the flames slowly making their way up to the tapestry and the timber roof. One group of soldiers, complete with the young boy with his sore head, raced past with the leader shouting at him,

"This is what happens when I send a boy to do a man's work, you haven't heard the last of this."

Daniel and Craig froze as they thundered by, Craig whispered,

"What was this netting doing with your camping gear?"

Daniel grinned and replied,

"Some mates and I used it one day in the woods when we decided it would be a good idea to camp out with some cider."

"Did it work?"

"It must have, but to be honest that day is so hazy that I can't remember much, I just know that the next day I felt so ill that I told myself that it had been a bad idea and that I wouldn't do it again."

Hollie looked at both,

"You boys, can we concentrate on the matters at hand? . . . like getting out of here?" Daniel then noticed that the map had fallen from his coat and was on the track in front of them.

"The map," He pointed it out to Craig, "I have to get it, stay here."

The other group of soldiers that went south noticed that there were no new tracks and the Sergeant assessed the evidence,

"They didn't come this way, we have to turn back."

Daniel walked out to pick up the map leaving Hollie and Craig behind the netting. He put it in his jacket pocket. He was still in the middle of the track, as the soldiers came back and saw him. He froze to the spot, his heart pounding. They pulled up and three dismounted and marched up to him in. Craig and Hollie with horses at the ready could only watch.

The sergeant spoke to Daniel,

"Where are the other two . . . in the wood?"

He turned to the other three and gave the order,

"You three, find them!"

The three dismounted and went into the dense wood. Only twenty metres away from them Craig whispered to Hollie,

"Be ready to drop this net and ride."

Daniel looked the three soldiers up and down remembering his martial art training prepared himself mentally. One came up and grabbed his left wrist, Daniel grabbed his hand with his right hand, twisted it round forcing the soldier to the floor. The other stepped forward and Daniel let out a round house kick to his head, knocking off his helmet, then using his elbow he hit the other, on the back of the neck. The third ran forward, Daniel ran to him and jumped into the air. Daniel thrust a flying side kick, laying him flat to the ground, then he spun round expecting more, but they all lay very dazed and unable to stand.

Craig and Hollie dropped the netting and rode out to Daniel with his horse in tow.

The three soldiers in the wood hearing the commotion came running back. Daniel jumped onto the horse and swung round to see the three soldiers run straight into the netting, tripping up and getting tangled.

Daniel's eyes and ears were then drawn to the castle, which was spitting flames into the air,

"We can't go back for the treasure now."

They all watched the flames for a moment which grew with ferocity and it was clear that the castle was in the midst of being totally consumed.

"Let's get out of here fast. That fire is going to be like a huge beacon and attract more soldiers from miles around."

The three rode out at speed with the other three soldiers still scrambling around on the track.

Hollie shouted to Daniel,

"That was so cool Daniel, what you did to those soldiers."

Craig added,

"Breathe Hollie, breathe, now's not the time to go all gooey."

Daniel felt confused because one minute she was scolding him for being too rough on one soldier, then congratulating him on others, he put it down to Hollie having a woman's prerogatives to change her mind, but felt compelled to say something,

"Hollie what's the difference between what happened there and the other in the castle."

"Oh! Come on Daniel those back there were big soldiers, grown men with swords. The other was nothing more than a boy with no sword, he was only armed with a mug of water!"

Daniel understood what she meant, but shook his head and thought, 'I give up'. The other six soldiers were in front somewhere. They came upon the clearing and Daniel signalled them back into the trees. Craig and Hollie followed and they dismounted catching their breath. Daniel sighed,

"Sorry guys but the treasure hunting is off for now, I think we should get back and head for another . . . safer time, what do you think?"

"Good thinking." replied Craig.

Hollie agreed but did not like to admit that she enjoyed the danger even though it made no sense at all. They all remounted to continue, the weather was still cloudy but the rain stayed off. It was time to go home. The Summerhouse came into view and hearts warmed at the thought of home, until the young soldier with the bump on his head was in front of them. Daniel shouted to Craig and Hollie,

"Leave him to me."

Daniel raced to him, ready for anything, then pulled up close to him. The soldier drew his sword and looked into Daniel's eyes, and with conviction ordered,

"You are all under arrest."

He was now in command of the situation, "You will dismount and hand over any weapons you have."

Daniel smiled,

"Sorry mate the only weapon was that chair I broke over your head, that's back there, burnt to a cinder by now."

The soldier looked surprised,

"Burnt?"

"Yes the castle is on fire!"

The soldier's shoulders sank,

"Great, I will get the blame for that too I expect, and it's all your fault. Have you any idea how difficult it is when you're the youngest in the troop. I'm always given the worst jobs, mind you better that than a pike man, I suppose."

Hollie started to feel sorry for him, after all it was her idea to christen his head with a chair. So Hollie suggested.

"Let's take him with us . . . away from this war!"

Craig could not believe his ears and replied,

"Have you gone mad, he belongs here not in the twenty first century, he won't cope. Besides, Dad will go nuts and Mum ballistic."

Hollie thought for a moment,

"He might have skills that he could use in our time, it would be better than here . . . you hit him Daniel, we are responsible for this mess."

They could not argue with her, so Daniel asked,

"Look Mr. Roundhead soldier do you want to get out of this war?"

He looked confused, "Yes but . . . "

"No buts what can you do . . . work wise?"

"I am a roof thatcher."

"Sounds good to me follow us mate."

Hollie grabbed the soldiers arm gently and asked,

"You have family? If you come with us you will never see them again."

"What do you mean, never again? And besides no I have no family, my parents died when I was 10 years old. I was brought up by my uncle who was a Thatcher, but he was killed six months ago and I ended up as a soldier."

It took seconds for Hollie, Daniel and Craig to decide to take him home, with her Mum gone for the night it wouldn't be a problem.

He did not even understand the war, so he followed the three into the house and the doors were shut quickly. Daniel set the dials, Craig held onto the horses and Hollie held onto the frightened soldier. The dials glowed green, the house groaned and the soldier shivered with fear as the house moved into the twenty-first century. Hollie tried to explain what was happening and about the future. To her surprise he seemed to catch on quick, the future sounded better.

The house settled and Daniel and Craig led the horses out.

Craig turned to Hollie,

"You had better see Dad about our guest whilst Daniel and I take the horses back." Hollie responded with a reluctant yes, and Daniel and Craig led the horses back to the stables. Hollie asked the soldiers name, he replied,

"Richard ma'am!"

She felt it so quaint being called 'ma'am.' She was sure that her father would understand the situation. Richard looked mesmerised and lost, his world was gone, a new one around him. Hollie called for Simon, who came downstairs. He looked at Richard and asked,

"Sealed Knot in town enacting the Civil War? That costume is great, it looks very authentic."

Hollie tried to smile and replied,

"Actually Dad it is real. We brought Richard back from 1644, where we accidentally got him into huge trouble ... We were taken prisoners and." Her Dad stopped her with a signal of his hand and said,

"Hollie, say no more."

She smiled. Simon turned a funny shade of red, and she cowered as knew her father was about to unleash hell.

"Hollie what did I say about the Summerhouse.'

He paced up and down with his hands behind his back.

'It's not for fun and games, it's most certainly not for bringing strays home."

Richard looked at Simon, tongue tied. Hollie replied,

"Sorry but we were left with ... err ... no option, honest Dad ... he's a thatcher of roofs. Can't we help him? It's war back there, absolute hell."

Simon considered for a moment,

"Give me a moment to think things through. Just as well your mum is not home, this would take some explaining!"

He paused holding his hands to his lips as though to pray, then said,

"Hollie, my dear, it's not as easy as that. He is an alien to this time, having no National Insurance number, no Birth Certificate. . . . Also Hollie I don't really think it's fair on Richard, he is been thrown into a world he does not know or understand."

Richard said meekly "I'd love to see some of this life . . . it would be . . . so . . . exciting!"

Hollie could see Simon's point,

"That's true Dad, but what about the illegal aliens that get into this country now, they get documents on the black market, so can't we?"

"Absolutely not, I am a doctor Hollie. If I was found out I would be struck off, prison, who knows."

He felt guilty, as he knew Hollies' intensions were good, and in a perfect world he would do it. However Richard would pose too many problems, he hugged her, and he looked at Richard. He was so young, he had the makings of a nice young man, even a good soldier. Simon snapped his fingers,

"Got it, Hollie we'll let him stay for a few days . . . to recover from that head injury, but on going back he cannot divulge anything about his stay. He could be in danger of being burned at the stake, as a witch!"

Richard looked horrified,

"Oh no, sir. I'll tell no one of anything, I promise."

Some time later after Daniel and Alex went home, Craig and Hollie swapped Richard's clothes for some of Craig's, then took him for a walk around the neighbourhood. He was full of questions as they walked,

"So many castles along this road. No muddy tracks."

Hollie explained that the castles were houses and the roads covered the whole country, transportation was so much quicker. Richard was amazed when he saw a car,

"A carriage with people inside but no horses to pull it."

Then he saw a bigger red one with many more people inside. Hollie called it a "Bus. It takes people around the town and from town to town. Shortly afterwards the street lights came on.' Richard asked,

"Such big candles to light the roads." Craig laughed, then Richard asked,

"What happened to the fields, the deer . . . my home?"

Craig and Hollie went on to explain about progress, the population explosion, and Richard asked, "This population explosion do you mean like a cannon . . . exploding people?" Hollie laughed,

"No Richard, I mean that towns grew because more people are born than died, and people live longer."

They started to make their way back to the house. Richard would sleep in Craig's room and in the morning Hollie would make him a modern day English breakfast. They were walking up the path to the to the house when Hollie heard the sound of running water, she turned to se Richard peeing into a hedge,

"Richard you don't do that there, we pee in the toilet in the house."

"In the house." Richard was shocked. They went in and Craig took Richard to the bathroom and showed him the toilet, Richard asked,

"So you pee into this then carry it outside to empty it?"

"No, you pull this handle and water flushes pee and the other away." Richard laughed,

"That's clever, and this funny paper? What's that for?"

"That's for cleaning your bottom after you have done . . . a you know what!"

Richard grinned with relief,

"When Hollie said you all do it in the house I thought for a moment that she meant. . . . " Craig laughed,

"No we don't do it on the floor. . . . and this is for washing your face and hands," he said pointing to the basin. He pointed to the bath saying,

"This is for having a bath, washing yourself all over."

"Where's the well, to fetch the water?"

"No well, you turn these taps and water comes out, when you have enough water you simply turn them off again," Richard was amazed.

"You are so lucky having all this, water brought to you in the house."

They joined the family down stairs and Simon examined Richard's head.

"Well, Richard, it looks fine. In the morning I will put a fresh dressing on it and then we will discuss your return home."

After a meal they chilled out in front of a log fire, chatting and laughing.

Richard smiled at Hollie,

"This has been the best day of my life. You are all so lucky to be able to do this with your family in such warmth."

Hollie felt guilty, she had always taken home life for granted. She took his hand and replied,

"We envy what you have too, the green fields, trees and deer, clean air and a simple life, both times have their good points and bad."

Simon suggested that Craig helped him draw a bath, after all he was rather grubby,

Richard looked perplexed and replied,

"Draw a bath? I'm afraid, sir, I can't draw . . . or write."

Craig just put his arm round Richard's shoulders and said,

"Don't worry we'll make you have a good clean, then I think I will stay up with you and show you how to write your name."

Hollie thought it was an excellent idea and that she would join them later. In the bathroom Richard relaxed in a bath of bubbles that Craig had prepared for him. He had never smelt anything so fragrance. When he had finished he joined Craig in his room and Craig showed Richard how to sign his name. Hollie came in shortly afterwards and for the next two hours they gave Richard a crash course in basic lettering. He actually proved a quick learner.

That night Richard had the best sleep of his life in Craig's bed . . . sheer luxury. In the morning Richard sat at the kitchen table, tucking into a cooked breakfast. Craig had porridge, he had developed a taste for it since their time with Mrs. Bennett. Richard sipped at a mug of tea between mouthfuls. He had never had tea before, it was very nice he thought, however he preferred the water which came off the hills, which he was glad to see, that people still collected today to drink. As he ate he looked round the kitchen, his knife and fork were so clean, made for a king. His mug had a picture of Ben the Border Collie on it which he thought was very posh. To afford such luxury, he thought, Craig and Hollie must be very rich. Simon came through and greeted them, then he took Hollie to one side,

"Richard's head is looking OK, I think it will be alright for him to go back home today. Staying may cause more problems. He might see too much, even want to stay . . . I think it would be for the best, and there's also your Mum to think about."

When Richard finished his breakfast, there was a knock at the door. It was Daniel and Alex. They came in and Craig made a pot of tea as they sat round the table listening to Simon explain his thoughts on why Richard should go back that day. Richard listened, "You have been very kind and helped me a great deal, I don't want to be any trouble to you."

Hollie with a beaming smile replied,

"You are no trouble, but as Dad said, what you see here you will have to keep to yourself . . . our secret."

Simon stood behind Richard and put both hands on his shoulders, gave a gentle squeeze and said,

"We all want what's best for you and to take you home as soon as possible. It's for the best."

Simon looked to Hollie and Craig,

"Hollie take Richard to the Summerhouse and wait for me. Craig and Daniel we will need those two horses back here now."

Simon caught up with everyone just as they were bringing the horses back to the Summerhouse down the path. He was carrying a parcel, and said,

"I am going to put this mess right and help our young friend at the same time."

They stared at him in disbelief. He stood there wearing an officer's uniform of the Roundheads. Richard stood up and saluted.

"Sir, I never knew you were an officer sir."

"Neither did we," laughed Hollie.

Simon saluted Richard back,

"I have an old friend who lives near, who is in the Sealed Knot.

I borrowed this from him. Richard and I are going back to 1644, alone, to put things right. Richard, as long as you do as you're told and never tell what you've seen here, I'll make sure you'll be fine."

Hollie and Craig left the Summerhouse and Simon and Richard were swept back to 1644. Simon opened the door on 1644, and they rode out. Richard asked Simon,

"Sir, what am I to do?"

"You are to forget the house and what it can do, we have the only key. If you are ever in desperate trouble you are to go to the Priory and ask for Brother Samuel. He can get word to us, then we could come and help, if we can. In return for keeping our secret, I am going to make you look like a real hero, which will help your army career no end."

They rode closer to the castle and in the distance Simon could make out eleven soldiers. As they got closer they could see that their captain was reprimanding them, shouting,

"I leave for a few hours, not only do you lose my prisoners, but you also burn down Bronsil Castle! What am I to tell the General?"

One soldier pointed towards the track,

"I think we are about to find out. Isn't that one coming with young Richard?"

Simon whispered to Richard,

"My name, by the way, is Lord Thomas Fairfax from York, I'm on my way to Oxford, and I took your prisoners off you and left them with my men. I have now brought you back and instead to inspect the troops here."

Richard was shocked, but composed himself. As they got closer, the group of soldiers stood silent. Simon looked down at the captain,

"Captain, I am Lord Fairfax, from York. What the.hell is going on here? . . . Are your men responsible for the fire at Bronsil Castle?"

"Yes sir well . . . "

"Cromwell will hear of this."

The captain cowered,

"I am sorry my lord."

He hadn't heard of Lord Fairfax being in the area, he was also unsure what he actually looked like!

"Excuse me, my lord, I was not aware that you were due here."

He looked at Simon inquisitively. Simon felt uneasy but immediately took control of his nerves, sat upright in his saddle and raised his voice,

"You lost your prisoners too! This brave young soldier here re-captured them. He handed them to my troops who are just beyond the woods back yonder. He caught them single handily, the man's a hero, saved your bacon he did. We need more like him. Look after him, I shall be watching his progress and yours from now on."

The captain stood aghast and his men could hardly believe that the young soldier was rubbing shoulders with a lord. Simon shook hands with Richard,

"Young sir it has been a pleasure, I now must return to my men. Oxford is awaiting us. I bid you farewell."

He turned to the captain and leaned forward, beckoning him closer. The captain stepped towards him and looked up at Simon who then spoke in a quiet voice,

"Next time a senior officer speaks to you Captain be sure not act as you have just done. I am a generous man and will overlook it this time, however another senior officer or lord may not." Simon rode off back down the track.

The captain swallowed hard then turned and looked at Richard, "Soldier dismount."

Richard got down, feeling nervous and a little frightened. The captain looked him up and down and said,

"Well, young man, you certainly impressed Lord Fairfax. You are a better soldier than I gave you credit for. Promotion will be on its way to you very shortly and a better uniform."

Then he shook his hand and the other soldiers patted his back, glad to relieve the tension that had been in the air. Simon glanced back and was pleased to see the young man being accepted as an equal, even a hero.

Chapter 17

Simon stepped out of the Summerhouse to the present time. Alex had been brought up to date while he was gone.

Simon told them all about his adventure, they cheered and said in unison,

"Wish we could have been there to see that!"

Simon lifted his hand,

"No absolutely not. No more time travelling."

A shriek of laughter from the house drew everyone's attention. Mrs. Templeton was leaning through the open window,

"Hi all. I'm back . . . Simon what are you wearing? This is no time to be playing soldiers in the back garden with the kids! . . . Really, how old are you?"

Daniel winked at Hollie and motioned Craig to stand back, whispering,

"Where and when shall we go next? We didn't get the treasure, so shall we try again?"

"For now I think Hollie and I should help Mum and Dad with some decorating. Let's discuss the Summerhouse tomorrow, when Dad's not around."

Daniel and Alex made their way home, whilst Craig and Hollie went inside to help their parents. When Daniel and Alex arrived home their mother excitedly told them that they had been organising an appointment for the next day to visit a local auctioneer of antiques.

"Hello boys, your Dad and I are off to see that antiques man that you see on TV Tomorrow. It's possible that the collection of porcelain I have is worth a lot of money, so I intend to sell the lot to help us out of this financial mess."

"Sounds good Mum." replied Daniel. "Alex and I are just off upstairs to tidy our rooms."

Alex looked up at Daniel with shock, "Tidy our rooms, what for?"

Daniel put his arm round him and grinned a reply,

"Yes we are bro . . . " then whispering, "Trust me."

Their Dad, rubbing his hands together replied,

"OK, good lads. We will call you when dinner is ready."

Upstairs Daniel went on to tell Alex that it was in their best interests to keep on the good side of their parents if they were to keep going out every day with Craig and Hollie.

"Oh I see now, good planning, Daniel, I thought you were going mad wanting to do housework! . . . Shall we go with them to the auction and see how much they get?"

"Nice idea, however we did say we would meet Craig and Hollie."

"Sorry, forgot that. Do you fancy Hollie then?"

A flustered Daniel replied,

"Look at the mess under your bed, come on clean it up."

"Hit a raw nerve there eh! Bro."

After an hour with their rooms done, they went downstairs, Daniel asked his Dad if he could use the phone.

"Yes you can, but don't spend ages on it."

Alex walked passed saying,

"Daniel's got to call his new girlfriend."

"Leave your brother alone Alex." his Mother called.

Simon answered the phone,

"Hello. . . . Hollie in? Yes, hold on Daniel."

He then called upstairs to Hollie,

"Hollie . . . Daniel on the phone."

She ran down the stairs, took the phone from her grinning Dad and answered,

"Hi Daniel, long time no speak!"

"Hollie, Alex and I were coming to you in the morning but he wants to go with Mum and Dad to an auctioneers to get her collection valued . . . she wants to sell the lot. I thought maybe you and Craig might want to come along, it's not far from here and it might be an eye opener."

"Yes! Ok, Craig and I will come over in the morning."

"Great, be here by 9.30."

Then Daniel turned to Alex, who was pretending to play a non-existent violin,

"Alex get a grip, I thought with what we went through with Mrs. B and Coombs it might be interesting for all of us."

"Sure bro, I believe you."

The next morning Hollie and Craig got ready to go to Daniel and Alex's. Craig made sure he had the pocket watch he had off Mrs. B as he thought he might ask the antique dealer what it was worth and Hollie wore her pink heart shape brooch. They met up with Daniel, Alex and their parents and made their way to the dealers. They arrived at the auction house and the dealer examined the porcelain. He remarked that it was all good and worth a considerable amount. The vase that Daniel and Alex had given her was worth even more because it was in such an excellent condition. Daniel & Alex's parents were really pleased, and decided to walk around the auction-room 'window shopping'. The children cornered the auctioneer. Craig showed him his pocket watch. It was worth several hundred pounds. Craig was thrilled.

The man's eyes on Hollie, he said,

"Gorgeous my dear . . . your brooch I mean, may I take a closer look?"

"Yes of course."

Hollie took it off and he looked at it through an eye glass.

"If I am not mistaken this is by Faberge, this could be worth twenty plus."

"Pounds? . . . thought it might be more"

"No my dear I mean twenty thousand. It's very rare indeed."

All stood with mouths open in disbelief.

"Do you want to sell it?"

It took Hollie all of a minute to recover enough to answer,

"No, it's is very special to me. Maybe one day. Thank you though."

Craig looked at his watch and said he would hold onto it also. Daniel and Alex's parents come back and organised with the man to auction their collection. He suggested they put a reserve on each item, then see what happens on auction day which was the following week, Thursday. They left, and Daniel said to Hollie,

"You should put that somewhere safe and not wear it out."

"I know that now. Just think, this could pay for both Craig and I to go to University! You gave your vase to your Mum. That was kind, but why are they selling it?"

"Dad had been made redundant, the money from the sale will help lower their mortgage and help Dad set up his own business."

"That's a great idea, what type of business?"

"Decorating and stuff . . . Dad is great with his hands, he can turn his hand to many things really. He didn't want to stay in his old job anyway."

"You never know my Dad might just have some work for him. The house needs so much doing to it but he needs to return to hospital work, I will mention it to him when we get back."

"Thanks Hollie."

He put his arm round her giving her a hug. Alex and Craig saw this and both went arr! Daniel removed his arm quickly and they all got in the car and drove home. Craig and Hollie walked the short way home, as they got in Hollie went straight to her father and told him of Daniel's Dads intentions of setting up his own business. Simon was very interested at the thought of some of the restoration being done by someone else.

Later that day they all met up in the Summerhouse to discuss another trip, and the treasure they had not had a chance to find. Craig asked Daniel,

"What do you think Daniel, should we try going back for the treasure or not?"

Daniel sighed the thought was so tempting and wealth was something that he or his family did not have,

"Craig mate, I really don't know. That last trip was too close for comfort. If we go we must pick a safer date, so I suggest we go either long before the start of Civil War or long after it."

Craig smiled and nodded,

"Yes, we messed up the timing a lot, we should go to a time when the castle grounds are not overgrown. Hollie, over to you, what year shall we aim for?"

Hollie pulled out from her bag a pile of notes. She started to read them to the group, "Well, as we know the castle burnt down in 1644, except the records show a siege involving the Royalists troops. In the early 1600s, the Reede family were driven out by a restless ghost, possibly Lord Beauchamp's, that's the guy who buried the treasure."

Alex sat listening quietly then stuck his arm in the air, as if at school and asked, "Hollie why did he bury it in the first place?"

"As far as I can gather, he did not trust his relatives to look after his fortune whilst he went off to the crusades. He buried a box full of gold in or around the moat. He didn't returned from the crusades and so the treasure was never found."

Hollie went into drama mode and started to create an atmosphere as she told more of the story.

"The legend says that the knight's body was supposed to be sent back if he was killed, so that he could be buried in the family crypt. Only then would the rightful family heir receive the gold. Only part of his body was returned home from the crusades and never laid to rest properly. So a raven stands guards on the gold to this very day. Until all of his bones are laid to rest, his spirit will haunt the castle and its grounds. It's also said that his ghost can still be seen walking around the moat and castle trying to find everlasting peace."

Everyone shivered at listening to the chilling tale. What if it was true? What if the gold did exist? The knight was a very real person and very, very rich. It was the stuff that true adventures were made of, all these thoughts were going through their minds.

Alex's imagination was running riot after hearing the word 'ghost.'

He thought out loud, "Gold and Ghost . . . cool!"

Daniel asked,

"So when are you saying we should go, Hollie?"

Hollie looked at the notes, then up at the ceiling. She mumbled years to herself. The boy's looked at each other, then the ceiling wondering what she was looking at. She looked back at them, and smiled,

"Well, if the moat dried out in the early 1600's and the castle was burnt down in the Civil War in 1644, then we should go somewhere in the middle, say 1630. What do you think?"

As far as Craig was concerned as long as it made it easier to find the gold and avoid trouble he did not mind what year it was,

"As good as any I suppose, at least those soldiers won't be hassling us."

Daniel shrugged his shoulders and agreed,

"That is the main point . . . no soldiers, as long as we can get there and back in one piece, with the gold, or whatever it is buried there."

Hollie felt quite pleased that her research went down well with the group.

Alex stuck his arm in the air,

"So what was happening in 1630 then?"

"Well to be honest, I'm not sure. Shall we go and see?!"

He smiled at her flippant answer coated with confident undertones.

Craig stood with his arms folded, deep in thought, then he put them behind his back, rocked on the balls of his feet and addressed the group,

"Well, we are agreed on the date so when shall we go. I say tomorrow, how's that with you, Daniel?"

Daniel ruffled Alex's hair and replied,

"Hell! Craig what's wrong with today, what do you think bro?"

Alex raised his arms in a scary fashion and replied,

"Boo ghosts and goulies, let's go!"

Hollie motioned her hand in a calming way,

"Ok Alex we are not going ghost hunting, we had enough scary moments on the last trip, although, it would be fun, I must admit."

They were getting so engrossed in the prospect, that they did not hear the footsteps coming down the path towards them. The door swung open and Simon cast a shadow across the floor. With his fists firmly planted on his hips, he said,

"I hope this is not a meeting for another trip into certain trouble?"

Hollie and Craig fumbled for words and Daniel stood up, put his hands into his pockets, opened his mouth as though to speak but no words came out. Alex, however, found a few and replied,

"Yes . . . we're going hunting for lots of gold, ghosts and stuff."

All looked shocked at Alex's reply. Simon just folded his arms, looked down at Alex and said,

"Is that a fact young man? Can you fill me in on more facts, or have Craig and Hollie found their tongues now?"

Hollie stood up and went to her father and told him the whole story of the gold and the knight who buried it. At first he listened politely, then more intently when Hollie showed him her written research, including pages copied from a rare book dated 1901. This he found very interesting. He sat in the old armchair smiled and said,

"Well I have to say Hollie you have done well to research this, but allowing you to go chasing such dreams, I cannot condone."

Alex, who with a cheeky smile, stepped forward,

"Mr. Templeton you are right, but if you came with us that would be OK wouldn't it? I mean we can go and be back before Mrs. Templeton rumbled us."

Simon was amused by his wit and quick thinking.

"That is very true Alex. I must admit the thought of a treasure hunt is tempting." Craig and Hollie both jumped in with,

"Come on, Dad, we are going to a safe time and like Alex said Mum wouldn't know. Just think what we could all do with that gold, split equally obviously."

Simon thought of his youthful memories of adventure,

"Give me ten minutes. I will be back."

He ran back to the house and in the bathroom changed out of his painting overalls and put on, jeans and t-shirt with a old camouflage jacket. He called to his wife,

"Just off out with the kids for a minute, need to look at a sick horse."

"You're a doctor not a vet . . . well if you must, bring some milk on your way back, please!"

"OK, will do."

He dashed back to the Summerhouse making sure Shirley could not see him. Once inside he went up to the dials,

"If everyone is ready . . . What was that date Hollie, I will set the dials."

Simon set the date and the house did its magic and light show. All had become accustomed to this part, it was opening the shutters on the new world in an old time that was unnerving. The house became quiet once more, signaling they had arrived at their destination. Simon suddenly felt uneasy as he smelt the air, bringing back memories, mostly bad ones that he had long forgotten. Things like disease suddenly had a new meaning, he felt naked without his doctors bag and a nearby hospital.

Hollie opened one shutter, then said,

"Well here we are again. Actually it's pretty much the same."

Craig quipped,

"What did you expect, Hollie, a London taxi cab to take us to the gold?"

Simon grinned, put his arm round her and said,

"Come on then you lot, let's go. Pity we didn't have enough horses to go all round, anyway it will be a good walk from here. What do you say Daniel?"

"A good few hours I would say sir."

"Sir . . . I like that."

The clouds were dark but ahead looked clear. Daniel carried the metal detector, Hollie the notes and map, Craig a pack of food and the key, and Alex a camping compass.

They made their way in the direction of the castle. When they got to the woods Alex's compass gave them a rough bearing on the right direction to take. The wind whistled through the trees and seemed to be blowing in the direction that they were going. Daniel led the group with Simon at the rear, where he could oversee all members of the expedition. Craig felt that it was strange that they had not seen anybody else so far. Hollie tapped Daniel on the back,

"Daniel, any idea how far to go?"

He really knew how far it was, however he was out to impress Simon so he checked his map,

"I would say another half hour or more. See that hill rise there? Well it's over that and then another quarter of a mile or so, not far really."

Craig had been pondering their past trips and asked Daniel,

"I am starting to see why Samuel stayed here in these times, it is peaceful . . . but I would not say no to a bus right now, my legs ache, big time!"

The time seemed to pass quite quickly as they walked up the hill; and they were all glad that now it was all downhill to the castle. At the top they paused and looked around at the view. Simon remembered it all from his youth and how he and Samuel walked the hills, he addressed the group,

"From here you can see three counties. Over there in the far distance are the Black Mountains and behind us is a view we don't have any more. Now it's full of houses and trading estates. The sad thing is it will get worse as time goes on. Doesn't it look fabulous? Well that's progress I suppose."

His tone of voice was full of doubt at the prospect of further progress at the cost of countryside.

"Well come on gang, the castle is that way, isn't it Daniel?"

"Yes, just beyond those trees."

In the distance the castle loomed into view, looking abandoned. With only trees and crows for company, it almost seemed to call to them. Was it the Ghost of the Knight longing for human contact, or was it the cry of other lost souls which walked the hills. No one knew but there was a certain chill that surrounded them all as they drew closer to Castle Bronsil.

Chapter 18

They came upon the castle impressive entrance, it seemed abandoned by human life and had been for many years. Crows flew around the towers, a bridge spanned the moat which they crossed with caution.

Alex asked Hollie as he held her hand,

"Are you sure that we are not going to bump into those square heads again?"

Daniel laughed and corrected him,

"Roundheads bro . . . it's roundheads."

Hollie laughed too and squeezed his hand,

"No we should be OK, according to my research but keep your eyes peeled."

They all stood in the middle of the courtyard taking in the atmosphere. Craig looked around,

"Wow, it's like being in a movie of King Arthur and the Knights of the Round Table."

The crows flew in circles overhead, screeching as though to warn them of impending peril. Hollie shivered and hugged her Dad saying,

"This place is creepy, I don't like it, I feel as though I'm being watched."

"Don't worry, Hollie, we are all in this together. You will be quite safe, just keep your eyes open in case the bogey man puts in a appearance!"

"Oh! Very funny, let's just get on with it."

She looked around at the high walls of the castle and the two towers standing either side of the main gate. She could just imagine a Knight riding through the gate with his small band of men, off to the crusades, dressed in armour and the white tunic with a large red cross on it. She had seen pictures of The Knights Templar in history books and this fuelled imagination. She looked up at the top of one tower and thought she saw him, staring with armour shining in the sunlight, but instead it was a large black raven, glaring at her. He stood proud and majestic with a large strong beak; she instantly thought of the legend, the Knight whose ravens guarded the gold. Daniel looked at Mrs. B's map and stamped his foot,

"Well X marks the spot and that is right here."

They all looked at the ground which was hard and dusty. Alex moaned,

"Digging this with this spade will be like digging concrete."

Simon asked Daniel for the map. Daniel handed it to him.

"The X is clear in the middle of the castle, the hand written scribble underneath makes no sense."

Simon squinted at the writing and after a few moments replied.

"Elementary, my dear Watson, as Sherlock Holmes would say, X actually marks the spot where you start."

He suddenly had everyone's attention and went on,

"These letters are points of the compass followed by the numbers of paces you take in the direction stated."

He pointed to the first letters,

"This NW means North West, the number fifty, is the amount of strides you take. Daniel if you use your compass and stride fifty steps out in that direction, then follow the other three directions it should lead us to the spot where the treasure is buried."

He started to pace out fifty paces, the others followed closely, out through the gates. Daniel strode away counting out to himself,

"49, 50, now the next say's, S35 . . . south thirty five paces."

Daniel again took long strides until he reached thirty five.

"The next says NE70, north east seventy . . . one, two."

Daniel paced out the amount to seventy, then read the last instruction,

"N10, north ten paces, one, two, three, four, five. . . . Hold on!"

All stopped walking at Daniel's cry of frustration, they all looked ahead and saw what Daniel meant,

"If I keep going I will end up in the middle of the moat; surely he didn't bury it there! He's having a laugh!"

Simon smirked,

"Typical, I thought the idea of a treasure hunt was too good to be true."

Craig tapped Daniel on the back,

"Come on, Daniel, you and I have faced worse than this since becoming time travellers, let's go in together, and kick around. You never know, we might get something!"

"Yes we will, a rotten cold!"

Hollie clutched her heart in a very theatrical manner,

"My hero, bring me yonder pot of gold."

"Oh shut up Hollie." replied an embarrassed Craig.

Daniel looked at Craig and together they paced out the last five strides up to ten. By seven the water was above the knees, by nine was up to their stomachs, and by ten was nearly at their chests. Simon called to them,

"Careful boys. That is deep. Don't get caught up on anything or get stuck in the mud."

"Don't worry Dad we are good swimmers; mind you we will be careful . . . it is tricky under foot."

Daniel confirmed that,

"It is too . . . you take that side and I will take this, small steps and feel around with your foot."

They moved slowly around with the others looking on in anticipation. Simon kept looking all round for unwelcome company, but everything was quite quiet except for the occasional curse from Craig and Daniel as they kicked stones at the bottom of the moat.

Simon called out encouragement,

"You're doing well, boys, keep going. These instructions would only be a rough guideline, I mean 'paces' aren't that accurate."

Daniel and Craig looked at each other,

"Now he tells us, we could be in here for ages, and it's getting cold."

Daniel winked,

"Come on mate, five more minutes then we will call it a day."

Hollie asked her Dad,

"How long have they been in there?"

"Nearly twenty minutes, they best come out soon before they go numb from cold."

Five minutes was up and Daniel signalled to Craig to get out. Suddenly Craig vanished under the water, Hollie shouted to Daniel and he dived under, Simon rushed into the water to help Daniel pull Craig back up. Alex held on to Hollies' hand, both looked on helplessly. Hollie was close to tears. Suddenly Simon and Daniel appeared gasping for breath, and between them was Craig, held up by his armpits. They dragged him out, coughing and spluttering. Clutched tightly to his chest was a muddy box.

"Found this."

Alex punched the air,

"Way to go, Craig!"

They all turned their attention to what was a very rusty chest, about twice the size of a shoebox, with heavy metal straps holding the oak timbers together. Simon and Daniel took either end to move it up the bank. As they lifted it there was a creak and a clatter as the bottom fell out, and with it about a hundred coins. They were covered in green slime, and the smell of stagnant water reached everyone's nostrils. Simon reached down and picked one up, he took it to the water's edge to wash the dirt off.

Craig looked in disbelief, "Nothing but very dirty old pennies, no gold bars or jewelry.

Simon walked back to them rubbing the old coin,

"No it's not gold bars, Craig, or jewelry, however these are gold coins!"

"Really!?"

"Look for yourself."

They started to clean the coins off, each taking a handful, and rubbing them vigorously.

Craig was deep in thought and his Dad asked,

"Penny for them? You are miles away, near drowning scare you?"

"Yes, a little but as soon as I went under my hands found the box, almost as though someone wanted me to. Dad I felt as though someone grabbed my hands and put them on the box, I held onto it and felt hands lift me."

Simon smiled,

"Son that was Daniel and me lifting you. We dived under and brought you out."

Craig nodded,

"I know that Dad, but I felt I was lifted out of a hole at the bottom of the moat and handed to you and Daniel. Dad, I opened my eyes and saw the face of a man."

By this time everyone was listening to Craig.

"Go on Craig, tell us more," asked an excited Alex.

"He wore a helmet and armour I think with a white thing and a red cross across his chest . . . well that's what I think I saw."

Hollie ruffled the hair on his head and told him that it was just shock, his mind playing tricks. Alex had other ideas,

"Come on Hollie, you said that the ghost of a Knight haunted the castle, now that ghost has just saved Craig . . . It's a good ghost looking out for us."

Simon laughed,

"Come on you lot, it's time we went. We have been safe up to now, let's not push our luck. We have a precious cargo now, so we had better be careful. These are desperate times and we have a long walk back."

Craig and Daniel felt the excitement fade as the thought of another chase with soldiers or robbers. Craig also couldn't get the vision of the Knight's face out of his mind, it was quite haunting yet not threatening. They put the coins into the two backpacks, Simon carried one and Daniel the other, then started the journey back, heavier and wetter. As they marched off a raven sitting on one of the castle towers opened its wings and glided over their heads to a tall tree ahead of them.

With the gold weighing heavy in the backpacks, Simon and Daniel soon worked up a sweat. They started to climb to the top of Midsummer Hill, Simon wondering whether the gold was worth it, as his back was aching badly and they still had a long way to go. The view from the top was spectacular. Daniel checked his watch, it was 3 o'clock. Their clothes were drying in the afternoon sun. To distract from the pain Simon started to give a brief history lesson that he remembered from being a young boy living in Malvern.

"This, Craig and Hollie, is Midsummer Hill, it's an old encampment and it was believed that it was here that Caractacus, who led the Britain's against the Romans, was captured and taken to Rome. You would have thought they would have executed him, but in fact he became good friends with the Emperor and lived in luxury to a ripe old age."

Above him, the raven flew into a tree, peering down through the branches. They had listened but gave no reply as they just wanted to get back home, especially Craig and Daniel who were feeling dirty and muddy and smelly. Hollie and Alex being dry, were quite enjoying the walk until Daniel called out from the rear that he could see riders. Simon cried out,

"Quickly, into the trees before we are spotted."

They hid as Daniel pulled out his binoculars and looked through the bushes at the oncoming riders. He passed them to Hollie,

"Are those King's men?"

"No they're not, but I don't think they saw us because they're not galloping this way, they're heading north."

Simon took the binoculars,

"Well Hollie is right, they actually look more like rich landowners out hunting . . . there would be wild deer around here, maybe even boar. That's why it became known as 'The Chase'. It was an area for hunting by royalty, gentry and general super rich. Let's get going, we don't want to be seen."

Above them the raven took off and flew over the riders, as if making sure that they went on their way, then it flew back to the group, and circled as they hurried through the dense woods. Craig with the Knight's face still imprinted in his mind asked Simon,

"What should we do with this treasure now Dad? I mean, how do we explain how we got it?"

Simon pondered this,

"Good point Craig, it really would be treasure trove, I think. Selling it could be a problem as treasure found belongs to the state."

They listened to this and Daniel spoke for all,

"But we found it, and Craig nearly drowned getting it! So what do you suggest we do with it?"

"The answer to that is simple . . . I don't know!"

They carried on walking, confused that even Simon was unsure what to do. What started out as an exciting find, which they had gone through so much to get, now their spirits were dampened. Above the raven watched the group, occasionally squawking as though to let its presence be known.

They were making their way through the wood at the bottom of the hills heading North West according to the compass Daniel was holding, when the raven flew down close over their heads in front of Alex, and landed on the ground. They all stopped in their tracks as the bird stared at them with eyes like black pearls. Its beak was large, its feathers were the deepest black and it stood its ground, unafraid. They were tall humans and it was a bird a fraction of their size, yet in sheer presence it towered ever them with pride and fortitude. Then as if by magic . . . in total amazement, eyes staring in disbelief, their mouths fell open, as the raven slowly changed into a towering knight astride a white horse with flaring nostrils. It had eyes that seemed to penetrate their very souls, as it stomped the ground with its hooves. Each one of them felt unable to move, glued to the spot. Even Simon felt himself shake with fear as the horse stamped at the ground as though to charge. Hollie grabbed Alex's hand and her Dad's as Craig grabbed Daniel's which made him even more worried! Craig stepped back and whispered,

"It's him, the man in the moat!"

He wore armour and a white tunic with a red cross on his chest, a large sword in its scabbard hung from his waist. His face was chiseled with high cheek bones and through his beard his mouth looked stern and thin lipped. His eyes resembled those of the Raven's and his body seemed to be lit by a soft white light that gave off a clean, cold, chill, he spoke,

"Two persons among you have gold coins which belong to me. They were left for rightful heir, which you are not. They must be returned."

The horse again stamped the ground, its nostrils flared and snorted, the knight's armour glistened and jangled whilst his sword looked threatening even though it was still sheathed. All were captivated by the apparition that seemed very real as was their fear.

At this point Craig found his voice,

"I nearly drowned finding the coins . . . no one else was going to retrieve them . . . they've been there for a few hundred years."

Everyone, including his Dad wished he had not said that, as the knight looked very imposing, even if he was a ghost. The knight paused for a moment,

"A few hundred years you say young sir. Has it been that long? I have walked and waited for my family to return but they have not."

His eyes were filled with sorrow, Hollie stepped forward and once again as she did for the young soldier, Richard, felt pity.

"We did not mean to steal your treasure. We didn't know that it belonged to anyone."

The knight smiled and his now blue eyes looked down on Hollie,

"That may be so young maiden, you weren't to know that I cannot be at peace until it is in the rightful hands, and my bones are laid to rest."

Simon then moved forward,

"We are trying to understand, and we would like to help, but you would have to tell us how."

Daniel lifted the heavy backpack off his back and lay it on the ground,

"Shall we take it and throw it back in the moat?

The knight stayed silent, staring, his armour shining light upon the group like the stars of the night. Simon turned back as if going towards the moat. The knight raised his hand,

"Stop! . . . On one condition. I will let you take a portion of the gold if you carry out two tasks for me . . . First task, you will give me a Christian burial. The second task, half of the gold you will take to the monks at The Priory."

He pointed in the direction of The Priory, then continued,

"I have seen much blood spilt in War and never seen much Peace. The monks are the same in the Holy Land, helping people every day.

163

Half of this gold would help them a great deal. I don't want it to fund more war, bloodletting or tears. I want it to bring smiles of happiness and tears of laughter."

He paused, and all were deep in thought of his meaningful words, except for Alex who was captivated by the Knights sword, it was decorated beautifully he thought.

"Do this for me and the rest of the gold is yours to do with as you please, as long as it is for peaceful ends."

Simon was having trouble taking it all in, hoping that he would awake and find that it was all a bad dream. Daniel and Craig could not believe that they would have to stay in muddy, damp clothes even longer. Alex on the other hand could not believe his luck; treasure and a ghost in one morning, how cool was that!

Hollie nudged her dad,

"Come on, Dad, we must do this for him."

Simon tried to overcome his fear and smile, and nodded,

"Looks as though we have no choice."

They all started to walk in the direction of the knight's pointing finger. Craig was the last to turn and as he did he caught a glimpse of the knight turning back into the raven. Its black silky wings stretched out as it took to the sky and flew above the group. Craig admired its graceful beauty and wondered if they were doing the right thing. Alex looked up at the raven, it flew low and Alex thought it resembled a modern day plane a fighter/bomber with stealth and power. He then decided that the raven was one very 'cool' bird with slick aerodynamic body lines.

Nearly an hour had passed as they came close to the Priory. Simon wondered how he was going to approach Samuel. Because they had gone back further in time, Samuel would not yet have lived their last meeting. Simon decided he should stay out of the way so not to shock his old friend, and besides, he did not want to stay any longer than he needed to, talking about the old days. He was muddy and cold and wanted to go home and have a hot bath. Craig and Daniel on the other hand were feeling quite excited now, and being young weren't aching all over. The raven squawked and landed in front of them and turned back into the knight. Alex could not get over this, he wished he could fly too!

The knight looked to Simon,

"Take the one sack of gold to the priory and hand it to a monk"

Simon signalled to Daniel,

"Daniel will take the sack he has on his back."

"Why me?"

"I don't want to get caught up in a trip down memory lane because I will only be repeating everything that I told him the other day when we were here last!"

Daniel saw the truth of that and said,

"Yes of course, forgot that."

Daniel turned and walked the short distance to the main gate and through it to the Priory door. He knocked with the iron knocker. It boomed out a deep sound, and after a few moments footsteps could be heard and the door opened. It was Samuel and Daniel smiled,

"Do you have a large bowl, box or a sack, as I have something in the bag for you."

Samuel looked confused, but went off to fetch one, and came back moments later, "Will this do? What is it you have for us, food?"

Daniel put the sack over his open backpack and tipped the contents from one to the other. Samuel could tell by the sound that it was money, his eyes lit up,

"A donation. That is so kind."

Samuel looked Daniel up and down and asked,

"You are not from around here are you?"

He looked in the sack, his face went pale and his knees weak. He looked at Daniel, "This is a very great deal of money. May I ask how . . . why?"

"It's not mine, it belongs to a very wealthy man who wants you to have it. He used to live in the castle on the other side of the hill."

Samuel looked puzzled,

"The castle has been empty for some time . . . I would like to thank the man. Where is he?"

Daniel felt awkward. He put the backpack back on,

"Well, you see, he sent me because he couldn't come as he is dying. He is an old man . . . a very old man in fact."

"Well, you must thank him from all of us here, and we will pray for him."

"I will Samuel, you take care now."

Samuel looked surprised,

"How did you know my name, have we met before?"

"No not yet, but we will . . . given time."

Samuel pondered at his reply which did not make sense. He took out one of the coins, and looked at the date. It was very old and quite rare. Looking to Daniel who was walking away, he spoke to himself,

"Very old coins, a young man, a stranger who knows my name . . . he says we will meet again one day . . . Interesting."

Daniel stood in front of the knight out of sight of The Priory,

"Well I have given the monk the gold, he was very pleased and surprised."

The knight sat back on his saddle,

"But you still have the bag on your back"

"My dad bought me the backpack on my first camping trip, I wasn't going to leave it, I emptied the gold coins into a sack that the monk had. He was very pleased to receive so much, in fact I think he wondered if it was hot . . . I mean stolen! Besides why would anyone steal gold to hand over to a monk?"

"WE just did . . . I mean it wasn't ours in the first place, and they will do good things with it." replied Alex.

"I had a few good ideas too!" quipped Daniel

The knight looked down at Alex, and smiled,

"Honesty, a very good virtue for someone so young. You will receive a special gift before I leave."

He then spread his arms out stretched and became the raven once more and flew high, leading the way, with the others following.

Chapter 19

They all had mixed emotions on the gold. Simon was not too bothered, getting something for nothing had never featured in his life and he could see the problems of turning the gold into real money back home would be a very big problem. Daniel and Craig both felt that they had worked hard to get the gold and that they deserved it. Alex was contemplating what the gift promised by the knight could possibly be. Hollie summed it up by saying,

"Well people, I think we did a good deed today. Not only have we saved the soul of a dead knight but we may have saved the lives of many by giving the gold to the monks to help the poor, we should be proud."

The rest were not so sure but within minutes all were in agreement that indeed they had done the right thing.

It had been nearly an hour before the raven flew back down to the front of the group, and became the knight once more. The knight looked tired,

"I would like to thank you all for your help. As for the burial, there cannot be one without a body. I feel sure now that if a prayer is said by you all, then I may rest. If you would form a circle around me we can begin."

"What words or prayer would you like us to say?"

"The Lord's prayer."

He then looked down at Alex,

"I promised you a gift, and when I leave you shall receive it, my most treasured possession. I will not be needing it where I am going. Look after it and it will look after you, if you should ever need my help call upon it and I will come."

The group lowered their heads and started to recite The Lord's

Prayer, feeling shivers up and down their spines. With lowered heads they could only see the horse's feet, around the hooves gathered a white mist that shone. With each word the light grew and the cold became warmth. A sense of wellbeing came over everyone and Simon felt peace cover the group like a warm blanket. As they finished the prayer with Amen, they lifted their heads, and he had gone.

"I liked him . . . pity he couldn't have stayed longer."

"He was really tired." replied Simon.

"Knackered more like" said Daniel.

The mist cleared revealing the knight's sword stuck in the grass standing like a large cross. Craig looked to Alex and repeated the knight's words.

"Treasured possession for you to look after Alex."

Alex's eyes were wide, tears welling up, no one had ever given him such a gift, especially their very own prized possession. He pulled it from the ground and felt like King Arthur himself, making all of them smile as he pushed it up high into the air,

"Thank you sir."

He studied the sword, running the palm of his hand up and down the blade, being careful not to cut himself. There was an inscription on it that he could not quite make out. Everyone around stood a little closer to look. Daniel turned to Simon,

"I would have thought it would be impossible for a ghost to leave a solid object such as that, I mean . . . he was a ghost, as in not living, breathing, flesh and blood, but that sword is real!"

Simon agreed,

"True Daniel, but let's face it . . . nothing is what it seems . . . for instance only a few days ago if someone was to tell you that you could go back in time using an old shed, would you have believed it"

He laughed,

"No."

"Right people, let's be off home."

Once back inside the Summerhouse Simon set the dials, whilst Daniel and Craig admired the gold coins once more. Hollie looked at the sword with Alex, trying to read the inscription. She squinted and read the words slowly.

"I think it says . . . For Justice and Truth, Morglay will protect."

Daniel looked out of the shutter and announced,

"Lady and gentlemen next stop twenty first century with all mod cons, please mind the step on exiting, we hope you have enjoyed your trip to the past and please travel with us again."

Simon laughed, and opened the door,

"I'd best get back and help your mum, and let's all change out of these damp clothes."

He and Craig ran inside the house to change, leaving the others in the Summerhouse discussing Alex's sword. Inside Mrs. Templeton saw them come in and remarked, "Your clothes are all wet."

Craig quickly replied,

"Yes Mum, we got caught in this shower . . . must go, and get changed."

They quickly ran upstairs to their bedrooms, she looked out through the window, the sun was shining. She looked up the stairs, then back out the window at the blue sky then muttered to herself,

"Boys will be boys I suppose, I don't think I will bother to ask."

Meanwhile in the Summerhouse the others were discussing the sword inscription. Daniel read the words,

"It looks as though its name is Morglay and it will protect you . . . well, let's face it if you have the strength to pick it up and swing it around, I dare say it would protect, but alas, little Alex boy here, will have a bit of a hard job doing that, with his muscles being the size of acorns."

Hollie laughed,

"Oh! Don't be cruel Daniel, it could be magical."

"Shall I rub it and make a wish?"

Daniel smiled,

"Go on then bro, but make it a good one at least."

Alex rubbed it and said,

"I wish for another sack of gold."

They sat quiet and waited, but nothing happened.

"Never mind Alex."

Daniel stood up and put his hand out to help Alex up,

"Come on squirt we best get off home, but first you had better cover that sword with some of that old sacking in the corner. We don't want to be stopped by the police for carrying an offensive weapon."

Daniel pulled Hollie up off the floor,

"This bag of coins best stay with you until your Dad decides what to do with it."

Daniel and Alex started the short walk home.

"Hey, Alex, fancy a bar of chocolate on me from the corner shop?"

Alex's face lit up, and they both turned into the road with the shop Daniel holding tightly on to the sword. They were yards away when a man came running out of the shop, closely followed by the owner shouting,

"Stop thief."

Daniel instinctively stood his ground, and tried to deflect him with a Judo throw, but he was too slow. The bulky thief crashed into him, their bodies slammed together making Daniel loose grip of the sword. It spun up into the air and Alex ran to catch it. The thief staggered to his feet and, he ran at Alex like a thundering juggernaut out of control. Alex held the sword out, closed his eyes, and in a feeble act of defiance shouted,

"No . . . Stop."

The thief slammed into Alex. It was though he had run into a brick wall. His eyes crossed and glazed over as he crumpled to the ground, out cold. Daniel got up and staggered to Alex in slight shock, his little brother had just floored a six foot crook. The shopkeeper stopped running and put his hand on his heart, panting heavily. He stood looking down at Alex, and mumbled,

"Blimey, it's like David and Goliath!"

Alex looked at him and replied,

"Just lucky I guess, it must have been an aftershock after my brother tackled him!"

Moments later a police car was coming up the road with sirens blazing, the shopkeeper waved his hands in the air to indicate to them.

Daniel put his hand on Alex's shoulder,

"Well done bro, but we had better get out of here, that sword and police do not mix well."

To the shopkeeper's bewilderment they both ran off and headed to their home. The police arrested the still dazed thief, and put him in the back of the patrol car, then took a statement from the shopkeeper. He told them that two boys stopped him,

"Like I said officer, I chased this guy out of my shop, up the road, the one lad grabbed him and they both tumbled to the ground. Then the thief got up and ran into the other smaller lad, and fell to the floor, out cold, he was! The little one was the only one left standing, odd that!"

The policeman looked puzzled by the story, but wrote it down word for word,

"Lucky we were only a few roads away, so we were able to get here quick. Pity the boys didn't hang around longer."

The shopkeeper neglected to tell them that he knew the boys, and where they lived. Keeping things simple was his way, and he didn't want them to be hassled with statements . . . Justice had been done, after all!

Daniel and Alex collapsed onto their beds. Their parents were out and had left a note saying that they would not be back until six that evening, After Daniel had caught his breath, he went to Alex's room,

"Alex, cast your mind back half an hour to when I tackled the six footer. I was holding the sword then, but he smashed into me like a train, I have the bruises to prove it. Then you have the sword, he comes at you, and knocks himself out . . . How?"

"I don't know Daniel . . . Honest, I caught the sword, I saw him run at me, so I closed my eyes and hoped for the best. Bam! That was it! The thing is Daniel, I felt nothing, it was as though he hadn't touched me."

Daniel thought for a few moments,

"Right we've had enough for one day, don't you think? Let's relax, wait for Mum and Dad, have a snack, shower and change. We'll think about this tomorrow and talk to Simon."

Later that evening the boys were sitting on the veranda and Alex began to open up to Daniel and tell him a secret and a fear that he had had for the last two months at school.

"I wish I had the ability to do that to someone else." said Alex

"Do what?"

"Knock someone out, there's this boy at school David Yates who keeps picking on me with his two mates, they're brothers, and they back him up all the time, Yates and his Mates, we call them at school."

His bottom lip quivered,

"On the last day of school he punched me hard and stole my pocket money . . . I will get bigger won't I?. I'm not a coward Daniel . . . it's just that he is bigger than me, I wish I could meet him in the street with my sword and stop his bullying."

Daniel feeling very concerned replied,

"Chopping his head off with that sword would stop the bullying alright, but you will be in real big trouble . . . how about if I have a few words with him, I will sort it."

"No Daniel it has to be me, I have to stand on my own two feet."

"I understand little brother, let's go in and have an early night."

Daniel was about to leave Alex's room when he thought of his brothers fears and knew how it could eat away at you, so he turned and quietly said with honesty,

"Alex, I just called you little brother, yet today you took down a guy bigger than me. Ok! I know the sword has some sort of power, but at the time you didn't. But like a big man, you stood your ground, and made me proud."

Those words meant so much to him, so he leapt off his bed and gave Daniel a huge hug. Daniel ruffled his hair and turned and left the bedroom, then from the landing he called back to Alex,

"Of course you realise that you're still my squirt though!"

Alex nodded and smiled.

Chapter 20

The following day Daniel and Alex overslept, as did Craig and Hollie, Simon however was up early painting again. Through the night he had decided to suggest to Alex that he store the sword until he was older, as for the gold coins he was undecided. Daniel woke up and went into Alex's bedroom to find him dressed, bed made and the sword lying on it with Alex kneeling next to the bed, as though praying.

"You alright Alex?"

Alex jumped and replied,

"Don't creep up on me, thought you were Dad, don't want him finding this!"

"I wonder if there are any other tricks it can do for you"

"Don't think so, I held it before I went to bed and wished that in the morning I was as big as you or bigger, but when I woke my feet still couldn't reach the bottom of the bed. I wished to be strong and tried to lift my bed, but I couldn't budge it. Let's get off to Craig's, Mum and Dad are off to the auction today, Mum's porcelain goes under the hammer."

"What? Break them?"

"No squirt, that means it is sold today"

They both laughed and got ready to walk to Craig's, Alex wrapped the sword in the sacking cloth that he had used yesterday. It did not take long before they were walking to Craig and Hollies', Alex was unusually quiet, deep in thought.

"Come on Alex, penny for your thoughts?"

"Make it a fiver and I'll tell yah! Ha, Ha . . . it's nothing really Daniel, just been thinking about this sword. It's got power but it also could be worth money which Mum and Dad could do with at the moment."

"Yes Alex I know but, it was a special gift to you, and they're selling the pottery today. It could give them enough for their plans."

"Yes I know but what if it doesn't?"

"Well let's not worry about that now . . . tell you what, how about if we ask Craig and Hollie if they would like to go to the auction, might be fun.

They got to Craig and Hollies' house and they all sat at the kitchen table. Alex and Daniel told them all of what had happened on the way home the day before. Simon joined them and listened intently. Alex looked to him and asked,

"What do you think sir?"

"Well, the Knight left it to you specifically and you were the first to touch it, so it looks as though it protects you only. But, Alex, you can't carry that thing around, it is rather large."

Alex nodded and agreed that he wouldn't try carrying it around, unless for a specific reason. Daniel then told them of the auction. Hollies' thoughts drifted to the brooch Mrs. B gave her, she asked Craig,

"Craig shall we go? It would be nice, don't you think?"

Daniel stood up and walked around the kitchen,

"Are we all going to go the auction? It starts in twenty minutes."

Hollie put on her brooch, and Craig pocketed his watch and they walked the short distance to the auction house. They found Daniel's parents, and after brief pleasantries they found the auctioneer who remembered them from before. They reminded him about the brooch and pocket-watch, and asked whether they could put them in the auction.

"No, not now, it's too late, auction starts in ten minutes, they need to be given a lot number and be valued properly. These really should go on our website first to attract the right buyers. Stay and watch the auction and at the end we will photograph these pieces and do the necessary paperwork so they can go into next week's auction. This will also give you time to think about it and make sure you want to sell . . . talk to your parents about it too."

They re-joined Daniel's folks and watched each sale go under the hammer. Alex felt a little bored and sat on a wooden stool. Time and time again the auctioneer's hammer marked the sound of another sale, Hollie held Daniel's hand as his Mum's collection was presented as the next lot. The auctioneer read out an impressive description of the various pieces. The bidding started, hands holding wooden paddles with their identification numbers, were constantly going up indicating to the auctioneer who was putting in a bid. The air in the sale room was becoming electric as one by one the items reached a sale, until the vase which Daniel and Alex had given their Mum came up. The auctioneer announced,

"Ladies and Gentlemen the next lot is number 103 a Royal Worcester Vase in exquisite condition. We have eight phone lines bidding and a starting bid in the book. I will be starting at four,"

Daniel squeezed Hollies' hand and said,

"Four hundred pounds that's brilliant."

The auctioneer continued,

"Four, four thousand pounds."

Daniel's eyes widened, Alex nearly fell off his stool and their parents were numb and in shock. In minutes it rose to five thousand . . . Five and Half Thousand, the bids just kept flowing as were the tears in their Mums eyes. Alex joined Hollie and held her other hand. Craig felt the watch in his pocket and wondered how much it would fetch. It came from the same period.

"The bid now stands at six and half thousand pounds, do we have anymore?"

A woman on the phone with the last remaining bidder nodded and the auctioneer announced,

"The bid now stands at £6600 do we have any more bids?"

There was silence until one paddle was raised into the air.

"£6700, thank you Sir."

He then looked to the phone bidder, the woman was listening to the other person on the end of the phone, then she nodded.

"£6800, any more bids ladies and gentlemen, any more bids?"

The man with the paddle shook his head and the auctioneer with a beaming smile announced,

"Sold to our American bidder on phone number three."

The hall erupted with applause and Hollie spun round and kissed Daniel who proceeded to go red. Craig patted Daniel on the back and Daniel's parents excitedly totted up the total that the collection sold for. Daniel and Alex approached their Dad and asked what was the total,

"Boys, your mum and I want to thank you for that present, the vase, it was the cream of the crop, we have a total of £9000, enough to set up the business."

"That's so good Dad." said Daniel.

His mum asked through her tears,

"Where on earth did you get that vase, it was in such good condition. Anybody would think you had brought it back from the factory."

Then she laughed and Daniel touched his nose,

"Of course I did mum, just keep it to yourself."

It had been a long day, standing around on their feet. Daniel and Alex's parents went home whilst they stayed with Craig and Hollie who had their watch and brooch digitally photographed for the website of the auction house. They had decided that it was the best course of action, the money would come in very useful. When they had finished with the additional form filling, they all went on to the Summerhouse. The conversation turned to the gold coins, Craig spoke his feelings on the matter,

"We should take a vote on what to do with them, do we auction them, remembering we'd have to explain where they came from. That will not be easy and we may not end up with the true worth because they would be classed as treasure trove. Hollie over to you."

Hollie had researched the internet for the necessary information and had notes written down which she started to read out.

"Well it would seem that the treasure belongs to its rightful owner. If they cannot be found it belongs to the landowner. If there isn't one then it's basically split between the finder and the state . . . well at least that's the way I read it on the net."

She paused and looked at the confused faces.

Daniel confessed, "It's not as easy as we thought then, not

finders keepers, so to speak, in fact we might not see a fortune as we first thought"

"That's right, and I think we might be better off talking to an expert first. Dad said he would talk to a friend of his who may know one."

Craig clapped his hands together,

"Well that's that then . . . it will be days before we know any more, mind you we could do something else instead."

"Well you might think I am mad, but what if we took it back in time and did some good with it . . . you know, improve other people's lives."

Daniel looked confounded,

"You mean give it all away? after all we went through to get it, I mean you nearly drowned!"

"Yes I know, and you and Dad saved me with a lot of help from a stranger who was a ghost who owned the gold . . . He may have let us keep it, but I'm not so sure we should keep it for ourselves." Daniel was not convinced,

"Daniel mate, we benefited a lot by our first trip to Mrs. B, which you passed on to your parents. We have benefited too, how much we won't know until next week. So now I think we should give something back."

Simon had been standing at the door and heard all that was said. He entered, which made them jump, then spoke,

"That's a very kind and honourable thing to say, but maybe you should put it to the vote. Before I act as referee in this decision I think I should tell you that I have spoken to my friend whose brother is an archaeologist. He is willing to come next week and look at the coins, but the decision is yours."

They all thought for a moment then Craig announced, "Right, group, let's vote, all in favour to give the gold back to people in need raise their hands."

Craig, Hollie and Alex raised their hands spurned on by the thought of doing good, Daniel did not. Craig then asked,

"Those against and want to keep the gold."

Daniel raised his hand, then got up and walked out and sat on the step of the Summerhouse. Simon signalled to the others to stay whilst he went out to see Daniel. He walked out calmly closing the doors behind him, then sat on the step next to Daniel. Simon started to speak in a calm and quiet voice,

"I understand, Daniel, I was in your shoes once. I am guessing that you see the others with things of value, Craig who has a watch, Hollie with her brooch and Alex has the sword with amazing power. You got an old suit: not exciting I will admit, but you both had the vase, which you gave to your parents. That was most generous of you, but now you have nothing."

Daniel looked at him and smiled,

"My share of that gold would give me enough to get my own place and set up a business."

Simon saw his reasoning and replied

"I understand Daniel, however look at it this way you say you want to set up a business; your Dad is setting one up, he is going to need help. I know that if I was him I would want my son at my side. As for your own place, wouldn't it make more sense if you were working together to live under the same roof?"

Daniel laughed and put his hands up,

"OK you win . . . yes you're right."

They both stood to go back in,

"If you want Daniel we could just split it. You take what is your share." said Simon

"No Sir, we went into this as a group of friends and it stays that way . . . I've just changed my vote."

They all shook hands, except for Hollie, who walked up to Daniel and kissed him on the cheek.

Simon went back inside the house and left the others in the Summerhouse,

Craig asked,

"Well anybody got an idea of a time to go?"

Hollie stuck her hand in the air,

"Yes, I think we should at least wait until Dad's expert friend has looked at the coins, and as for a time to go to, a time that is safer, and no war!"

To which Alex stuck his hand in the air and said,

"I second that motion, those square heads, they were everywhere!"

"Roundheads . . . it's roundheads Alex." laughed Daniel

"Well whatever. They just seemed to pop up everywhere, let's go back and see Mrs. B."

Daniel voiced his thoughts,

"There is a lot of time to play with, I mean we could go to when the Summerhouse was first built or why don't we try a more recent time?"

"We have all been so obsessed with the distant past that we haven't considered the recent past. What about going to the 60s or 70s, the time of the Beatles. My Dad's got all their records, it was a time of change they say, and I have heard it said that the expression, 'Teenager' was invented then."

Alex looked confused and asked,

"If teenagers were invented then, what were they before?"

Everyone laughed at Alex's question except Daniel, who patted his head,

"Well bro, according to Dad they were 'Boys' until they reached the age of 21, then they were given the key to the door and they were Men."

Craig asked,

"Come on gang where are we going then and for how long?"

"60s" replied Daniel.

Hollie clapped her hands and said,

"I like the idea, what do you say Craig, shall we? We could just go for a morning, less chance of anything going wrong. We could get a taste of what is was like in the rock and roll years."

That was it, Hollie had just sold everyone on the idea of going to the teenage revolution era of the 60s. The days of Mary Quant and miniskirts, the original mini car and scooters, the Beatles, Rolling Stones.

"Go on Craig set the dials and put that key in. Let's roll into the sixties."

Craig set the dials and they all started rock and roll dancing. As the inside glowed green from the stones, it added to the atmosphere as though they were disco lights. Hollie jived with Daniel, and Craig and Alex danced around. Craig grabbed Alex's hand and swung him round, then lost his grip and Alex fell into the dials, Craig picked Alex up and both fell about laughing. Daniel and Hollie joined in the laughter, then the green lights faded and all was still.

Alex asked,

"Bags me out first to the swinging sixties."

They ran for the door and outside, up the path to the road. The house seemed quiet, no one home. They opened the gate and stepped onto the path.

Alex was a bit puzzled,

"Swinging sixties didn't have horse drawn carriages did it? What's that woman wearing? It's not a mini dress, it reaches the floor."

Daniel pulled Alex back inside through the gate and ordered.

"Back to the Summerhouse, this is not right." The others followed.

Chapter 21

Once inside, Craig pointed to the dials and said,
"When Alex fell against the dials they must have moved instead of 1960, we are in 1860 . . . oops!"

Hollie grinned, "Boys will be boys, and make a mess of things, but never mind we could still go and have a look around."

Daniel felt dubious but went along with Hollies' suggestion,
"Ok! On one condition . . . we only make it brief . . . give ourselves one hour then back here. The house seems empty now but who knows who might come home."

They agreed to that. Alex looked at the dials as Craig removed the key.

"Craig, when you remove the key no one else can use the dials, but if owners of the house come in surely they will see the dials."

Craig looked at him and suddenly wondered why on earth he hadn't thought of that. Daniel looked to Hollie,

"Hells bells, he's right I never gave it a thought."

Alex was standing looking through the window,

"Hey, Guys we may be about to find out, here comes the gardener I think."

Daniel looked out in horror,

"Perfect! . . . just perfect, everyone hide,"

There was nowhere to hide at all, the gardener opened the door and came in. He went to the corner of the room and leaned against the missing false wall and picked up something. He turned and walked out, but when he stepped out a spade appeared in his hand, and he walked away. They all looked on in disbelief,

"He couldn't see us, he lent up against the missing false wall, he could not see the dials, us, or anything."

The others agreed, but they could be seen once they left the Summerhouse. Craig whispered,

"He's still out there, we can't just go out, what shall we do now?"

They all agreed that they should leave, but were split on destination. Hollie and Alex wanted to go to visit Mrs. B, and Daniel and Craig were still in sixties mode, Daniel had quite a bit of sixties music on his I-pod and had been playing it earlier to Craig. Daniel turned the dial back to the same date they left Mrs. B,

"Ok Hollie we go back to say hi then off to rock and roll years . . . deal?"

"Deal." replied Hollie.

The lights again glowed green and the stones sparkled as they were once more taken back to the 10th August 1952. They all shot out and up to the house and knocked on the door, Hollie said giggling,

"This will be a big surprise for her."

The door opened and Mrs. B stood there and through tears she smiled and said how good it was to see them again, Hollie asked,

"You've been crying what's wrong?"

The tears still rolling down her cheeks she asked Craig,

"Be a love and make us all a pot of tea."

"Sure sit down Ma I'll do it."

He could not believe how he had just spoken to her, but it felt natural and right, he saw her as a Granny.

"It's Harry, I'm afraid he's dead."

Everybody was lost for words except for Daniel who asked,

"What happened? He was so fit."

"He was murdered, stabbed through the back . . . in the line of duty, such a waste of a good man."

"How on earth did this happen, Coombs wasn't involved was he?" ask Daniel.

"When he was awaiting trial he was released out on bail, he knew it all depended on Harry's testimony. When it came to trial his lawyer fought hard and got him off on a technicality . . . I think that's what they call it."

Through gritted teeth Daniel said,

"Technicality my foot, I would love to put my foot up his . . . "

"So would I Daniel, my love" interrupted Mrs. B.

Craig passed out cups of tea, Mrs. B gave him a broad smile and a wink.

Daniel held his cup of tea up as though to make a toast,

"Well group its goodbye to rock and roll years, and hello to this here present. We, Ladies and Gentlemen are about to go Coombs hunting, but this time we make it stick and make him pay, because we are going to get him our way."

They all toasted and Craig walked up to the side of Daniel and asked,

"Ok partner how shall we do it?"

"Craig, could you go back with Alex and get us some supplies to do the job and some of our coin, thirty or so, we won't get them back of course, as they'll become state evidence. It'll be worth it though to catch that murdering thief."

Mrs. B clapped with excitement,

"Oh good, sounds just like a military operation, it's such fun when you come round."

They could not help but feel happy to see her smile again. Craig and Daniel sat down and made a list of things to bring back and started to hatch a plan. Hollie and Alex told Mrs. B of the adventures they had had since they last saw her. Daniel and Craig bounced ideas off each other of how to catch Coombs red handed.

"If Mrs. B has Harry's house keys we could use it to lure Coombs."

Daniel turned on his chair to Mrs. B,

"Have you got a key to Harry's house? If you have can we use it to catch Coombs? "

"Yes I have. Yes you can, but how? What is your plan, Daniel?"

"Well, we could have someone there posing as the new resident with some antiques for sale. They take it to Coombs for valuation but refuse his efforts to buy it. Hopefully he will be lured to go to the house and steal the goods. We contact the police of a thief entering the property. We take pictures of him in the act and hold him until the police get there. He gets arrested, caught red-handed, and if the prosecutor has his wits about him, he will have another look at the past accusations. "

Mrs. B clapped happily,

"It's brilliant, but Daniel . . . for him to steal after he was caught before would take something real special. Also I can't think of anybody who I would trust to carry out such a task."

"We have a King's ransom in the shape of gold coins, but as for people, No! How about you Craig? Is there a good doctor and his wife in the house?"

Craig shook his head at first until the penny dropped.

"Dad . . . and Mum . . . well, yes, but Mum knows nothing."

Then Mrs. B stood up and walked over,

"Don't worry dear, I will put her at ease. We can have a good chat over a cup of tea, before you start catching the bad guy."

Craig had visions of his Mum coming to terms with Time Travel and what they had been up to, and the danger they'd been in. He turned to Hollie,

"Hollie could you pick up these few things from home and Mum and Dad.

"I will ask Dad, just give me a little time." Hollie said.

"It will be Dad's choice whether Mum comes with you, he is the one that has to fill her in on everything, or decide not to. He's kept his secret for so long, he may not want to tell, we'll have to see."

Hollie made her way with Alex back to the Summerhouse to go home. Hollie set the dials and the green glow signalled the trip forward in time as Craig and Daniel looked on from the garden. Craig turned to Daniel,

"Well she won't be too long. By the way it has just occurred to me, remember that when we were in the Summerhouse and that gardener guy came in and couldn't see us or the dials?"

"Yes?"

"It means that we could leave that key in there and it would be safe if only people from our own time can see it."

"Your point being?"

"That time we lost it, then nearly got captured trying to get it back, being chased by roundheads all over the place . . . for nothing. We could have just left it in the house."

Daniel looked glum and nodded,

"That's life, one big learning curve. Then again we did take the young drummer boy back with us, and the horses. The Summerhouse certainly has secrets we still don't know about!"

Mrs. Bennett, was eagerly awaiting Craig and Hollies' parents. Hollie and Alex arrived back home, Alex wasted no time in getting the things on the list, while Hollie went from room to room looking for Simon. She followed the sound of a radio blasting out old sixties music, it was The Rolling Stones playing 'Time is on my side', Hollie smiled at the irony of such a record being played at a time like this. She entered the room to see her parents painting, signalling to her father to come onto the landing. Hollie proceeded to explain the plan to catch Coombes with his help and Shirley! Simon agreed in principle to the plan but pointed out that explaining this all to her Mum resembled Maths lessons in Algebra, it made no real sense.

However a voice from behind them begged to differ and said,

"The problems with Fathers and Daughters is that they think that Mums don't know what's going on. Well, I don't really know—but I know it's something—and I want to know . . . I am willing to go along with it, as long as I get some help with the decorating of this house. If we could afford it I would get a decorator in to do the whole house."

So the lengthy, complicated, unbelievable explanation began. Shirley was shocked and excited . . . and a little disbelieving!! Go—with—it—was her thinking . . . Why not?

After changing clothes they all headed to the Summerhouse.

Shirley put her arm through Simons,

"So Mr. Time Traveller of a husband, what happens now?"

"Hollie, you know the date, set the dial and let's take your mother into the past."

Shirley looked at Simon and smiled,

"It was a great wind up, but come on love, let's get back and do some painting."

As she finished her sentence the house was filled with the green light and Shirley felt movement under her feet. Her eyes widened as she clung to Simon,

"Is this for real?"

"Yes it is, we have just gone past the time you were born and beyond."

Hollie turned to her mother,

"We are here Mum, I know this is going to be a lot to take in but be patient."

Shirley tutted,

"Hollie I am not a child, I can deal with most things and situations . . . even for me this is a 'Wow,' I will behave in an adult manner."

Hollie opened the doors and they walked out,

"Oh my! It's true! Look at this garden, Ooh! And the house looks great!"

She ran up to the house, Hollie looked at her Dad,

"Yep! That's Mums way of coping in a quiet adult manner!"

Mrs. B greeted Shirley at the back door and Shirley blurted out,

"You must be Mrs. Bennet, I've been filled in about you, as much as time allowed . . . It's such a pleasure to meet you—where are Craig and Daniel?"

Mrs. B led the excited Shirley through to the kitchen and she saw what the house used to look like. It was perfect in every way. She turned to Simon,

"This is just how it should look."

Simon and Shirley sat at the kitchen table with everyone and Daniel went through the plan.

At the end of Daniel's brief, Simon pointed out a small problem,

"It's a great plan, Daniel, however when the police arrive to take Mr. Coombs away, we can't be witnesses because we are not of this time. Besides that they will know that it was Harry's house and no one else's."

Everyone saw Simon's point, but Shirley thought of a possible solution,

"It's no problem, they catch him breaking and entering to steal. We only have to entice him there, not be there ourselves. If Mrs. Bennett says that Mr. Coombs knew of the gold coins all along, it would add to the circumstantial evidence that Mr. Coombs had something to do with the murder."

Mrs. B smiled,

"My, your Mother's good! What a team we make. I think a cup of tea is in order." She asked Craig to make it, Craig got up, disgruntled,

"Why is it always me that makes the tea?"

"You do it so well dear." replied his mother.

Shirley looked round the kitchen with its traditional décor of the forties, then looked at Hollie,

"Now I see why you wanted to have the kitchen in traditional colours. It has a lot of style and simplicity, it's gorgeous."

They spent the next hour bringing Shirley up to date on all the events. Later in the afternoon Simon and Shirley were taken to Mr. Coombs shop to pose as sellers of rare gold coins. The others waited around the corner with Mrs. B in a small café.

Once in the shop they both pretended to look at the many antique pieces on sale. Mr Coombs came from behind a curtain, behind the counter at the back of the shop. He rubbed his hands together, not because it was cold but because he could sense another dodgy sale of his items, which were mostly stolen goods.

"Good afternoon Sir and Madam, can I be of assistance?"

His demeanour made Shirley's skin crawl. Simon walked up to him and put a small bag on his counter. It rattled. At first Mr. Coombs was unimpressed, another collection of old coins would not be worth a lot. However, when Simon pulled out one coin and placed it in the hand of Mr. Coombs his eyes lit up, then he composed himself,

"Are there more of these?"

"Yes, thirty in total."

"That's good . . . very good . . . you see these coins are not worth a huge amount, but in volume . . . You see many people believe them to be gold but in actual fact they are not, manufactured before the war as souvenirs. If they were real then the quality would not be so perfect. They have some value . . . maybe £12 each at most. I would be willing to buy them if you wish."

He tried his best to convince them that they were not worth more.

"£12? Well I was hoping for more than that and have reason to believe they are worth more, but let me sleep on it. If you decide that you can give a better price then you may reach us at this address. I am afraid we have no phone at the moment as we have just moved in."

Simon gave him a piece of paper with Harry's old address,

"Please call by any time, not this evening though as we are off to London for a Medical Convention and won't be back until tomorrow afternoon"

Coombs took the paper and replied,

"Oh! but I will. They are very nice and I will try to find a buyer for them. I may be able to offer you a little more. Do have a pleasant evening in London and leave the coins somewhere safe. Undesirable elements of our society may think that they are gold, I wouldn't want you to attract such danger from such thugs. I do have a safe here, if you'd like to lock them in it . . . I'd give you a receipt of course."

"That's very thoughtful of you, but no need I will, of course, lock them up, they're too heavy to lug around."

Simon and Shirley left the shop and met up with the others, briefing them on what was said. It was agreed they would have a bite to eat and wait until dusk, then move onto Harry's house. This waiting time was full of chatter, mostly Shirley hearing of all the details of the group's exploits and how they met Mrs. Bennett and Harry. Shirley was stunned and partly horrified, but quite proud of her youngsters with undertones of jealousy that she had missed out on so much!

Chapter 22

Later on at Harry's house Simon found an old oak tea caddy just the right size to fit the bag of coins in, and placed it on the coffee table.

"He shouldn't miss that . . . don't want to make it too obvious, but if he takes the bait . . . we'll have him!! He was very interested, almost dribbling on the counter. I imagine he realized straight away that these are worth a lot."

"Enough to gamble on prison?" asked Craig.

"Oh yes." replied Simon.

Daniel interrupted,

"Excuse me for butting in but I think we had better put all lights out and take up positions. Craig and I in the garden with one radio, and everyone else in the back room. We will let you know if or when he arrives, and as soon as he's inside, Mrs. Bennett be ready to call the police, giving them the excuse that as executor to Harry's estate you were here sorting things out. You nodded off and were awakened by Coomb's breaking in, once the police are here we leg it. Have I missed anything?"

"Actually Daniel you have organised everyone very well . . . your Dad would be proud." Replied Simon.

Moments later they were all hiding. Hollie with her parents, Mrs. B next to the phone and Alex in the back room. Outside Craig and Daniel hid among some bushes in the front garden, next to a side gate. Daniel had bolted the door so Coombs had to either break through it, or a window. This left the others safe in the back of the house. Outside Craig and Daniel sat quietly with their radio ready. Minutes turned into half an hour, and then an hour, then two. It was nearly three hours before a shadowy figure could be seen at the front gate . . . it could only be one person. He opened the gate, came up the path and made his way to the side gate. In the moonlight Daniel saw his face. It wasn't Coombs!

He tried the gate then walked back to the front door. Daniel whispered on the radio to the others that it wasn't Coombs but still a thief, and for Mrs. Bennett to call the police. She immediately got on the phone. The man looked through the bay window and then he moved towards the front door. They heard a pane of glass in the front door being broken, and the door being opened. Mrs Bennett had just rung off from whispering to the police as the man walked in, they all listened carefully. He went straight to the front room where the tea caddy was. He rummaged through a few drawers in a sideboard—and then scanned the room quickly until he saw the tea caddy. He immediately picked it up . . . tried to open it—what Luck—it wasn't locked! He saw the bag inside and without opening it he turned heading for the door, just then catching his foot on something, and hitting the floor face first the bag landing just behind him, a number of the coins rolling out across the floor. Simon whispered,

"Yes! . . . Hopefully that will slow him down 'til the cops get here."

Hollie and Mrs. B both gave the thumbs up sign. Where was Alex? Simon could do nothing but hope that he was OK. The man was still grovelling around on the floor; he had found the coins and was feeling around for the box. He then thought to open the front door and using the moonlight to find it. He did and felt around putting his hand on something round.

"Got you, my beauty, you will make me rich."

"Will I indeed!" came a reply.

He was holding onto the boot of a six foot policeman holding a truncheon in his hand.

Mrs. B switched on the light,

"Thank you Officer, I was here sorting out Harry's things when I heard a noise, it was this fellow trying to steal poor Harry's coin collection."

The thief was still looking around, and the policeman asked him,

"Lost something sir? We've been on to you for a long time, you won't be getting out of this one."

He looked at Mrs. Bennett then at the policeman as he stood up saying,

"It wasn't my idea, that Coombs put me up to this."

The policeman read him his rights and put handcuffs on him,

"Well, it would be in your favour to tell us all about this Mr. Coombs."

"We're both thieves, but at least I didn't kill anyone ... and I'm not going down for that."

Mrs. Bennett and the policeman looked at him, shocked at his revelation,

"Who did he kill?"

"That old copper, Coombs did it, and I will testify ... under the right circumstances and conditions. It will be worth a 'deal' for me, I'm sure."

The others at the back were all elated, not only did they have a thief, who Coombs recruited but Coombs fingered as the killer. The policeman asked Mrs. Bennett to come to the station in the morning to make a statement. The thief was taken away with the gold coins as evidence. Mrs. Bennett closed the door. Simon, Shirley and Hollie rushed from the back room and called out for Alex, but there was no reply. There was a knock on the door, they shot back into the back room. Shirley grabbed Simon's hand,

Mrs. B opened the door, it was Daniel and Craig shivering,

"Had you forgotten we were out there? It's freezing!"

The others joined them, Hollie had her back to the stairs cupboard when it was pushed open.

Alex came out holding the bag of gold,

"I hid in there when no one was looking, when I saw that he was heading for the door, I crawled out and tripped him up and whilst he was flat on his face I took the bag back, left the ones on the floor though, for the cops."

Simon patted his shoulder,

"Well done Alex."

Daniel was not so impressed,

"You shouldn't take risks Alex, for all you know he may have had a knife."

"True Bro but I had all you lot to back me up, plus this."

Then he pulled out the sword from the cupboard,

"I used it to trip him up and if he had turned on me I would have been protected by it or have used it."

All were quite shocked by his ingenuity and cunning, then they all headed off back to Mrs Bennett's house. Craig's face was full of concern, his eyebrows low as Hollie put her arm round him,

"What's troubling you?"

"I'm not happy that Coombs is still free and at home, what if he catches wind of what's happened to his partner in crime?"

"Look everyone, Craig has a valid point, what if he does try to make a run for it before the cops get there, after all he's probably expecting this guy back at any moment now with the gold."

Simon stopped walking,

"That's more than a valid point. Mrs. Bennett could you go back to the house with Hollie and Alex? Call the police and tell them Coombs address, in case the thief starts clamming up. They already have your statement that you were the last to see Harry with Coombs. Meanwhile, Shirley, Craig, Daniel and I will go to Coombs house check up on him."

They got to Coombs house and quietly sneaked down his footpath to the house, as Mrs. B and the others went on to her house further on up the road. Whilst Simon and Shirley watched the front door, he did a very quiet radio check with Daniel,

"Receiving you Simon, I'm at the back door it's very quiet, no lights on."

Meanwhile, Mrs. B, Hollie and Alex got in, Alex put his wrapped up sword up against the wall in the hall, and Mrs. B went to telephone the police. Hollie put the kettle on. Alex was just walking past Mrs. B as she got a reply, and identified herself, when a voice bellowed,

"Put the phone down."

In the doorway was Coombs. In front of him was the shaking Hollie . . . at her throat was a kitchen knife.

Mrs. B took Alex's hand,

"Please don't hurt her, I lost my husband and both boys in the last war I could not stand to witness more senseless loss."

"She won't die as long as you do as I say . . . You see I know what your Summerhouse is capable of. I was quite happy until you and your copper friend decided that mine had to go, put me behind bars, and dismantled the dials."

Mrs. B still holding firm onto Alex asked again,

"Please let her go, I will do anything you say."

"Indeed you will, I want the rest of those gold coins, come on I know you have them."

He had a smug grin on his face, as he went on to tell her how he saw through their plan.

"You see when I sent 'Brain of Britain' to break into the house of those friends of yours, it occurred to me that it was the address of that copper friend. I do my homework, and make it my business to find out as much as possible about people that I deal with. It was as obvious to me that you and your 'future friends' had planned this. That's right I know who they really are! Your copper friend took away my lifestyle, and that is why I took away his life, poetic justice you could say."

Alex pulled forward and cried out,

"It's murder, not justice, he was a nice old man just doing his job."

Coombs grinned and snarled,

"You said it. He was old! Past his time, so get me the gold, then I will be on my way using your Summerhouse."

Alex knew that only they could use it as the key could not be seen or used be anyone else, unless they had their own key. As though reading his mind, Coombs added, "Oh! Yes of course, don't worry, I still do have my own key."

Alex dismayed at Coombs reply walked over to his sword, beside it was the bag of gold, he was tempted to pick up the sword, but he picked the gold and took it to Coombs.

Hollie started to cry slightly, Mrs. B said,

"Let her go now, you have your gold."

Coombs, with his knife still firmly against Hollies' throat and arm wrapped tight across her chest, motioned to Alex to put the gold in Hollies' hands, saying,

"That's it, Hollie, you hold on to that bag as though your life depends on it, because it does. You drop that bag and I will slice your throat."

These words cut deep into Alex's heart; although young he had the heart of the knight that gave him the sword. Mrs. B also started to quietly shed a tear and was feeling weak with all the stress. Coombs sniggered,

"Best sit on that chair Granny before you drop dead."

This only antagonised Alex even more. He was burning with rage, as Coombs dragged Hollie to the back door saying,

"And as for you Hollie, you are coming with me, as insurance."

Meanwhile at Coombs house the others had almost given up. They had gathered back at the front gate as a police car pulled up, the policeman got out and said,

"Mrs. Bennett has been on the phone, but was cut off. She need not have bothered I was on my way to make an arrest. That thief, Samms has given loads of evidence against Coombs, sang like a bird on the way to the police station. So, is he still inside?"

Simon shook his head,

"No, we have been all round the house and it seems empty."

The policeman's face went pale,

"Her phone call, thought it was odd, where is her house?"

"Next door . . . next house along up the road."

They all started running to the house, Daniel and Craig burst through the door, just as Alex went through the back door. They saw Mrs. B and asked if she was OK.

She pointed to the back door shouting,

"Coombs got Hollie at knifepoint, and the gold, he's going into the Summerhouse and taking Hollie with him."

They rushed out closely followed by all the others including the policeman. They found Coombs holding on to Hollie with his back to the Summerhouse, facing him was Alex with his sword in hand. The others stopped and listened as Alex demanded in a unusually deep voice,

"Let her go, and you will live."

Daniel could not believe his ears, he looked more closely then asked Simon,

"Is it me or is that the knight's ghost standing on the same spot as Alex."

Simon did not answer, but Craig did,

"Yes it is, it's as though they have merged together."

Coombs snarled back at Alex,

"For a little brat you have guts, but now go away and play."

Alex's eyes widened more, he felt six feet tall.

Alex's entire body seemed to be consumed by the vision of the knight becoming strong and clear in all his splendour. It was not just the sword that glistened now, his armour, helmet and his chain mail seemed to radiate a pure light. Coomb's knees felt weak as he looked upon this formidable opponent holding his sword out towards him.

The knight demanded,

"You will leave her be, or face the wrath of my sword."

Hollie summoned up all her strength, flicked the bag of gold over her shoulder which hit Coombs in the face. He lost his grip and she ran to Daniel. Coombs stared at the knight as he stooped to pick up the gold,

"Leave that too, it belongs to another, its rightful heir."

"No. No, it's mine, I am taking it."

He ran brandishing the knife at the knight, the knight with fire in his eyes, screamed out a battle cry and thrust his sword forward, almost up to the hilt through Coombs chest. Coombs sank to his knees, his eyes open wide, gasping for breath. Everything fell silent as he slid back off the blade. Blood dripped from the tip of the sword.

The policeman looked as though he had seen a ghost, which indeed he had. The knight turned slowly and spoke to Simon,

"This gold is cursed and destined for its rightful heir. Protect your family and return this bag, the six coins that are missing will remain missing. God speed to you on that journey and bless you with good health. Then the knight and his sword faded away and Alex was stood in his place. He collapsed to the ground.

Simon rushed to him in a panic, searching for a pulse on Alex's neck, then his wrist. Hollie burst into floods of tears, as his small body lay motionless. Simon started to give artificial respiration.

Mrs. B joined them, and saw what was going on, she screamed,

"Not my little Alex, Oh! Please No!"

Simon continued to pump at his chest, calling his name.

"Come on Alex, come on, breath."

Then a small ball of light came from nowhere and shot into Alex's chest, he coughed and spluttered.

"Thank you." said Alex.

Simon smiled through tears,

"That's alright!"

Alex still weak smiled back,

"I was saying thank you to the knight."

Simon looked puzzled,

"He's gone Alex, the knights gone."

"Yes I know, but he told me that in exchange for the sword he would give me an even better gift."

"What was that Alex?"

"Life."

Simon thought for a moment and realised that indeed it was the best gift one can give.

"It sure is, that's why I wanted to become a Doctor. I think what happened to you was too much for such a small heart and your body could not take it. But I believe the knight knew this, so he took the sword back to give your life back."

Craig looked down at Coombs body,

"Look at Coombs, the blood and sword wound has gone."

Simon moved over to Coombs,

"I don't believe it. There isn't a mark on him! It's as though he just died of a heart attack."

The policeman stooped down to look,

"Well in that case that's what will go in my report, after all I've seen tonight I'm surprised I didn't have a heart attack myself! I think it is best that I keep the report simple. He tried to resist arrest and had an attack. I will call a doctor to confirm it."

"And I am a witness to that fact also." said Mrs. B.

Then she turned to Simon and said quietly,

"It's been a traumatic time for your family, you had best get them home."

The policeman walked up to the house to phone for the duty doctor. Daniel and the others filled Alex in on what had happened,

"I did all that and no one had a camcorder . . . typical!"

Then they all went up to the house and awaited the doctor's arrival.

Craig made the tea saying,

"Every time I seem to make tea the group gets bigger, it's turning into a right party!

An hour later the doctor had been, and gone, taking Coomb's body away. He confirmed 'natural causes' in the death of Mr. Coombs, which was a great relief to everyone. They made their way down to the Summerhouse, Alex held Mrs. Bennett's hand and Hollie held her Dads. Craig bantered with his mother and Daniel carried the gold. When they were stood outside the house Daniel addressed the whole group,

"What shall we do with this gold, I say we take it back, we should do as the knight asked."

Hollie walked forward,

"I think Daniel is right, I am not normally superstitious but I am inclined to agree."

Simon seconded it,

"Yes, but who is going to take it back?"

Daniel put his arm round Hollie and said in a theatrical manner,

"WE shall go into the valley of death and delivery ye gold into ye murky depths in ye moat . . . then be back in time for a supper!"

Then they gave each other a high five.

Chapter 23

Mrs. B felt tears well yet once more as she said goodbye to Daniel,

"You and Craig take care when you go."

Then Mrs. B went round everyone in turn saying goodbye. One by one they each went into the Summerhouse. Shirley kissed Mrs. B and thanked her for everything, then Mrs. B watched them close the door on the forties.

The Summerhouse settled back in modern times. All were tired from what seemed like a long day, even though they had returned to the time they had left, which was early morning, Simon yawned and said,

"Feels as though I am suffering from jet lag! Forgotten about that side effect." Shirley smirked,

"What else is there to find out about your murky past then? I think I might have a nap."

Simon agreed and they retired to the front room and collapsed into the armchairs, still fitted with dust covers dotted with dried white paint. Craig and Daniel sat on the lawn in the morning sun and discussed returning the gold, whilst Hollie and Alex went to collect Ben and take him for a walk. Daniel pulled at the green grass and played with it in his hand,

"Well Craig, shall we go today or tomorrow? How shall we go, horseback or bike?"

Craig chuckled,

"Today, later, on horseback. I do think the bike may attract too much attention, although it would be fun, but best not,"

"Horses this afternoon then." Craig nodded.

Daniel was getting up to leave for home when Craig started,

"Daniel, you know what happened with Alex and the Knight."

"Yes, really strange . . . why?"

"Well nothing really, it's just that it makes you wonder what on earth else we could run into. I mean, that was like being in a Hollywood movie, except it was for real."

"Well, yes it was, and I don't have a clue what else could happen. I am just glad that Alex came out of it Ok. He can't remember much of anything really, that's probably for the best that."

Craig smiled and nodded,

"Wish I could say the same for Hollie, that's why she went with Alex to walk Ben, it helps her in times of trouble. She gets that from Mum, she always says that if you have a lot on your mind, instead of blowing a fuse, go for a walk."

"Sensible woman your Mum, my Dad always said that a good walk was wasted unless you had a dog with you."

"Thanks Daniel, yes she is a good sort, and adults do come out with some good stuff from time to time."

"Anyway Craig, Hollie and Alex are back with Ben, so we'd best get off back home. I will come back in a few hours with the horses and we will shoot off and take that gold back."

Craig and Hollie both went to their rooms. Hollie fell asleep on her bed. Their parents were snoozing in the armchairs. Craig sat on his bed thinking about all that had happened in the past ten hours. When Alex and Daniel arrived home, their parents were both out. Alex collapsed onto his bed and fell asleep, whilst Daniel had a shower, then made his way to the farm to pick up the horses. He didn't feel a bit tired, the sun was out and he looked forward to riding. It had been two hours since Daniel had left when he returned to Craig's house. He put the horses in the Summerhouse one by one, then he went back up to the house and knocked on the back door, Hollie answered it with a broad smile,

"Hello stranger."

"Hi Hollie. Is Craig ready?"

"Yes, just coming. Daniel could I come too? After all you will be going to where we've just been and we know it's relatively safe."

Then Craig appeared behind her and butted in,

"The plan was just Daniel and I go."

"Oh! Come on Craig, we can double up on a horse, or I could double up with Daniel."

Daniel looked very unsure about the idea, but when Craig saw this he confirmed, "Ok, I suppose you could double up with Daniel . . . what do you say, Daniel." Daniel felt cornered,

"Yes OK . . . Sure! Why not?"

Craig went and told Simon and Shirley that they were off to take back the coins, and his parents gave him the third degree in being safe and quick. Simon embellished his concern,

"And no stopping off in some other time to see what life is like . . . straight home."

"Yes, Dad, I promise."

Then all three set off down to the Summerhouse. Craig set the dials for the year required and as the house did its magic, Hollie could not help but stare at Daniel. She had never really fancied a boy before. Craig could see it, and felt a little odd because he had always thought that when Hollie got a boyfriend, he would be taking her off his hands, leaving him to do what he wanted.

Now that was likely, he wasn't so sure that he liked losing his sister and best friend. The house settled and the lights dimmed, signalling time for them to step out once more into the past. Craig and Daniel each took a horse and led them outside. Hollie followed. Outside there were dark rain clouds, with a distinct chill in the air. Luckily they had left their backpacks in the Summerhouse from the last trip. Hollie put on a lightweight waterproof jacket. Craig got Daniel to hold his horse while he got their jackets,

"Just as well we forgot our packs in there."

They all mounted with Hollie holding onto Daniel. Craig moved his horse on a few strides, however when Daniel tried to get his to move the horse had other ideas, much to the amusement of Hollie. She leant forward and asked,

"Would you like me to drive?!"

Daniel gritted his teeth and replied,

"He's just being awkward today."

"He is a mare . . . a She"

They dismounted and changed places, whilst Craig was quietly laughing to himself. They slowly moved off with Hollie in total control of the horse, and Daniel looking quite uncomfortable.

It was not long before drops of rain could be felt, the wind rushed through Hollies' hair which flew back into Daniel's face. Taking the trip did not seem like such a good idea now. The wind started to pick up as the bag of gold swayed back and forth to the motion of Craig's horse. After about an hour, Craig could see something on the road. At first he thought it was the branch of a tree, when he was only a short distance from it, it moved. Craig called to Hollie,

"Hold on, Hollie, there's something in the road."

They slowed down and as Craig pulled up beside the bundle, it moved and moaned. He got off his horse knelt down and pulled away the cloth. The cloth was a cloak, underneath was the very pretty face of a young girl. She had long dark hair and an angelic face. She slowly opened her eyes,

"Please help me."

Craig could tell that she was exhausted and frightened. He helped her up to her feet asking if she was injured. She shook her head. Daniel and Hollie dismounted. Hollie took the girl's arm as Craig had the other,

"Help me get her on my horse, seems she is trying to get away from something."

They all set off again with the girl's arms around Craig, her head resting on his back. They trotted slowly, so Craig could ask the girl questions,

"What is your name?"

"Jane."

"Do you live near here?"

"Not far."

"Who or what are you afraid of?"

"The local magistrate and his men."

Simon on hearing the word magistrate felt nervous,

"Why are they chasing you?"

"They think I am a witch. That could mean being put to the ducking stool."

"Ducking stool, what's that?"

"You're obviously not from around here then? They tie you to a chair on the end of a plank and duck you into a pond of water. If you drown you are innocent, but if you survive you are guilty . . . because only a witch would be able to survive the ducking stool, they say"

Craig swallowed hard and quipped,

"Everyone's a winner! Well you will be OK now, I know you're not a witch. I can tell . . . it's a gift."

"That makes you a witch!" Jane replied

Craig stuttered and coughed, much to the amusement of Daniel and Hollie who were listening. Jane asked,

"You are dressed in an odd fashion. I can tell you see . . . it's a gift."

Craig smiled at her humour,

"We are not from here as you observe . . . where we come from everyone dresses this way."

Jane paused,

"You have come a long way . . . from a different time, in the future, you see I can see the future . . . that's why they called me a witch."

Craig was amazed at Jane's perception, then she added,

"Of course I'm kidding! I can't see the future, only I know the future that I am from, which is 2052."

Everyone heard that and weren't sure whether to believe her or not until she said, "You see that is the year I moved into the Brant and found the Summerhouse. Did you board up the dials behind a false wall?"

Craig was feeling very perplexed and replied,

"We didn't board them up, we only uncovered them, how many trips have you made?"

"One. Well it will be if I get home. Hopefully with your help I can. I have been here for a week or so, had to change clothes to blend in. But I got too chatty and someone reported me for speaking like a witch. I ask you, do I sound like one?"

Craig grinned,

"No. Are you on your own then, and how old are you?

"Yes on my own, and I am 16."

They were all so amazed that they were not only talking to a fellow Time Traveller, but one that was living in their house in the future. Daniel commented to Craig,

"This is mind blowing! Let's get these coins dropped off, and get back before this magistrate turns up."

Jane decided not to question them about the coins, she was just so relieved to have met them. It began to rain slightly heavier as the four riders speeded up, heading south alongside the hills for about nine miles, then heading south west over Black Hill to the castle. It was much slower than before, because of the rain, and both horses carrying two riders. As they reached the top of Black Hill a sudden gust of wind caught everyone by surprise and made their eyes water. They descended the hill to the forbidding looking castle. Jane's eyes were closed as she catnapped against the warmth of Craig's back with her arms locked tightly around him. She managed to stay more or less upright. Craig handed the coins to Daniel and signalled for him to ride ahead and throw them into the moat, at the spot where they had found them. Daniel and Hollie rode off around the castle out of sight, Daniel taking one last look at a fortune. Hollie looked up to the one tower where a Raven looked down on them. Daniel tossed the bag into the water.

Hollie patted his back,

"Well done! That was a very accurate throw."

She then looked again to the tower. There, instead of the raven stood the Knight. He held a hand in the air as though to wave. Hollie returned the wave with a smile. She noticed that his sword was at his side, its hilt sparkling in the sunlight against the grey sky. As they rode back she pondered the thought of how long he was to stand guard over the gold. His intentions, although honourable, seemed futile, as his immediate family had long since gone.

On returning to Craig and Jane they found them in deep conversation. Jane had been telling Craig a little of the future, which Craig repeated to Hollie in a very excited manner

"Hollie, in the time Jane comes from they have computers built into the school desks, and they all have these ace canteens with all sort of foods. Their school day is an hour longer, there's more Science and they have to stay on an extra year."

Daniel winced,

"Wow! Thought the future was supposed to improve."

Hollie then nodded,

"I think if it helps us get a better future then it can't be bad, besides I rather enjoy Science."

Craig looked to Hollie,

"It's Nano science that they teach a lot of, all about small stuff."

Daniel interrupted,

"Look people we really should make tracks, keeping an eye out for these people that were after Jane, then we have to make sure she gets home safely. That's a point, do you have a key?"

"Yes, here see, around my neck."

It looked identical to Craig and Hollies' key.

"It is ours, where did you find it then?"

"It was behind the false wall with the book and a note signed, Craig and Hollie."

They rode off back the way they had come. It would be several hours before they would reach the Summerhouse. The weather was not improving, the wind raced through the trees. As the rain hit their faces it stung like needles, it was making them very cold and miserable. Daniel pointed out,

"Look at it this way, with the weather being this bad it might keep any others out of our way."

"This is true, only utter idiots would be out in this weather . . . that means us!"

Then a huge clap of thunder shook the ground beneath, the horses reared but they managed to control them. The sky became darker and darker, and the rain became heavier. The track slowly turned into mud and the rain seeped through their clothes, chilling them to the bone. Another thunder clap shook them again and a fork of lightening hit a nearby tree, cutting it in two. The smell of burning wood and the light from the flame spooked the horses yet again, this time they bolted. They galloped out of control, Craig's horse losing its footing and stumbling, sending Craig and Jane flying through the air. Craig landed in a pool of mud and Jane hit a tree stump . . . she lay motionless, covered in mud. Daniel and Hollie dismounted and rushed to Craig, then ran to Jane . . . she was not moving. Craig wiped the mud from her face. She stirred, blood poured from a head wound.

Above the noise of the storm Daniel shouted,

"Let's get her on the horse, we must get her back to the Summerhouse then to your Dad . . . this looks nasty."

They struggled to get her on, in front of Daniel, because she was feeling weak. When they got to the Summerhouse Craig and Hollie each took one horse and Daniel carried Jane. There was no time to waste. With horses inside, Craig set the dials. The Green Mans eyes glowed, the sound of thunder disappeared and then they were finally home.

Chapter 24

Hollie ran into the house and fetched her father who brought his medical bag followed by Shirley who carried towels and a cushion. Shirley put the cushion behind Jane's head, then Simon examined her. Craig and the others filled Simon and Shirley in on the journey's events, as they dried themselves off. Simon stood back after bandaging Jane's head,

"I have put sterile strips across the cut, together with a bandage, the bleeding has stopped."

Jane, nursing her head, thanked them all. Craig told his parents of what Jane had told them of the future and that they had hidden the dials once more behind a false wall. Simon thought for a moment,

"That's under fifty years from now, I wonder what happened to us, and Craig and Hollie."

Jane, holding her head, replied,

"Well I found a note from Craig and Hollie saying that whoever should use it, should take great care and not try to alter the past, as some things are meant to be. And I heard my parents say that the last people to live in the house, you presumably, retired to Scotland."

Simon smiled and held Shirley round the waist, said,

"That's been a dream of ours, when that time comes. Fabulous countryside, people and fishing."

Shirley added,

"Plus your grandfather came from there, not forgetting your favourite tipple."

Jane's head was hurting; as Simon suggested that they leave and let her rest before returning home to her own time"

Later they all made their way to the Summerhouse making sure that the she had the dates right, and all said farewell.

Craig was the last to say goodbye, and kissed her gently on the cheek,

"Might see you some time, forgive the pun."

She giggled, then smiled and the door was shut, the familiar green glow seeped through the cracks of the doorframe. Everyone started to return to the house, Shirley suggested,

"You lot need a hot shower, Daniel, you are our guest so you go first."

"That's very kind, thanks."

Hollie looked disgruntled,

"That's hardly fair, shouldn't it be ladies first?"

Simon put his arm round her and replied,

"You get to baptise the en-suite, whilst you all have been gone the plumber has been in to connect the plumbing."

Hollie closed the door of the en-suite and turned on the shower. The room soon filled with warm steam which was a blessing after the cold rain. Craig could hear Daniel singing badly, in the hot shower in the bathroom. He heard the front door bell ring.

Simon answered the door, it was Alex who rushed by quickly saying,

"Hello Mr. Templeton, just need to see Hollie quickly."

"She's upstairs in our room."

Before he could say anymore, Alex was at the top of the stairs and straight into the room. He called her name,

"Yes I'm in here Alex I won't be . . . " Alex opened the door.

Hollie let out a short scream and Alex closed the door quickly, and proceeded to go very red faced. Downstairs Shirley came racing through from the kitchen and asked Simon,

"What on earth was that?"

"That was Alex getting an eyeful of Hollie in the shower."

Alex started talking to Hollie through the door of the en-suit.

"Sorry Hollie, just wanted to tell you that the auction is on tomorrow afternoon. If you want to take your brooch, best give them a ring."

Just then Simon and Shirley came in followed by Daniel, wrapped in a towel and drying his hair,

"Who screamed?"

"Hollie." replied Simon.

"Why?" asked Daniel

"She saw Alex at the door."

"Well if I saw a hideous little creature at the door, I would scream too."

Alex folded his arms and replied,

"I am not hideous. As soon as I saw she was in the shower I closed the door."

They all burst out laughing as everyone saw the funny side of it.

Then Hollies' voice came from the en-suit requesting,

"When you have all finished laughing at whatever it is, can you leave me in peace?"

A short time later they all gathered downstairs. By this time everyone knew of the impending sale and the story of Hollies' brooch and Craig's watch. Hollie told her parents how the last time at the auction house they took photographs of both items so to put them on the internet, if they did decide to sell. Hollie asked Shirley to phone them,

"You have such a posh voice, Mum. How, now, brown cow . . . Very la-dee-da . . . How do-you-do!"

When they arrived at the auction house the next morning they were met by the dealer who was very excited. There had been a lot of interest shown on both items. Inside the sale room there was a buzz of chatter and people holding catalogues and magnifying glasses, closely examining all of the items for sale. One man dressed in a tweed suit, and a pair of brown brogue shoes that you could see your face in, walked round and round a chair, tutting as he went. He stopped, looked at the reserve price of the chair in the catalogue and remarked quite loudly.

"Good Lord it will never sell, it's fake."

Hollie was impressed that someone could tell at a glance that it was fake. A little old lady saw it, she gently caressed the aged wood frame of the delicate looking chair. Hollie felt obliged to tell her about what she had seen.

"Excuse me but I think it's only fair to say that I saw that man examine it and say that it was fake. I think he's a dealer."

The little lady looked at her with the clearest blue eyes, she smiled, "You are so kind to point that out. You are quite right, he is a dealer. He's been a dealer for some years now, but not as successful as his father old Mr. Coombs. Well I say successful; he was, until he ended up having a heart attack, overwork they said. Young Coombs always tries that trick of trying to convince everyone something is fake, so he ends up the only one bidding. He thinks we were all born yesterday. This is a genuine mid-eighteenth century mahogany chair. Beautiful back, pierced and swept up at the corners."

Hollie was in shock that a descendent of Coombs still lived in the town and dealt in antiques. Hollie passed the news on to the rest of the group. This kept them entertained for a short while until the auctioneer started the proceedings. Hollie could not take her eyes off Mr. Coombs, nor could Craig, Daniel and Alex. Craig remarked

"Have you noticed that this Coombs is a bit of a geek?"

Coombs saw them looking at him and smiled. One front tooth was gold. Daniel replied to Alex's comment,

"24 carat geek."

With the auction under way Alex found himself wandering around the items of the sale room. He spotted a tea set like the one Mrs. B had, it brought back memories. After a hour Craig's watch came up as the next item to be sold. The whole family were glued to the spot listening as the price went up with each bid,

The auctioneer called out,

"£500 for this very nice pocket watch with chain, do I hear any more bids?"

A man put his program in the air and the auctioneer acknowledged him with, "£600 thank you sir, any more bids ladies and gentlemen, this really is a fine piece in superb condition. £700, thank you madam, £800, thank you sir."

The bidding continued as more joined in the battle for the pocket watch. Craig was astonished, his parents amazed. Daniel looked at Alex,

"I feel glad that we were able to help Mum and Dad with that vase and raise money for Dads business."

The auctioneer called out again,

"£1000 . . . 1300, the bid stands at £1300. Do I hear anymore bids ladies and Gentlemen?"

Then one after the other bid came flowing,

"1500, 1600, 1700, £1800."

The bids were between two people, the other bidder shook his head, then changed his mind and stuck his paddle in the air again signalling a bid of £1900. The other was sweating heavily as he also carried on. The auctioneer called out,

"The bid stands at £2200, do I hear any more? Last time ladies and gentlemen, going . . . Going . . . Going . . . Gone. SOLD."

Craig was numb with shock and his parents were overjoyed, Shirley was jumping up and down. Simon squeezed his shoulder,

"Craig you would do well to put that away and save it for the future."

"Sorry Dad, but no, I won't be doing that, you see I have something in mind, I want to finance services of a decorator to help with the house. Daniel's dad is in the business! You two can do with the help, especially once you are back at work."

Simon was stuck for words, but Shirley wasn't.

"Oh Craig, that's such a wonderful thing to do! Thank you."

Hollie grabbed his hand,

"That's so thoughtful Craig, just for that I will share half of what I get for the brooch with you."

"Thanks Hollie, but you don't have to."

The auctioneer announced her brooch as the next item.

"Next item is a brooch, lot number 175, by Faberge, pink in colour and quite charming. A lot of phones booked for this one ladies and gentlemen. I will start the bidding at two thousand pounds."

The hall went quiet for a second, then all hell broke loose as one bid followed the other. The Templeton's watched open-mouthed. Daniel whispered in Hollies' ear,

"Good luck!"

The auctioneer called out time and time again and the bid went higher,

"£7000, £7500, £8000."

One by one the bids slowed down, with only one left on the telephone.

"£13,000, are there any more bids, £13,500, thank you sir, £14,000, thank you Madam. We are £14,000 in the hall, any more bids."

Then a signal from the person manning the phone meant that it went up yet again, the auctioneer called out,

"The bid is on the phone at £14,500, are there any more bids? Any more bids ladies and gentlemen, for the last time, going once, going twice, Sold."

People started to applaud as it wasn't often that a sale was so exciting. Hollie looked at Craig,

"Well that's just over £7,000 I owe you."

Then Craig replied grinning,

"Just make it £7,000, Hollie, don't worry about the small change."

It was an hour or so later that the group were home again. Their lives had been made a great deal better by the sale of items all produced by the Summerhouse and its powers. Craig feeling a little guilty, spoke to his Dad.

"Dad, we are not as bad as Coombs are we? I mean we have used the Summerhouse's powers to gain things for ourselves."

Simon put his right hand on Craig's shoulder,

"Craig, we did not steal off other people or murder anyone. We simply have profited from gifts from a thankful and kind lady and found gold coins . . . which were given to a good cause and the other half put back in the moat. Most people would have kept it, so no, Craig, we have been quite honest and not abused the powers of the Summerhouse."

Alex joined in the conversation by adding,

"There are the six coins the coppers took away as evidence."

Simon sat down and replied,

"That makes it worse, because it probably means that those were taken by the taxman . . . one way or another!"

Craig shouted from the kitchen,

"Teas ready, all mugs and made with teabags."

"As much as I enjoyed Mrs. B's fresh breakfasts, I could not get used to the bits of tea leaves left at the bottom of the cup."

As they drank their tea they all thought that this was just the beginning of a brighter future. They also knew that another journey to times gone by was inevitable.

The adventures had changed them all in one way or another. As they made their way home they all talked of their plans for the future.

The Summerhouse stood in the summer sun and seemed glad that it had been given life once more, even the Green Man seemed to have a twinkle in his eye. Unbeknown to all, the Summerhouse held a deeper secret, one which Craig and Hollie were destined to find out about. The Templeton's, and the Barnaby's lives were destined to never be the same again. The past had only just begun, and Simon's past could someday catch up with him. Would it . . . because as they say, what goes around, comes around!

Book 2

A year was to pass before they ventured again through the summer house. They thought they had experienced most of what it had to offer, seen different times in history and met its challenges, but they couldn't be more wrong, they had only skimmed the surface.

A young girl with a very special talent was to enter their lives, opening a whole new world, and other people who were out of this world.

Craig, Hollie, Daniel and Alex were older and wiser, however history was to become bigger, and the future was about to become larger than life!

Made in the USA
Charleston, SC
26 April 2015